S0-BRW-107

Previously published Worldwide Mystery titles by
PENNY GRUBB

THE DOLL MAKERS
THE JAWBONE GANG
LIKE FALSE MONEY

WHERE THERE'S SMOKE

PENNY GRUBB

W❂RLDWIDE®

TORONTO • NEW YORK • LONDON
AMSTERDAM • PARIS • SYDNEY • HAMBURG
STOCKHOLM • ATHENS • TOKYO • MILAN
MADRID • WARSAW • BUDAPEST • AUCKLAND

If you purchased this book without a cover you should be aware
that this book is stolen property. It was reported as "unsold and
destroyed" to the publisher, and neither the author nor the
publisher has received any payment for this "stripped book."

Recycling programs
for this product may
not exist in your area.

Where There's Smoke

A Worldwide Mystery/November 2015

First published by Robert Hale Ltd.

ISBN-13: 978-0-373-26967-9

Copyright © 2012 by Penny Grubb

All rights reserved. No part of this book may be reproduced
or transmitted in any form or by any means, electronic or
mechanical, including photocopying, recording or by any
information storage and retrieval system, without permission
in writing from the publisher. For information, contact: Robert Hale Limited,
Clerkenwell House, Clerkenwell Green, London, EC1R 0HT, Great Britain.

This is a work of fiction. Names, characters, places and incidents are
either the product of the author's imagination or are used fictitiously,
and any resemblance to actual persons, living or dead, business
establishments, events or locales is entirely coincidental.

® and TM are trademarks of Harlequin Enterprises Limited.
Trademarks indicated with ® are registered in the United States
Patent and Trademark Office, the Canadian Intellectual Property Office
and in other countries.

Printed in U.S.A.

WHERE
THERE'S
SMOKE

PROLOGUE

WAVES SLAPPED AGAINST the low sides of the boat, salt water splashing in the darkness, pinpricks on Vitoria's skin. The night air cut across her, emphasizing her sense of isolation, but she felt no fear, just an exhilaration she held tight to herself. Too soon to celebrate. The man with her, her pilot for this last short stretch, cut the motor, swivelled the tiny outboard free of the water and pulled a pair of oars from the floor of the craft. As he did so he glanced at her as though wondering if the move would alarm her. Maybe it would have if she hadn't understood every word of the quick fire exchanges before she'd been pushed out into his care. As they'd helped her make the precarious step into the smaller boat over the churning oily blackness between the two craft, she had pretended to need their exaggerated sign language.

Get your bag...hold tight...step here...step there....

Away from the wake of the bigger vessel, the sea was barely choppy but the tiny size of the boat exaggerated the swell.

Vitoria looked intently into the darkness ahead, straining to make out the line of the cliffs against the night sky, curious for her first glimpse of the beach where they would make landfall.

A single lamp swayed gently, almost lost in the gloom. She might have missed it if she hadn't been looking. The man at the oars had glanced behind to see

its reassuring presence and then simply bent his back
to the task of taking them ashore.

It was Vitoria, facing the direction of travel, who
saw the lamp ignite a string of lanterns, a ribbon of fire
along the pebbly shore.

Alarmed, she leant forward, tapping her companion's
arm, and pointed: *Look behind you*, knowing it was the
sign to pull back, to abort the landing. His head shot up,
his stare hard into her eyes. She saw suspicion flare as
though he perceived everything about her in that moment. Then he glanced over his shoulder before lowering his gaze and continuing to pull on the oars, taking
them closer to the blaze of light.

Confused she looked at him, then at the beach. The
extra light showed two figures in silhouette jockeying
for position at a barbecue that suddenly spouted red
hot embers. Had she misunderstood the instructions
she'd heard repeated out there in the deep water? Had
she walked into some sort of betrayal at the last hurdle?
After her first alarm, she sat back. What could she do—
jump out and swim? Hardly. Nor could she wrestle the
oars from him and turn the boat herself.

A jolt as they scraped on the pebbles. It almost threw
Vitoria from her seat. At once, the man at the oars leapt
up, grabbed her arm and all but threw her out into the
shallow water. Without his iron grip she would have
fallen. 'Go…go.' His hands flapped, miming speed.
Go with speed.

Off balance, the freezing water above her knees, Vitoria clutched her bag and stumbled towards the beach.
The pull of the water dragged at her legs, threatening
to lift her feet from under her as the waves swelled.
All her concentration focused on balancing over the
pebbly surface, but she heard the scrape of the oar, and

glimpsed the man in her peripheral vision as the pull of the waves turned her sideways. He stood in the boat, his face contorted with effort as he used a single oar to push himself free of the shallows and back out to sea.

A few metres in and she was stable enough to take a proper look towards the beach. The water lapped round her calves and her feet were numb with cold. The figures at the barbecue, now distinguishable as a man and a woman both dressed in worn jeans and floppy T-shirts, looked out into darkness, blind to the drama played out in the shallows. If she'd had any doubts about the instructions given her pilot, they evaporated at the consternation greeting the sight of her wading ashore. He should have turned his boat silently, kept her aboard, and allowed the sea to swallow them into the night.

For a moment, they just stared, then they started towards her.

Not knowing if she should be frightened, but having no way to avoid them, she carried on. She was all but out of the water now, no more than ankle deep. They stood back beyond the reach of the highest of the waves, waiting for her. Vitoria looked down, concentrating on the sludge at her feet, careful not to fall at the last moment.

She glanced up when the woman spoke. 'We were just having a barbecue on the beach, no law against that.'

As she stepped up beyond the line of the last of the waves, Vitoria saw the intended recipients of this well-rehearsed, badly timed line. Two men in British police uniforms, who had yet to speak, yet to ask a question of anyone, approached from the other direction. It wasn't a sight she wanted to see, but she couldn't help feeling reassured, because what real harm could come at the hands of the British policeman of the story books, the affable Bobby with his absurd hat. The first of them was too young to fit the stereotype and his face was far from friendly, but she almost smiled.

Then she looked behind him. His companion was older, his expression grim. He stared with distaste at the unkempt couple and their barbecue forks. Then he glanced at Vitoria and looked her up and down. Briefly, their eyes met.

In that fleeting moment, for the first time, Vitoria was afraid.

ONE

ANNIE GLANCED AT the time as she saw her quarry cross from the far side of the road and merge with the throng outside Farringdon station. She fell into step some way behind him, scrutinizing the top of his head where one tuft of dark brown hair stood at an angle. They would be in the midst of a dense crowd in a few seconds and the top of his head might be all she could see. Not that she had real concerns about losing him. It was a routine surveillance that had been assigned to someone else. She wasn't yet sure why she'd insisted on taking it over. It was just a feeling that something didn't add up.

The man she followed accepted a free newspaper before turning into the station. A few paces behind, Annie waved away the proffered pages. She was less than two metres from her target as he pushed through the turnstiles, and she made sure that a dozen bustling commuters separated them as they made their way down to the platform in amongst London's Friday stampede for home. A train pulled in as they headed down the stairs. Annie kept a close eye on the man ahead as he moved with the surge of the crowd.

Then it happened. As she timed her leap for the doors, hearing the beep-beep-beep of imminent closure, seeing her quarry squeeze aboard further along, something caught her foot. She fought to keep her balance, all her unease about the case flooding to the fore. Attack in a dense crowd could mean a hidden blade…

But in the fraction of a second her instincts readied for fight or flight, she realized it was chance. A child's buggy awkwardly angled…a flurry of apologies from the woman who'd entangled her…the thunk of the train doors closing, leaving her behind. Such a stupid thing, losing someone on the Underground; a real beginner's error. She ducked her head so her escaping quarry wouldn't clock her face as the carriage sped past.

And as she turned, she saw him.

He stood on the platform, momentarily exposed as the crowd thinned, then was swallowed up again as the next surge surrounded him. He had his back to her, his head buried in his newspaper. A moment's confusion. Had she been wrong; glimpsed someone else squeezing their way into the train?

No, nothing so simple. The answer was plain in his stance, the way his back was to her, his too avid interest in his newspaper. He had leapt out at the last moment. She hadn't been following him at all. He'd been leading her. Her spine tingled as people pushed through onto the platform. The all-pervasive rumble of trains, the hiss of air-brakes, the general clatter of a system that moved thousands of commuters across miles every day had been her cloak of invisibility. It had just become the camouflage behind which anyone might be hiding within arm's reach of her. The hidden blade in the crowd became a real possibility.

She made herself stay still until the next train hurtled in and clattered to a halt. Moving with the crowd, she edged forward. A line of disembarking passengers wrestled their way through the narrow gap left by those waiting to board. Well-practised, Annie used her small size to advantage, snaking through the pack, ducking under outstretched arms and jamming herself just inside the door, claiming this prime position as her own.

It was hard to see through the press of bodies, but she made out the distinctive tuft of hair. Her quarry had crammed himself in further down the carriage.

As the doors slid closed Annie pushed her foot forward to plant the bulk of her steel-toe-capped boot in their path, bracing herself for the jolt as they banged into her foot. The doors reopened. She watched for any signs of anyone getting on or off in this moment of reprieve, and saw nothing but a trio of commuters who threw themselves down the last of the stairs and dived aboard, just as the beep-beep-beep sounded again, with an impatient 'Stand clear of the doors'.

This time, Annie snaked her whole body out between the closing panels and took three strides to bury herself in a group crowding up from the mainline platform, hurrying along with them as the train carrying her quarry pulled out.

As she marched out of the station, she pulled her phone from her pocket and rang back to the office. 'Pieternel, don't go till I get back. We need to talk.'

'I thought you'd gone home, Annie. We'll nip across for a drink, then. Where are you, anyway? What's up?'

I need to know just what in hell's going on, she thought, but said only, 'Tell you when I get there.'

ANNIE'S SENIOR PARTNER, Pieternel, latched immediately on to a point Annie considered irrelevant. Raking her hand through her hair in a characteristic gesture of annoyance, she said, 'But you know you can't take on these jobs, Annie. Not until you're fit again. What if anything had happened? We wouldn't have been covered.'

Annoyed in her turn, Annie snapped, 'I'm fine.' She

hated reminders of the events that had led to her being at the wrong end of a boot to the head, to the weeks in hospital, the worry she'd caused. She'd been well enough to be back in the field for months, but the insurance company medics insisted she wasn't and Pieternel was terrified of being caught without cover. Going back to the case, she said, 'I told you there was something wrong with this one. It doesn't add up.'

'Come on, ninety per cent of our clients walk through that door with their own agenda. It's why they come to us, to protect their secrets. It's why they pay over the odds, and we're getting a good premium on this one.'

'Too good.'

Pieternel's eyes narrowed. Annie knew her senior partner would sail close to the boundaries of their professional code with regard to the legitimacy of a client's motives when a big fee was offered, but equally she and Pieternel had worked together for long enough not to ignore each other's instincts. They moved through the office as they talked, checking that the desks were locked, the computers off, as the noise from the street outside swelled from commuters hurrying for home to party-goers coming out to play. 'We were assuming a pressure group, right?' Annie ticked off the points on her fingers. 'And that we're working for some official outfit that wants it all at arm's length. Fair enough, but why not tell us who they think these guys are? Why the pretence?'

'Maybe they genuinely don't know.'

'I don't buy that.'

'OK.' Pieternel blew out her cheeks in a sigh. 'What now? I'm not letting it go. We aren't doing so well that we can chuck out this sort of repeat business.'

'Let me run with it. I'll get at them from a different angle.'

'No way. You'll run a coach and horses through all our insurance cover.' Pieternel reached out to tap the security code into the alarm system and they headed for the door.

'Then you'll have to do it,' said Annie. 'We don't have anyone experienced enough to throw to these sharks. When your quarry knows you're following and does everything to make it easy for you, it's time to back off. You'll get nothing useful and you might end up under ten metres of concrete at a road junction.' Annie's mind flashed through the scenario. The less-experienced operator, seeing it as a stroke of luck that the guy wasn't on the train; being led along to somewhere quieter, perhaps a door left temptingly ajar; an opportunity too good to miss. And then? They'd lost someone once; someone who'd been out doing an errand for Annie. Casey had been a friend as well as a colleague. She'd have been relaxed, job done, making for home when she was taken unawares, not seen the blade, her body burnt beyond recognition to disguise the crime. Annie didn't want that to happen ever again. This was a big case, far bigger than the contract which dressed it up as routine surveillance for mundane and rather woolly reasons. Annie knew, and Pieternel knew, that the huge fee didn't match what they'd been asked to do. They were unofficial subcontractors several steps removed from someone who didn't want to get their hands dirty.

'Oh, and here's a thing,' Pieternel said, as they stepped out into the night air. 'You remember that outfit you used to work for in Hull? One of the sisters called up for you this morning. God, I'm looking forward to a drink tonight.'

With that she left Annie, mouth agape, staring after her as she dodged through the traffic and headed for their usual Friday-night drink-after-work bar. The Thompson sisters from Hull? She had no idea they even knew where she was. They'd never tried to get in touch, not even during her long spell in a Glasgow hospital when they must have heard what had happened to her. Suddenly nothing about today added up. She felt perplexed and uneasy, as though an opponent had out-guessed her.

Pieternel was already at the bar ordering their beers when Annie caught up. 'Which sister and what did she want?' she snapped, then watched as Pieternel, her mouth open to reply, paused and threw her a puzzled look.

'I'm not sure. I think she just introduced herself as one of the Thompson sisters.'

Annie shrugged. 'It doesn't matter. It'll have been Pat. They used to do that on the phone. *It's one of the Thompson sisters.* Like gangsters. What did she want?'

Pieternel raised her glass to her lips and drew in a mouthful of the rich dark liquid. 'You,' she said. 'They want you to go back and do a job for them.'

They carried their beers to a table by the window. Annie shook her head. The idea that Pat had been in touch after all this time to ask Annie to go back and do a job for them was absurd on so many levels.

'That's ridiculous. I'll give her a ring tomorrow and see what it's really about.'

'Ah, well, there's a thing. She said not to. She doesn't want her sister to know just yet.'

Annie sipped her beer, savouring its cool velvety smoothness. That was the Thompsons all over, Pat keeping things from Barbara; Barbara stifling all progress with her cautious outlook. She pushed the memories away and returned to the case in hand.

'What are we going to do about this surveillance? Are you going to take it on?'

Pieternel shrugged and nodded. 'Looks like I'd better. But listen, the Thompson woman wants to do everything through a London-based agency so that her sister doesn't get wind of it. Here's the number.'

Something in Pieternel's tone snapped Annie's gaze to her senior partner's face. 'Hang on! You haven't said I'll do it, have you? It makes no sense for me to chase a two-bit job in the north-east with all we have on here.'

'Think about it, Annie. You're stuck behind a desk until you get your health clearance. You're not exactly paying your way. Wouldn't you like a bit of a change?' Pieternel glanced around as she spoke, not meeting Annie's eye.

Annie stared, dumbstruck at this betrayal. Sure, she'd been a long time in hospital and convalescing afterwards. It had been a serious injury. She might have died. And she'd done her best to be at full throttle for months now. It was hardly her fault they had such wary insurers. 'A pittance of a fee from them isn't going to make a difference.' She heard the sullen note in her own voice.

'Pittance?' Pieternel leant forward, lowered her voice and told Annie how much Pat had offered.

'For just a few weeks! They can't afford that.' Annie felt the weight of her bottom jaw.

'Maybe someone else's paying. Whatever…they're keen to get you up there. We can hardly refuse.'

'Or someone wants me away from here.' As Annie voiced the thought, her eyes met Pieternel's, where she saw her own puzzlement reflected. It couldn't be anything to do with the dodgy surveillance because no one could have known she'd be involved. She hadn't known herself until a couple of hours ago. She tried to catch the thoughts that flitted through her head.

'Coincidence,' said Pieternel. 'It has to be. It can't be anything to do with...anything...'

Annie heard Pieternel's voice fade into uncertainty. She feels it too, she thought. That insecurity of someone else pulling the strings, massaging the agenda behind the scenes.

'Listen, whatever the Thompsons have cooked up, I need to stay properly in touch with the office. None of this ducking under the radar, dropping out of sight stuff. And you need to keep me up to date on what's happening here. If this is some ploy to get me out of the way, we need to know.'

'Of course we'll keep in touch, Annie. I'm going to need your input, but the timing of this Hull job's just a coincidence. Don't get paranoid.'

Annie's gaze focused somewhere in the crowd now building between them and the bar. Her hand reached out to raise her glass to her lips. As she tipped the liquid into her mouth, she thought of the man on the station, buried in his paper, pretending not to see her, and about this unexpected job that would take her hundreds of miles away. Pieternel was right. It must be coincidence. How could the two things be linked? But her misgiving remained. Something didn't add up.

TWO

MONDAY, MID-MORNING and 200 miles away, the scene gave Annie a sharp contrast from the cityscape that usually surrounded her. She crawled her car along the bumpy track that twisted towards her rendezvous. After her rushed departure from London and the long drive through the morning traffic, the calm felt unnatural. London quiet was always accompanied by the background bustle of the city at some level.

She had reached Hull after a crack of dawn start and had been at the Thompsons' office by 9 a.m. only to have to wait the best part of an hour before both sisters arrived in a flurry of speculation as they saw her pacing up and down by the door. By their own admission neither had expected her actually to show up. Barbara fished for details of the contract she'd signed. Annie stalled, knowing a row would ensue once Barbara found out how much they were paying her. By the time Annie had dragged their attention on to the job she was here to do, it was to learn that she had better hot-foot it out of the office if she were to make it to the meeting with the client.

'It's nothing you can't handle,' Pat tossed after her. 'Drugs…kids…right up your street.'

And now she was here in the middle of nowhere. A battered Range Rover sat alone at the end of a track that had widened into an irregular surface criss-crossed with tyre marks. She pulled her car to a halt beside it, killed the engine and looked around. The dirt roadway along which she'd driven snaked back past a large, square stable block and on out of sight between fenced paddocks. Ahead lay a vast open expanse, a rickety sign at the corner labelling it a 'Lorry Park'. To one side nestled a long one-storey building, functional rather than attractive, that tailed off into a derelict-looking annexe at the far end. No sign of life from the blank doors and misted windows. Ahead, a wide footpath meandered away over the crest of a gentle hill.

A tall, angular woman climbed out of the other vehicle and Annie went to meet her.

'You must be Jean Greenhough.'

The woman stretched out her hand to shake Annie's. 'How do you do, Miss Thompson. Good of you to come.'

'No, my name's Annie Raymond. Pat Thompson brought me in to work on your case.'

The woman gave her an apologetic smile. 'Yes, I understand… I didn't mean… I know it can't take priority. Had Miss Thompson made any initial enquiries? She said she would.'

'Let's start afresh,' Annie said. 'I want you to assume that I know nothing at all. How about telling me about this place, for starters?'

The woman looked taken aback, but Annie smiled reassuringly and listened as she explained that this was the back way in to one of Yorkshire's busiest racecourses, in easy reach of Hull, York and Beverley. The racetrack wasn't visible from this off-stage area but on race days it would be packed with horses, boxes, grooms and all their paraphernalia. Today it was a deserted wasteland.

'This is where we're having the camp,' she ended.

Again Annie smiled and nodded, not wanting to admit to how totally clueless she was about what this woman wanted.

Since she and Pieternel had spoken on Friday night, she'd sought answers to this strange call from her Hull past and found none. Pieternel had signed a contract whose co-signatory was Vincent Sleeman. Annie had laughed outright at that.

'If that's Vince Sleeman's signature, I'm a domestic goddess. He hates my guts. If he gets wind of any of this, he'll have me out of there faster than you can blink.'

'That's what you're to say if anyone quizzes you, you were hired by Sleeman. But apparently this Sleeman guy's ill, really ill.' After a pause, she'd added, 'They paid for you in advance.'

'I know.' Annie remembered how their eyes had met briefly, Pieternel's gaze searching her face the way hers had Pieternel's. They both wanted to know what on earth it was in her that the Thompson sisters needed so badly.

And now she stood in the back of beyond, face to face with the client Pat had brought her halfway up the country to work for.

'Tell me about this camp,' Annie said to Jean Greenhough.

'There'll be thirty odd kids here next week. There's always a bit of messing around. Someone gets hold of a few bottles of beer or something. They go mad on the last night, but we turn a blind eye if they don't go overboard. They're on the brink of adolescence. You have to cut them some slack.'

'And what's different this time?'

'A young man approached me a few weeks ago, said

there would be drugs at the camp. Class A drugs. That's way beyond pushing boundaries. That's well over the line.'

'Did you know him?'

'No, he was a stranger. He said he knew the supplier and didn't think it was right to involve kids.'

'Describe this man to me.'

The woman narrowed her eyes as though visualizing him. 'He was black, slim, tall for his age. Twenties, I'd say, hair all different lengths, sticking out. Jeans, T-shirt, the usual thing.'

'You didn't manage to find out who he was, I suppose?'

'Yes, he gave me his name, but only if I promised not to tell anyone.'

Annie looked closely at the woman in front of her. She could just about buy the young guy with a conscience, but struggled to imagine him trusting Jean Greenhough with anything as precious as his real identity.

'You're not going to tell me, are you?'

'I don't break my promises.'

Annie suppressed a sigh. 'What made you go to the Thompsons?'

'I didn't at first. I went to the police. Promises don't count when you're reporting a crime. They looked into it, and a man called round to see me, a Sergeant Greaves. He said it was a kids' feud. The lad turned out to be one of the kid's cousins, trying to get him into trouble.'

Annie tried to read the woman's expression. 'And…?' she prompted.

'I…uh… I'm not convinced there isn't more to it. Someone recommended the Thompson sisters to me.'

Annie drew in a deep breath and looked around at the fields imagining them packed with shrieking kids. There was no job here; certainly nothing to justify dragging her 200 miles. The words played in her head like a jingle she couldn't shake off.

…doesn't add up…doesn't add up….

THE WIDE CARRIAGEWAY that took her back into Hull cut its path through a landscape of sweeping green hills and fields. Annie remembered this road with its free-flowing traffic. It relaxed her as she drove. Hunger gnawed inside her. With the early start and all the rushing about, she hadn't stopped to eat or drink. The office back in Hull held no promise of anything better than cheap coffee, but that was where she headed. This business must be settled right away.

She decided she would stay on for the rest of the week to justify some sort of fee. In all conscience, they would have to pay back a part of the advance payment.

The buzz of the phone cut into her thoughts, and Annie stretched her thumb sideways to the button on the steering column as she threw a glance at the screen. An unfamiliar mobile number.

'Hello. Annie Raymond.'

'Hi, Annie. It's me.'

Annie struggled for a moment to put a name to the voice. Then she remembered and laughed. Christa Andrew was one of their regular temps, a bit of a loose cannon but a sharp operator, whose familiar bouncy tone was muted as though she was keeping quiet in a church. 'Christa, how are you doing? What are you doing?'

'Walking in your footsteps.' That same lowered tone, and did she now detect a hint of unease? 'Pieternel asked me to cover. Something's not right, Annie. I'm following this guy. Haven't got his name yet, but he has this funny bit of hair that sort of sticks up and…'

'I know who you mean,' Annie interrupted, feeling the smile wiped from her face as her body tensed. She looked ahead for somewhere to stop. This call needed her whole attention. 'What's happened? Where are you?'

A prickle of apprehension ran through her as Christa described the trail she'd followed. It wasn't exactly the door left temptingly ajar that Annie had envisaged, but was the brink of something nasty nonetheless. She was thankful that Christa had been worried enough to call.

'Get away from there. Don't hang up, keep talking to me but get back. Now. You're being watched. They're leading you in. Be quick, Christa.'

'But if they're watching me, I don't want them to know I've sussed them.'

'For God's sake, Christa, get out of there! We don't know who we're dealing with.'

'OK… OK…but I'm not going to…' A pause, during which Annie held her breath. 'That's it. I'm playing dumb. I'm going the wrong way. I'll pretend I've missed the trail. I should have known, you know. This guy leaves a track that a kid could follow. He waits if you get too far back. Did you know that? I just thought…'

'Christa, these are not amateurs, whatever they look like. Whoever they are, they're using us. You have to get out of there. Where are you now?'

'I'm back near the main road. I'm looking all puzzled, like I can't understand where I've gone wrong.'

The wide road ahead of Annie climbed towards a roundabout. She accelerated towards it and turned left, off the main carriageway, breathing out her relief as she found herself on a road where she could stop. The isola-

tion of the few buildings now ahead of her matched uncomfortably with what she listened to from the phone.

'It's OK, I'm back on the main street now. I'm...
Oh my God!'

Annie felt her teeth clamp tightly shut as she heard
the exclamation, but Christa's tone held wonderment
rather than fear. 'What,' Annie hissed. 'What is it?'

'He's followed me back. I can see his reflection.'

'Christa, you must get away. Get yourself—'

'I've got it!' Christa cut across her. 'I need to phone
someone, Annie, but I'll ring you back. I'll get the ar-
rogant bastard.'

'No, Christa...' but the phone had gone dead.

Annie called straight back, and thumped her fist on
the wheel in frustration at the sound of Christa's voicemail answering her.

She felt helpless and too far from the action. 'Christa,
you *must* ring me as soon as you get this.'

That was her decision made at any rate, she thought
as she restarted the car. Back to the Thompsons', dump
the file, give Pat a brief run-through, and then she'd
be off. She could be in London in a few hours with no
hold-ups. As she set off Annie clicked her London office number into her phone.

'Annie here,' she rapped out as soon as the phone
was answered. 'I need Pieternel. It's urgent.'

'Sorry, Annie, she's in a meeting. She'll have her
phone off.'

'This is urgent. Interrupt her.'

'But she's not here. She went to the client.'

'Which client?'

'I'm sorry, she hasn't put it in the diary. I know, 'cos
someone else rang for her only a minute ago. She just
rushed off out. You know how she is.'

'OK, thanks.' Annie felt tension build in her shoulders as she clicked off the phone, and tried consciously to relax her muscles as she concentrated on the drive back.

As she pulled up outside Pat and Barbara's office her phone beeped. She grabbed it out of its cradle and pressed it to her ear. 'Christa?'

'Uh… It's Mrs Greenhough. Jean Greenhough. We met less than an hour ago.'

Annie pulled in a breath, swallowing an urge to cut the call without words. There was an underlying hysteria to the woman's voice.

'Listen, I'm expecting a call. I'll ring back, or I'll get Pat Thompson to ring you.'

'Please, I'll be quick. Just thirty seconds.'

'OK, but if my other call comes through I'll have to cut you off.'

'I…uh… I told you I wasn't happy. This business about it being one of the girl's cousins. It wasn't. I was sure it couldn't be and I've just talked to her mother.'

'Then I think you should go back to the police.'

'I've just rung. The man told me to ring if I were still worried or if I heard anything else.'

'And…?' Annie prompted into a small pause. Jean Greenhough sounded upset.

'He was really quite short with me. He said he'd never said it was a cousin. It was a college friend of the cousin. He said he'd get on to him and tell him to stop messing me about or he'd be up for wasting police time. And he…he said I'd to be careful or I'd be in the dock next to him. I… I've never been in trouble in my life. Not so much as a parking ticket. I thought about a complaint. He was so curt with me.'

'A complaint's a lot of hassle. Sleep on it.'

'But police officers usually go out of their way to be polite.'

'Yes, they usually do,' said Annie, leaving unsaid the words *with people like you*, her ears straining for the beep of another incoming call. 'Probably he's just having a bad day.'

'It's made me more worried about it all, not less.' Jean Greenhough's voice betrayed the beginnings of desperation…that she'd somehow fallen foul of the law herself…that Annie would desert her.

Annie's mind was too full to find any crumb of comfort. She said, 'Sorry, I have to go. I'll…someone'll get back to you.'

She climbed out of her car and headed for the office. Halfway up the narrow staircase and her phone rang again. This time it was Christa's number on the screen.

Annie pressed the phone to her ear as she turned to sit on the stairs. 'Christa, where are you? Are you OK? What's happened?'

'Chill, Annie, I'm fine. I'm heading back now, going to tell Pieternel what I've done.'

Annie felt relief, but also a hollow sensation that wasn't just hunger. Christa's tone was smug. What had she done?

'My kid brother has some mates who hang round there. I called them up.'

'You can't use kids, Christa. You'll get into real trouble. We've told you before about sticking to the book.'

It exasperated Annie that Pieternel could be so prissy about the insurance cover in relation to herself, yet give a job like this to someone like Christa, who would routinely use the dodgiest of techniques, which now apparently included recruiting minors to do the dirty work for her.

'Yeah, I know. Anyway, I played dumb, got myself a burger and hung about eating it, eyes down, all gloomy. I was scared the man might give up before we were ready. Anyway, one of the guys called back. He was all set, so I got up and went through the mall, you know where I mean. And I knew the man'd go the other way to make sure I saw him.'

Annie heard the triumph in Christa's voice; she was intrigued now to hear more. Recriminations could wait.

'So Laces is in amongst the crush at the far side and soon as the man was in the crowd, Laces nicks his mobile.'

Annie held back from asking Laces' age and gender, or whether Christa had the least idea what trouble she could make for them all, playing Fagin. At the same time her mind turned to the information they might abstract from the man's phone.

'Did you find out who he is, who he's working for?'

'I didn't go near it. I don't want Laces in trouble. While I weaved about looking in shop windows, almost seeing the guy, acting like a real dipstick, Laces put a tracker in it. Then I make like I've spotted the man and I dive back on his trail. So he heads off out again, bangs into Laces on the way and bingo, his phone's back in his pocket but now we can follow him remotely so I just piss off first chance I get.'

Annie felt her mouth curve to a smile. She couldn't approve of Christa's methods and their cover would be blown just as soon as the tracker was discovered, but now they could report back the man's movements.

Christa might be a loose cannon, unreliable as hell, but she was a wily operator and she'd known just when to call Annie to check out her instinct that something was wrong with the job. Maybe it was foolish to worry.

All she need do now was get herself back on the spot directing things from nearby. She would call Pieternel this evening and sleep on her decision about when to leave. Maybe she'd give Pat and Jean Greenhough a day or two more.

'HI.' ANNIE TOSSED out a general greeting as she pushed open the door of the Thompsons' office and was pleased to see Barbara, her coat on and zipped, look up from where she bent over her bag, tucking papers into it. Perfect timing. As soon as Barbara left Annie would have the full story from Pat.

She said nothing more until she could hear the sound of Barbara's retreating footsteps down the staircase.

'There's nothing to the job,' she opened, 'but the Greenhough woman's going to need some reassurance. Maybe even have someone out there to keep an eye on things. It's up to you. You could talk her into making a job of it or not, as you want.'

Pat shrugged. 'Your call. Do you want to do it?'

'No, I don't. I need to get back to London.' She watched Pat for any reaction to this, but saw none. Pat was engrossed in something on her computer screen.

'I was thinking of going back today. Now.'

'Uh huh.'

'OK, come on, what's all this about? What have you brought me here for?'

Pat looked up, surprised. 'The horsey job,' she said. 'Why, what did you think?'

'What's horsey about it, apart from it being on racecourse land?'

'It's a pony camp. Didn't she tell you?'

Annie shrugged. 'She probably assumed I knew. But I didn't mean that. You didn't bring me all this way for that. It's a nothing of a job. Either of you could have done it unless you've got so lazy you can't be arsed to shift for anything that takes you out of the office any more.'

Pat's eyes opened wide. She gave a half-smile. 'Hello, what's rattled your cage? If you didn't want the job, why come all this way?'

'Because...' Annie began and then stopped. Because of how much you're paying us, were the words on her lips but she held them back. For the first time she considered Barbara as a possibility. No one had been specific about which Thompson sister had been in touch. One of the Thompson sisters... Miss Thompson...she doesn't want her sister to know... She'd assumed Pat because it made more sense, but Barbara had always remained Miss Thompson for business purposes. Could it have been Barbara? Barbara had never liked her, never even acknowledged that she was good at the job. And Barbara would be very wary of crossing Vince Sleeman.

'I heard that Vince is ill.'

Pat gave her a hard stare as she changed tack but said, 'Yes, hard living caught up with him.'

'What is it?'

'His liver's packing up.' Pat clicked at her keyboard, then pushed it aside and levered herself to her feet.

'That's serious then?'

'Oh, I think he'll be out of hospital again in a few weeks. His number's not up yet. Not quite. But yes, this'll be the death of him. Leah's fuming.'

'Who's Leah?'

Pat looked surprised. 'His wife.'

It was Annie's turn to be surprised. 'Vince got married? When?'

'1980. Didn't you know he was married?'

Annie was amazed. Vince had been married longer than she had been alive. But then, she'd never known him well. He was just a slightly sinister figure haunting the sisters' lives and business dealings. 'I suppose it must be tough for her,' she said at random, imagining an elderly woman with iron-grey hair accustomed to a lifetime of fading into the background.

'Well, yes,' Pat said without malice. 'It'll change things when he pegs out.' Pat reached for her coat. 'I've people coming round this afternoon, so if there wasn't anything else.'

'Yeah, OK.' Annie wanted to tell Pat how much her company had shelled out to bring her north apparently for nothing, and about the hotel she was booked into at their expense just to find out whether Pat knew, but what if it were Barbara? She reciprocated Barbara's dislike but would keep her confidence, not knowing what on earth the hidden agenda might be. She would stay until tomorrow; get Barbara on her own and give her a chance to come clean. It occurred to her that the scales might finally have fallen from Barbara's eyes about Vince Sleeman. Maybe she wanted Annie's help to wrest back control of the firm once Vince died. But it was hard to generate any real curiosity. Her real business was 200 miles south of here.

'If you're off to London, post the keys through the door,' said Pat in farewell as she made her way out.

Left to herself, Annie looked around the spartan office. Typical of Pat to treat so casually her reappearance in their lives and the possibility that she might be gone again by nightfall.

She ought to call Jean Greenhough one last time, and there was Pieternel, too. Christa's enthusiasm might get results but had to be curbed before she went too far. Annie decided they could all wait while she went back out and found something to ease her hunger pangs.

She locked the door, went down the stairs and out through the shared lobby where she listened to the bustle of the downstairs office, wondering who was in there now, what they did, remembering the wonderful coffee they used to brew and share in the early mornings.

Stepping outside was like coming out of a cave into the light, especially on a bright day. She blinked as her eyes adjusted and felt the breeze, cool on her face, as a tantalizing whiff of frying bacon caught her nostrils, and she wondered if the sandwich bars she remembered would still be there.

A man had been standing against the wall. It took a second for her to register that he was in uniform. At the sound of the door he turned and, with a shock that rushed the blood to her face and neck, she recognized him.

'Scott,' she said, hearing the surprise in her voice, as she looked him up and down. For several years, she and PC Scott Kerridge had conducted an on-off affair that had tailed away into an uneasy friendship after he became engaged to someone else, determined upon the settled existence that was anathema to her. The physical attraction between them had not immediately died and had led to resentment against her from Scott's new partner.

In the fraction of a second that their eyes met after she had spoken his name, Annie took in his thickened waistline, the hint of slack skin round his face, and knew there was nothing left of the attraction that had once made him irresistible to her.

He'd clearly been waiting for her. She wondered what he wanted; who had told him she was back.

As he stepped close, he put up his hand as though to stop an embrace she hadn't thought of making.

'Annie.' His voice was cold. 'I know why you're here. For old time's sake, I'm warning you. You have no idea what you're getting into. Leave it alone. Leave the area. Go back to London.'

Taken aback, she said, 'I'm about to. That's what I've just told Pat.'

'Good.'

With that, he spun on his heel and marched away.

As Annie watched, slightly open-mouthed at the unexpected encounter, she thought of a man with a tuft of hair out of place, of Christa and Pieternel, of Jean Greenhough and her baseless fears; of all the reasons she had to leave.

Her gaze tracked Scott Kerridge as he crossed the road, climbed into his car and drove away; followed the path of his car down the street until it turned out of sight. And for the first time since Pieternel had told her of the call from the Thompsons, she experienced a real gut-deep desire to know why she'd really been brought here.

THREE

ANNIE DROVE UP the ramp into the car park that occupied the first six floors of the Premier Inn tower. Bypassing the lift, she made herself jog up the stairs to the 7th floor reception and restaurant, savoring the light and airy space after being cooped up in the Thompsons' office.

A smiling waitress led her to a table by the sweep of glass that looked out over the Humber as it stretched its banks wide on its way to meet the North Sea. Recession? What recession? she thought as she looked out on to a prosperous landscape. So much had changed since she'd been here last. The angular roof of the Deep, the aquarium whose silhouette she'd once mistaken for a sinking ship, was dwarfed from this height, but its entranceway bustled with customers.

She felt perplexed by the events of the day, as though someone had tossed her a handful of brightly coloured jigsaw pieces and dared her to guess the full picture. A couple of hours ago she would have dismissed the Hull end of the puzzle, but Scott's intervention had changed everything. Why had he warned her off? He couldn't have had the pony camp in mind. Who had told him she was back? What did he think she had come here to do? She recalled the deserted car park behind the racecourse. Jean Greenhough was no fool. She too was infected with the jittery unease of someone aware of strings being pulled behind the scenes.

Her gaze wandered over the panorama of the waterfront. Downriver, the fat ferries would be herding passengers and vehicles into their capacious bodies, ready to set off on their overnight journeys to Holland and Belgium. Seven storeys down, tidal waters pushed their way up the estuary, creating a surge up the River Hull, through a hidden underbelly of the city where the Thompsons eked out an existence, and on into rolling countryside where spring tides threatened floods miles inland.

The waitress returned bearing a steaming plate. Annie needed no urging to enjoy her meal as the smell of the rib eye steak flooded her mouth with saliva and she realized just how hungry she was. For a few moments she surrendered to the succulence of the beef. If she were to stay she would eat her way right through the menu. But she'd yet to answer the question, why was she here? The little she knew didn't fit with Scott's clumsy intrusion. She had to fill in some gaps.

She pulled out her phone and rang Jean Greenhough. The woman was tremulously grateful to hear her voice, almost tearful in her expressions of gratitude that they hadn't abandoned her. Annie pushed for the whole story again; the young guy who'd approached her; the supposed grudge match between cousins; the link back to college friends.

'You know you have to give me his name now; the name he gave you, anyway?'

'Yes, of course. It was Lance Mailers.' The name meant nothing to her. She scribbled it on a scrap of paper.

'And the cousin, the one who's the link back to the kids?'

'I don't know. I thought I did, but when I checked…

it didn't add up. The policeman, Sergeant Greaves, said he couldn't give me any names. I understand that, but I know all the kids…all the families… I don't feel I can go back to him now. I mean, I know they're busy. Real crimes to deal with. But I was so worried.'

Nothing concrete, thought Annie. Nothing to get hold of; nothing to justify the level of worry in Jean Greenhough's voice. But as she listened, spearing a mushroom and swirling it in the sauce that smothered her steak, it was Christa Andrew all over again. Christa had seen nothing, heard nothing overtly wrong, but something had spooked her enough for her to ring Annie to check. And now she recognized the same in Jean Greenhough. Not that the woman recognized it in herself.

'I'm sorry,' she kept saying. 'I know I'm worrying over nothing, but—'

'I don't think so, Jean,' Annie broke in. 'Something's going on here. You're right to be worried.'

Jean's relief was palpable. 'I can't tell you how much better it makes me feel to hear you say that. I really need your help.'

'You need someone, but there might be a problem in it being me.'

'If you need to be discreet, I can arrange for you to have a billet out here. No one need know.'

That hadn't been what Annie meant, but she sat back for a moment, picking up a chip and crunching it between her teeth. An out-of-the-way bolthole might be useful.

'Sit tight,' she said. 'Wait for me to get back to you.'

A SHORT WHILE after saying goodbye to Jean Greenhough Annie had Pieternel on the phone. She asked about the man who was desperate to be followed.

'I sent Christa out again, told her to act wasted and to follow and lose him. She said it wasn't easy. Meanwhile, we're clocking just where he goes. Nowhere remarkable as yet, but we'll have a name for him by this evening. I'll send her out again tomorrow and then I'll report back; give them his details and all his movements for twenty-four hours. Everything. The places we followed him and the places he went when he got fed up trying to keep Christa on his tail.'

'Is he going to swallow it? How incompetent does he think we are? He must have known I'd clocked him when I ran out on him.'

'Yeah, it's a risk. That's why I'm not going to play it more than a day more. Christa's good at looking wasted. He probably thinks she's all we can afford.'

'And…' Annie prompted into a pause.

'I don't know. Something's not right. I'll give it a couple of days, then report back to the client, see what reaction I get. How's it going with you? Have they really brought you all that way so they don't have to get their feet muddy?'

'I don't know, either.' Annie told Pieternel about Scott, about Jean, about her misgivings about the whole set-up. 'I'm going to get Barbara on her own tomorrow,' she ended. 'Looking back, I think she was putting on an act for Pat this morning. It didn't register because I wasn't expecting it.'

THE NEXT MORNING neither sister showed up at the office. Annie waited until mid-morning and then rang Pat.

'Are you coming in today?'

'Yeah, later. Are you still here then? I thought you'd pissed off back.'

'I'm just off now. I came in to leave your keys.' Annie wasn't sure what made her speak the lie.

She rang Barbara's home number.

'Oh, it's you. Pat said you'd left.'

'Well, I haven't. Not yet. I want to talk to you before I decide what I'm doing.'

'Talk about what? Why?'

Annie listened carefully. Was there anything under the slightly irritable tone Barbara usually used when talking to her? She couldn't say for sure. 'Were you planning to come into the office today?'

'What's it to you? I'm off out shopping for an hour if you must know, and after that I'm working from home.'

'I want to come and see you. We need to talk.'

'About what?' Barbara asked again and Annie wasn't sure if she heard an underlying panic or if Barbara was just amazed at this unprecedented request.

'I need to know what's going on; why I was brought here. The real reason I mean.'

She cut across Barbara's blustered denials, saying, 'I'll see you in a couple of hours,' and rang off.

Whilst in the office Annie searched round, flicking through the filing cabinets, checking the desks, switching on the PCs and going through the firm's emails and online documents. For someone accustomed to thorough searching at lightning speed, an hour was more than enough to go through everything the office had to offer. She was left with looking for loose floorboards, things secreted in the toilet cisterns and hidden safes, but even being this thorough she was done long before Barbara would be home from her shopping trip. And all she'd uncovered was the detritus of a stagnant business.

She decided to kill time by walking. It would give her some fresh air and exercise and remind her of the days she used to walk everywhere in Hull. Three-quarters of an hour, she judged, would get her to Barbara's door.

WALKING RAISED HER spirits and she increased her pace, keeping deliberately to the back streets, trying to remember the cut-throughs and short cuts she used to know so well. Twenty minutes from the office took her to a narrow street in a run-down area not far from the river.

This part of her route was quiet. Buildings awaiting demolition rose directly from the narrow pavement, their walls hemming her in along this deserted stretch of road. No CCTV, no office workers looking out, just blank walls and boarded-up doors. A little further along a makeshift fence skirted an old cemetery, and somewhere nearby was the River Hull. She could hear the background splash of tidal waters slapping against some obstruction.

It was the sound of a car that alerted her; a background hum that had been the baseline to her thoughts. How long had it been on her tail?

As she turned to look the engine roared. A blur of flashing headlights swerved towards her.

Blind instinct took her into a dive out of its path. Broken tarmac rushed to meet her, shredding the skin up her arm. She scrambled to find her feet.

A high-pitched shriek charted the scrape of metal against brickwork as the car mounted the narrow pavement and screamed along the side of the building where she'd been walking.

She was barely up on hands and knees when she heard the crash of the gearbox and the engine's reverse whine.

No escape…no doorways…no hope of outrunning it.

The abandoned cemetery was all that broke the blank face of the high walls. She leapt at its corrugated-iron fencing, pulling herself up, careless of the blood that ran from her hands as she grabbed at the sharp edges.

With a deafening crash the rear end of the car rammed the panel below her and she clung desperately, hearing the air forced from her lungs in an involuntary scream.

For a second the damaged panel hung in the air, as though about to fall back into the road taking her with it. She scrambled over the top and threw herself towards the unkempt ground with its lopsided gravestones, hitting her arm hard on a splintered fence post.

Off the road. But nowhere to go.

She had seconds…as long as it took them to get out of the car and come after her.

Her eyes took in the whole of the scene. The spread of the old graves, tangled undergrowth too thin to hide a rabbit, patches of bare earth and rubble. A slope down towards the river. The faraway buzz of voices… the sound of traffic. There was access to another road somewhere down there. But she had only seconds to act.

Careless of broken glass and sharp edges or the stinging of the cuts she'd already sustained, Annie grabbed as big an armful as she could of the loose earth and rubble at her feet and flung it towards the slope. A second armful followed as tears coursed down her cheeks from the pain.

As the debris she'd thrown crashed and skittered down the slope and out of sight, she dived sideways and crammed herself back against the fence, away from the broken panel, wriggling face down into the tangle of briers and nettles.

Hardly breathing, she listened to the fence panel

being ripped aside as her pursuers forced their way through and sped towards the sounds of the tiny avalanche. She identified two people racing past her and off down the slope towards the river, but she had no idea how many had been in the vehicle. What if there were three, one waiting with the car? She was in no shape to stand up to a child, never mind whoever had driven that car at her.

It felt like hours later that she heard their footsteps crunching back up the slope, but in her mind she'd been counting from the moment they'd rushed by and knew it was barely a couple of minutes.

They were panting, out of breath. She could only rely on staying perfectly still and that they weren't looking for her here.

'...must have had a car down there,' she heard one of them say.

'Yeah, well, we can...' The voice disappeared in the clanking of the fence panel being pulled aside.

ANNIE WAITED UNTIL she heard the car start up and pull away, the purr of its engine now marred by the rattle of something loose from its incursions into the wall and the iron sheeting. She forced herself to her feet, taking a shaky step forward to prise open a gap in the fence panel and tried to get a clear view of the car as it disappeared down the street, but it was gone.

She brushed herself down as well as she could and clambered back out on to the road. It felt horribly exposed on the street where they'd tried to run her down but it was the last place they'd expect her to be. Grimacing against a sharp pain that jarred her left leg on every footfall, she broke into a jog to get out of the narrow alley of buildings.

Maybe she should call Scott. She thought about his warning and about Jean who had herself been warned off by one of Scott's colleagues. And what would she say? She'd seen nothing of the car or the people in it. She needed to know what was going on and Scott wasn't the person to tell her. She needed to get to Barbara.

Barbara might not like her, but she'd provide the means to clean her up and must surely now tell her the full story.

In half an hour she was at Barbara's front door, knocking loudly.

The door swung open and Annie faced a man she recognized as Barbara's son.

'Hello, I'm Annie. We met once a few years ago. I'm here to see Barbara. She's expecting me. I called her a couple of...'

She felt her smile fade with her words. Even before the man spoke, Annie read his expression.

'You haven't heard,' he said.

In a sudden rush, fluid gushed from Annie's nose and she looked down to see blood, bright red, splash on to her jacket. She scrabbled in her pocket for a tissue and clamped it to her nose as his words came at her in fragments.

'...in hospital...on her way to the shops...hit-and-run.'

FOUR

ANNIE RAN COLD water into the small sink and dunked her T-shirt, though the blood was dried in now. Leaving it to soak, she laid her jacket on the makeshift counter and sponged it down with a wet flannel.

Outside, dusk crept to the edges of the lorry park. Jean Greenhough's car had disappeared over the rise, leaving Annie alone at the racecourse with access to a tiny bedroom and primitive facilities.

Jean had been horrified to see her; every exposed stretch of skin criss-crossed with scratches from the brambles, her forearm red raw from the rough tarmac, and dried blood down her front. Her arm ached and a multicoloured bruise spread out from above her elbow.

Within half an hour of leaving Barbara's house Annie had a call from Pat, telling her about Barbara's accident; that she must stay on; the firm needed her.

She hadn't let on she already knew, but asked after Barbara's injuries—serious but not life threatening—then said no, she was on her way out of the city. Again, she wasn't sure why she lied to Pat, but knew she needed the space to get her head together.

Jean Greenhough had offered her an out of the way place to stay that no one need know about, but before getting in touch with her Annie had taken a circuitous route back to the Thompsons' office, watching the road, the office doorway and the pedestrian traffic before nerving herself to walk across and get in her car.

The men who'd chased her had seen her leave the office on foot. No reason they should know where her car was parked or which it was. Even if they had access to official records, they wouldn't find her name attached to it. No one who worked for Pieternel was that easy to trace.

In case of tracking devices, she headed for the Clive Sullivan Way and the route west out of the city, stopping at a roadside garage to fill up and check the car over. Once as sure as she could be that it hadn't been tampered with, she changed direction, rang Jean Greenhough and arranged to meet.

Now, here she was in the block that housed the grooms who stayed overnight when there were visiting racehorses in the adjoining stables. She was the only one, human or equine, in residence tonight. Her phone rang as she was rubbing at the material of her T-shirt. The screen showed the Thompsons' office number. Annie felt a rush of anger, not at Pat but at whoever had manoeuvred her into this position, and let the call ring through to voice mail.

Pat's voice was impatient but distracted, flitting from topic to topic. 'You've forgotten the damned keys... Ring me when you get this... Barbara's out of action for weeks... Vince paying for you anyway... Your blasted copper badgering me...' A heavy sigh, then a snapped, 'I don't see why you can't just stay on,' and the crash of the phone being slammed back into its rest.

Annie looked out across the lorry park, its edges now blurring into the fading light. She stretched her hands out in front of her, seeing the tremble in her fingers matching the shakiness she felt inside.

But there was one thing she was clear on. If someone was prepared to go to these lengths to force her out, then she was here to stay. She would find out what was going on, how it linked back to events in London and just who was pulling the strings.

As she curled up on a thin plank of a bed in a room that was little bigger than a cell, her mind skipped across her options. Who could tell her what she needed to know? Barbara... Pat... Scott...the mysterious Lance Mailers?

As sleep enveloped her, she wondered if she was right to trust Jean, a woman she'd met only twice.

ANNIE WOKE TO a spear of light through the small window, making her screw up her face and shade her eyes. The morning sun painted glistening edges to the view from the window and as she stretched the night out of her limbs, grimacing slightly at the ache from the battering she'd taken, her phone began to ring.

The Thompsons' office again, and early for Pat. It was just after ten. But Annie was ready to speak to her.

'Hi Pat. You're up and about early.'

'Well, of course I am. Barbara's laid up and there's no one else to do her work. Didn't you get my message? I need you back here. What are you playing at, running out on us? And I'll tell you something else: someone's been through the files. I can't cope with this lot on my own...'

Annie felt amazed. She was certain she'd been careful when she went through the office files. Pat must have sharpened up considerably to have noticed.

She pulled in a breath ready to speak as soon as Pat's rant subsided. Her first task for the day was to contact the hotel, to make sure they'd had their advance payment so she could keep the room on, but warn them she might be an absent guest. There was no evidence anyone had tracked her there, but she must be careful. After that, she and Pat had to have a frank talk. They could meet this evening.

'So?' Pat continued to badger her. 'When will you be back? There's chaos here. I don't even know what Babs was working on.'

On the point of telling Pat that, yes, she would be back; in fact had never left, the comment stopped Annie. *I don't even know what Babs was working on.* Pat and Barbara had always run the business together, albeit at loggerheads, but Barbara was now involved in something Pat knew nothing about—something that had brought Annie all this way. What and why?

A connection sparked. Her mind reran her last conversation with Barbara.

I need to know what's going on; why I'm here. The real reason.

Annie had rung from the office phone. Barbara had been at home.

Someone had heard them. The office phone was the more likely to have been tapped, but it could have been either or both.

'Uh…no,' she told Pat. 'I'm afraid I can't come back. I'm sure you can get someone from an agency. I have to go now. I'll post the keys.'

She clicked off the phone, knowing she must get to Pat face to face, but how and where? She needed her on her own, without alerting any hidden watchers. It wouldn't be easy.

Her phone rang.

'Don't you hang up on me,' Pat shouted. 'You've been paid. I know you have.'

Annie clicked the phone off, right off, and went

through to the tiny bathroom to get herself ready to meet Jean, who was due...she glanced at the clock... in less than an hour.

IT WAS DARK as Annie eased her car to the kerb. She looked around at the blank faces of the buildings on either side, a shiver running through her as the previous day's events echoed off the brick walls. This wasn't a great place to leave a car overnight, but she would have to risk it. Satisfied that no one was about, she clicked open the door and stepped into the night air.

She pulled her woollen cap down over her hair and ears and pulled up the zip on her dark jacket. Soft black trainers would deaden the sound of her footsteps once she was away from the light breeze that was the only sound on the street.

The car's indicators flashed with the click of the door locks, causing Annie to flinch at the way the vehicle advertised its presence. She walked down the pavement, keeping to the shadow until she reached a narrow alleyway between the buildings where the darkness pooled as the walls towered over her. She trod carefully here, braced for hidden obstructions, until the alley took a ninety-degree turn and showed the gleam of a streetlight from the road at the far end.

Out from the narrow path, Annie took a quick look up and down the street and headed for the Thompsons' office. She unlocked the outer door and went inside.

Upstairs, she looked with distaste at the uncarpeted floor and the worn cushions in the only armchair. Letting out a sigh, she thought that at least it would shine a better light on the stark grooms' billet where she would have to spend the next few nights.

Pat had rung half a dozen times during the day.

Annie had ignored the calls and the messages. Tomorrow she would be here when Pat arrived and they could at last have a frank exchange away from hidden listeners.

Moonlight, semi-obscured by clouds, shone through the window that overlooked the backyards, but wasn't enough to read by or do any useful searching, though she spent a minute or two looking through the recent paperwork on the desk, before leaving it and settling herself as comfortably as she could in the chair.

Drowsiness had just begun to catch hold when she found herself jerked awake.

Something…some sound had woken her.

She sat up, grasping the chair arms to pull herself silently to her feet.

They'd followed her after all. And she was trapped. She heard the click of the outer door closing downstairs. Whoever it was, they were inside the building. In a moment she was across the room, easing the window open. There was no way out, but she had to hope they didn't know that. She turned, strode softly to the office door and slipped out on to the landing.

She crept along the upstairs corridor before footfalls on the stairs froze her. She sank down into a crouch.

Peering out awkwardly, she caught the shadow of the intruder as he ascended. No choice but to wait and hope he fell for the open window. If he leant out to peer into the darkness below, she would have time to creep back down the stairs and away.

She saw the silhouette of a dark-clad figure rise up the staircase and head for the office door. Barely a creak of a floorboard gave away his presence. Thank heavens she hadn't been sound asleep.

She sensed rather than heard surprise at the unlocked

door, then watched the intruder head straight for the open window to look out.

At once she eased herself along the landing to the head of the stairs, one eye on the figure with its back to her leaning out to look into the night. The dim light of the moon outlined his shape and, at the point of turning on to the stairway to slip silently down, Annie stopped, smothering a gasp of surprise.

She stared intently through the open office door.

Then she stepped inside, deliberately clattering her shoes on the wooden floor. The figure before her spun round with a gasp.

She clicked on the light and said, 'Scott? What the hell are you doing?'

FIVE

THERE WAS SATISFACTION in catching Scott out; an affirmation that she was better at this stuff than he, despite his official status and warrant card. After an initial prickly exchange, where they each demanded to know what the other was doing and neither provided answers, they agreed it would be best to turn out the light and keep quiet in case anyone should report a burglary in progress. Annie suggested she make coffee for them both and Scott accepted with an ungracious, 'I hope you make a better cup than Pat Thompson.'

Annie shot him a glance, seeing his gaze run over the scratches that criss-crossed her arms and wondered if he'd clocked how recent they were, but said nothing as she made for the back office and clicked on the kettle. A better cup than Pat Thompson? When had Pat ever made coffee for Scott? In her mind, she ran through Pat's earlier message. *Your copper badgering me...* So Scott had been here earlier in the day and that was when he'd helped himself to the spare office key.

'You asked Pat to make coffee to get her out of the room, didn't you?' she asked as she passed him his cup. 'You went through her files.'

'Just the ones out on the desk,' he said with a shrug that acknowledged the futility of denying anything since she'd caught him breaking and entering. Annie thought about the full-scale search she'd undertaken, every drawer, desk and cabinet and not a trace left. He'd done one desktop and left a mess. But then the searches he specialized in were carried out under the auspices of a magistrate's warrant, with no need for stealth.

Settled with a drink in his hand, the pale moonlight showing his outline but not his features, Scott said, 'You told me you were leaving.'

'I did, but I came back,' she lied, trying to analyse his expression. How much did he know? 'Barbara's had an accident. Pat phoned me.'

'Huh! Some accident.'

'What do you mean?' She peered at him through the gloom. 'Wasn't it an accident?'

He shrugged. 'I did try to warn you to leave the job alone.'

'But what job? I don't know what's going on.'

It was his turn to stare at her across the dark office as though trying to work out if she were speaking the truth. 'Honestly, Scott, I haven't a clue. They brought me here for…' It seemed a bad idea to tell him anything, even about the pony camp. '…because they were short staffed, but I didn't get to know what jobs I was supposed to take on. I was on my way to see Barbara when she…' She gave a huff of exasperation and burst out, 'Why Barbara? Nothing goes on in this place that Pat doesn't know about. Barbara never works on her own.'

'Why did Sleeman bring in either of them?' Scott muttered.

Annie bit back her questions. He wasn't ready to confide in her. The intimacy they'd once shared was long gone. Whoever was behind this, it was someone who had deliberately brought Annie into the mix, and that wasn't Vince Sleeman. She glanced at Scott as he raised his cup to drain the last of his coffee. They both wanted answers and he thought Pat could provide them.

Even if Pat knew nothing, as Annie suspected, it would be instructive to hear Scott's questions. She wondered if she could persuade him to stay until morning. Putting her feet up on to a box of paper, trying to ease the dull ache in her leg, she said, 'So what have you been getting up to these last few years?' She tried for a light tone.

He turned to look at her, surprised, and gave a shrug.

'Go on,' she prompted. 'I'm interested. I'd say you're married with a couple of kids. A house in…hmm, let me guess… Beverley. You always liked Beverley better than Hull.'

For a moment, she didn't think he would play the game, but then he said, 'Closer to Wetherby. Twin boys.'

Not far from Jean Greenhough's stamping ground, she thought. 'That's quite a commute for you.'

He laughed. 'You haven't changed. Anyone else would ask about the boys, how old, what they're called. For you it's the commute.'

'OK, tell me about your kids. I'll bet you carry photos even on a jaunt like this.'

He laughed and they chatted desultorily for a while. She saw Scott's gaze wander about the room and once or twice he shifted in his chair as though about to stand up. Each time, she was ready with another question, until eventually he blew out a breath and nodded towards the PCs on the desks. 'Do you know your way around their filing system?'

'Yes. What are you after?'

A pause. 'Would you get me access and just let me look?' The first vestige of light had begun to define his features. He'd taken a key so he could come back at night to search the place. This wasn't the Scott she'd known. What had happened to change him so fundamentally in a few short years? Yet he didn't seem to have changed at all, and if not, what had driven the old Scott Kerridge to these lengths?

'Wait with me to see Pat,' she said. 'We both need answers. Let's tackle her together.'

'You said it was Barbara, not Pat,' he shot back, but he stayed in his chair.

ANNIE WOKE WITH a start. What was it? Scott? But no, he was lying back in his chair, mouth open, snoring gently. The noise came from downstairs. Suppressing a groan—every muscle and joint in her body seemed to have stiffened into a network of pain—Annie stretched out her foot and kicked Scott's ankle. 'Wake up,' she hissed. 'Pat's here.'

As she spoke she glanced out at the morning light and then at the time. It was far too early for Pat, but the huffing and puffing that matched the creaking of the stairs was unmistakable. As Pat pushed open the door Annie watched emotions chase across the woman's face, slightly flushed from the climb, brow wrinkled in annoyance at the early start. When her gaze lit on Annie, her eyes opened wide.

'At bloody last…' she began. 'What the hell's happ-?' She stopped abruptly as she saw Scott. Her gaze swung from one to the other of them as her eyes narrowed.

'Sit down.' Annie pushed the chair forward. 'I'll make coffee. We have to talk.'

'Talk nothing! I need to get Barbara's case files sorted out. At least you've come to your senses, but what's he doing here?'

'Yeah, OK, I'll help you out, but first we need to talk. We need answers. For starters, why am I here?'

As Annie asked the question she was aware of Scott's heightened attention. He wanted to know, too.

'Don't ask me,' said Pat. 'Vince brought you in to help out on that horse job.'

'Horse job?' Scott looked at Annie.

'Oh, that's nothing.' She waved it aside. 'Pat, you know it wasn't Vince. He hates my guts. He's the last person who'd call me in. And anyway, I heard he was at death's door in a hospital somewhere.'

'Yes, he is, but Barbara said...' She stopped and looked pointedly at Scott. 'Maybe we should talk privately.'

'I'm not here in an official capacity, don't worry. Annie can vouch for me.'

'You're working together?' Pat's glare swung round, but before Annie could open her mouth to frame an indignant denial, the phone rang. Pat reached across for it. 'Thompsons,' she barked, then immediately straightened up, her face frozen.

Annie strained to hear the faint gabble of the voice at the other end. Pat pressed the handset to her ear, turned and hurried out. As her footsteps receded down the corridor outside, Scott and Annie exchanged a glance.

Half a minute later, Pat was back. 'Vince isn't in hospital,' she said. 'He discharged himself an hour ago. If I were you, I'd make yourselves scarce.'

It was Pat's tone rather than her words that had Annie on her feet. 'Where's your car?' she asked Scott.

'I got a mate to drop me.'

'Come on. Mine's outside.' To Pat, she said, 'I'll be in touch. Don't ring me. Oh, and I'm not working with him and I can't vouch for what he's doing here. Not yet, anyway.'

They clattered down the stairs, Annie watching the street door, half expecting it to fly open, a gang of Sleeman's henchmen to crowd in. Outside, she glanced up and down the street. A couple of people strode in the direction of the town centre; a few more leant against walls, pulling on their cigarettes, sending clouds of smoke back up towards the office windows.

'Which is yours?' Annie heard puzzlement in Scott's tone. The only vehicles in sight were delivery vans.

'Back road. I cut through the tenfoot,' she rapped out, lapsing easily into Hull slang as she marched towards the alley between the buildings, gritting her teeth against the pain in her leg and hearing Scott's footsteps behind her, keeping pace.

As they made their way along the walled path, he spoke. 'She's shit scared of Sleeman. Did you see her face when she took that call?'

Annie answered him with a half-nod but said nothing. Pat had never been scared of Vince Sleeman in all the years she'd known her. Pat had never been scared of anyone. But Scott was right about that call, only it wasn't Vince Sleeman. The fragment Annie heard had been a woman's voice.

SIX

Scott sat across the table, his forearms resting on the plastic cloth, his hands cupping his mug of tea. Behind the counter at the far side of the room a man polished crockery whilst whistling tunelessly against the background chatter of the Lara King Show on Radio Humberside. They'd missed the breakfast rush and it was too early for lunch. For the time being, this roadside café was their private space. Annie listened to Scott as the smell of coffee rose from her cup, slightly bitter. She breathed it in, wanting the aroma rather than the coffee itself, and felt irritation as Scott's words washed over her. She was content to let him talk it out of his system, justifying his actions more to himself than to her, but now he tried to make out he'd followed her out because she needed his protection. You ran too, she wanted to say. We both wanted out before Sleeman's henchmen turned up. Hench-woman, she corrected herself, remembering the high imperious tone she'd heard barking orders at Pat.

Was it paranoia? Someone had tried to wipe her out less than twenty-four hours ago. Was she overreacting now? She remembered the look on Pat's face; the tone of her voice. Pat who was scared of nothing and no one. No, she wasn't overreacting. This was self-preservation.

Was this the moment to pin Scott to specifics? He was hardly in a position to deny her. Her phone buzzed in her pocket. She glanced down at it beneath the level of the table and clicked the ignore button. Pieternel. A reminder that they hadn't spoken since Monday night; a reminder too of where she was really needed.

'Who knows you're still here,' Scott asked, 'other than me and Pat Thompson?'

'No one,' she said. Pieternel didn't count.

'Will Thompson keep quiet about seeing you?'

She threw him a raised-eyebrows glance as she nodded yes. He knew Pat well enough to have no doubts.

'Then you could just leave. Come back with me like we planned, sort yourself out and then go.'

She gave a brief laugh but said nothing. *Like we planned?* Scott's plan, which she had no intention of going along with, was that they should both return to his house; the home he shared with his wife and twin boys. Annie hadn't asked, but assumed he had married the DC from West Yorkshire, the one with whom Annie had nearly come to blows a few years ago. No, she would drop him close to home and then head back to the racecourse. He was right about one thing though. If she were to go now, then whoever had been after her would assume they'd scared her off. Again she felt her phone vibrate an incoming call. She slipped it far enough out of her pocket to see it wasn't Pieternel calling back, but Jean Greenhough. Again she ignored the call.

Scott gabbled on, saying everything about nothing. If she wanted information from him, she would have to work for it, but did she want to know? This wasn't her mess. Barbara had called her in but hardly made her welcome. Pat seemed to be out of the loop. Pat? She thought about her ex-boss; the relief on her face when she'd arrived to see Annie sitting in the office; the fear that had flooded her face when she took that call. She reached into her pocket and cradled her phone.

Interrupting Scott mid-sentence, she stood up and said, 'Excuse me a moment. I've a call to make.'

Traffic streamed past the front of the café, its position on this main road securing its existence as long as it served food that was halfway decent. Annie leant against the wall, watching the scraps of straw and paper that eddied around the car park in the cool breeze, and clicked Pieternel's number into her phone. 'I couldn't take your call earlier,' she said. 'What's happened?'

'Nothing urgent. I wanted to give you the latest; see what you make of it.' There was laughter in Pieternel's voice. She sounded cheerful.

'Go on.'

'I reported in as planned. Gave them the guy's movements for twenty-four hours. Gave them everything except that he'd clocked us.'

'Were they pleased?'

'Ha! Good question, Annie. They should have been pleased, shouldn't they? And yes, he pretended to be, once he'd got over his shock. See, I had an idea I'd be handing him something he didn't expect, so I did it face to face. I've never seen someone work so hard to swallow back what they really want to say. Then it was all, ah yes, that's good, much as we expected. And he couldn't get rid of me fast enough.'

'What d'you think he really wanted to say?'

'A stream of profanity for sure. He was mad as mad. Did you meet him? No, you didn't. Old-fashioned city-gent type. The sort who doesn't do anger at work. Takes it all out on the family back home. I tell you, if he'd been armed, I'd have needed some nifty footwork to get out in one piece. Whatever it was they wanted, they sure as hell didn't get it from us.'

'So what did they want?'

'Well, I've been thinking about it. I reckon they knew we'd been clocked, maybe even had something to do with that themselves, and they expected a report from whatever wild-goose chase we were meant to be led on.'

Annie felt a prickle of indignation. 'Someone told them to expect a crap job from us.'

'Yup, and they came to the wrong outfit. They'll have to go elsewhere if they want a shoddy job doing. So that's that, whatever it was about. How about you? What's going on?'

'Quite a lot, but I can't go into it all now.'

'That sounds like you're going to stick it out.'

'I'll stay on for now, but if anyone chases me up, say I've come back to London, will you? I'll fill you in later. Hopefully I'll have something concrete to tell you. All I know at the moment is that Pat's in trouble. Bigger trouble than she realizes. I can't just desert her.'

Annie glanced through the window to check on Scott. He hadn't moved, so she made a second call. Jean Greenhough answered on the third ring. 'I don't have long,' Annie said, 'but I noticed you'd called me.'

'Can you get to the racecourse this afternoon,' Jean kept her voice low. Annie could hear shouting in the background. 'Lance Mailers has been in touch. He's coming to see me.'

'Not sure if I'll be able to, but get what you can from him and I'll catch up with you.' The pony camp was no longer high on her priority list, if it figured at all, but she wanted to keep in with Jean, because that out-of-the-way bolthole was going to be useful.

Annie re-entered the café and walked towards Scott. She needed what he knew, and wished she didn't feel so tired. It would be a relief to have an excuse to leave it until later, but she'd been behind the curve since she arrived in Hull and had to catch up.

'Scott, we need to talk. Seriously. About what's going on.'

'With respect Annie, I don't know if I can trust you.'

She smiled. He hadn't said, what the hell are you talking about? That was half the battle won. He stood up. 'Let's get home. I want to get out of these clothes. I'm sure you want to change too. I can probably find you something.'

'I have stuff in the car. Listen, Scott, is this a good idea? Your family…uh…wife?'

'She's at work. The boys are at the childminder.'

'Oh, OK. In that case, let's go.'

HALF AN HOUR later Annie found herself perched uncomfortably on the edge of a hard settee in Scott's living room. The security she'd felt in knowing that Scott's family would be out all day disappeared as soon as they pulled up outside the smart semi. It was exactly as she'd imagined. An estate of neat brick houses on a network of winding roads and cul-de-sacs. She saw curtains twitching as she and Scott walked up the path to the front door. He was oblivious to the scrutiny from neighbours who must be his wife's friends and confidantes. The phones would be going; Scott would get a call within minutes, thought Annie, or his wife might turn up in person.

She wasted no time as he sauntered back into the room from upstairs, now in jeans and T-shirt, towelling his hair. 'I'll tell you everything I know, Scott, but it's precious little. And I need you to be open with me. I'm mixed up in this thing whether I want to be or not. I don't like being the object of someone's target practice.'

She paused to see if he'd speak, but he remained in the doorway between living room and hallway, waiting for her to go on. 'I was called in to work for the Thompsons. The official line is that it's Vince Sleeman who's picking up the tab, but we both know that's garbage. I'm pretty sure it's Barbara, but before I could have it out with her, she was knocked down. And like you told me, it was no accident.'

'Well, I only said…'

'I already knew it wasn't an accident, Scott. You weren't telling me anything new.'

He leant against the doorjamb and looked down at her, as though weighing her words. 'But if you genuinely know nothing…?'

'That's not the point. I've been brought here for a reason and if I can stay out of the way of the people who don't want me to know, then I'm going to learn something very soon. The question is, do you want me to share it when I find out?'

'Of course I do. You'd be a fool not to. You're the one who's stepped into a trap.'

She stared up at him. He'd lost nothing of his ability to annoy her. She ran a couple of ripostes through her head. *If you want something from me, don't call me a fool… I could have your whole career on the line after last night.* Most of all she wanted to shout at him that he might think they had hours to play this out, but his wife could be back like an avenging fury within minutes. 'I'm going to find out one way or another. I'd rather have something from you to get me started or to keep me from asking questions in the wrong places, but I'll get to know, with or without your help. And you know I can open doors that you can't. But you can get at official records that aren't accessible to me. If this were all above board, Scott, you'd have the drop on me, but it isn't. You have to be desperate to have pulled a stunt like last night. If you're still the person I used to know, then we're on the same side. Let's work together on this before anyone else gets hurt. But if you don't want to, fine.'

As she began to get to her feet, she saw that she'd tipped the balance. It hadn't been so hard. He'd been halfway there to start with.

'Sit down, Annie. And we'll have one thing straight from the off. I've not told you anything. I've not even seen you. No one's seen us together.'

'Half the street watched us come in here.'

'I mean no one who matters,' he said impatiently, so she let it drop and waited for him to tell her what was going on.

For a moment, she thought he would come properly into the room and sit down, but he just shifted his stance in the doorway and took a deep breath. 'It was just over three weeks ago,' he began. 'A Sunday night. I went off on a fortnight's leave the next day. Do you remember Rob Greaves? He's been around for years. I can't remember if you knew him.'

Annie narrowed her eyes. 'Vaguely. Is he Sergeant Greaves now?' Jean Greenhough had mentioned a Sergeant Greaves.

'That Sunday night, we were out down Withernsea way when he had a call. Tip-off about something being landed on one of those remote beaches. We were nearest. It wasn't our case or our area. I should have been back home by then, anyway. I'd been taking a statement and some kids had got at the car. I was calling it in when I spotted Rob, so he took me back to town. We'd neither of us have been anywhere near usually.'

'Whereabouts?' she asked instinctively, but knew exactly where he meant.

'That's not important,' he snapped and Annie nodded as though deferring to him.

'What was it, drugs?'

'No, people. Illegals.'

'That's unusual.' When this had been her patch, she'd known of the landing site on a deserted stretch of the coastline. But it had always been drugs, small time, small operation. She'd never heard of people-smuggling other than sophisticated operations through the big ports. 'Did you catch them?' she asked.

'Yeah. We parked at the top and walked down; found two weirdos with a barbecue and a bunch of fairy lights. Hardly the weather for it. There was nothing to see. I thought we'd missed them but Rob spotted something.'

'Didn't you have back up? Coastguard or whatever?'

'It was all taken care of. We were just the skivvies called in because we were close by. I guess they didn't know exactly where the landing would be till the last minute. I don't know if they got the boat. It was all a bit of a rush.'

From the faraway look in his eyes, he relived the events of that evening as he described them to her. She wanted to tell him to come properly into the room, to sit down where she could watch him without twisting round in her seat, but she didn't want to distract his account. As she tried to picture the scene herself, she asked, 'Were you in uniform?'

He nodded. 'We walked down to the water. I didn't see her at first, then she just appeared out of the darkness…out of the sea…wading ashore like I don't know what. Fully clothed, big holdall thing.'

'Had she come from a boat, or waded out to get away from you and come back?'

'God knows. I couldn't see anything out there. You know how it is at night. Bits of lights playing off the surf. She didn't try to run or anything.'

Annie knew that people giving their own account often wanted to be selective in what they told her. She'd learnt to spot the pauses, the tiny gestures that signalled something hidden. Yet listening to Scott it was as though he was the one weighing every word of his story, trying to see what he'd missed first time round. It increased her sense of unease.

'So did you arrest them all?'

'No. We just took the woman back to town. Immigration wanted her. She was a cog in a bigger case. And like I say, I was off on leave the next day.'

'I can't see where I fit in to any of this. Or the Thompsons.'

'It was after I got back, just a week ago. I asked Rob what had happened to the woman. That's when he told me it had gone seriously pear-shaped and there was all hell on. He'd kept our names off the paperwork pretty much. He told me to keep quiet and keep my head down or we'd get caught up in it. Which I did…more or less.'

'More or less?'

'OK, I did a bit of digging, but I didn't like what I found.'

'Which was?'

'Nothing. All we'd done was fish her out of the sea and then hand her straight on. We didn't arrest her or anything. But there was nothing in the record to show we'd been there, that anyone had been there. I couldn't find her arrest, detention, anything.'

'Surely you asked someone.'

He was silent for a while, his expression troubled. 'I know I should have, but I talked to Rob and he said if I didn't leave it, we'd both be right in the shit.'

'Are you saying Rob Greaves is mixed up in it, whatever it is…was?'

'Hell, no. We were just in the wrong place at the wrong time. But something went badly adrift. I kept quiet because at first I thought I might be risking my job. I've a young family to think of now. But then, I thought if Rob and I go together and pick who we talk to, we can have this out properly. I put it to him. He said he'd been thinking on the same lines but he wanted to dig a bit further first. Like he said, no point throwing our careers down the pan. Turned out to be worse than we thought. The girl had been snatched and the word was there'd been a leak from somewhere, that they'd had inside help.'

'Any idea who?'

He laughed without mirth. 'No, but Rob and I had cut corners. I didn't want my name on it when I was due off on leave. It was only chance I was there with him. And he'd cut corners, too, with the paperwork. It might have looked like we'd been covering our tracks. The finger might have been pointed at me and Rob. That's why we've had to keep a lid on it.'

'And you're sure Rob Greaves isn't in on it?'

'No, of course not. Anyway, whoever helped to spring the woman knew more about the whole op than we did. It's a mess, Annie, and it wasn't anything I could risk getting tied up in. Did you hear about that undercover officer in Leicester a few months ago?'

She shook her head, but he went on as though she'd nodded.

'Well, it wasn't him they targeted, it was his family,

and it looks like there's a link. Believe me, when you've young kids, you don't risk them for anything. It's not our case. It was never really on our patch. There's a whole team somewhere on to it. It'd be madness to stir things up, knowing what we know.'

Or what we don't know, thought Annie, who felt she needed an hour alone to mull over this tangled account. 'So why are you chasing it up and where do the Thompsons fit in?'

'Rob came in last Monday to tell me he'd heard Sleeman was involved. He wasn't sure if Sleeman's mob had snatched the woman or were at war with whoever had. He said Sleeman had set the Thompsons on to it and they'd called you in. I knew you wouldn't work on that sort of case if you knew what it was, but I knew Sleeman would have kept you in the dark. That's why I came to warn you.'

'And that's why you looked through Pat's files. But Scott, it can't be Vince Sleeman. He's at death's door, and even if he wasn't, I'm the last person he'd pay good money to.'

'Pat Thompson wouldn't talk to me. Would she talk to you?'

Annie nodded. 'Yes, I'll get to find out what she knows. My worry is that she doesn't know much. I think Barbara's the key to this.'

'She's not going to be talking to anyone for a good while.'

'How bad is she? How do you know, anyway?'

'I checked with the hospital when I heard about it. She'll be in there a while.'

Annie wondered when and how he'd heard, but he looked so glum she couldn't help smiling. 'You always wanted to do it by the book. I guess the book let you down for once.'

Before he could respond, the phone rang. He glanced at the handset on a table in the far corner of the room, then briefly at Annie, before he murmured, 'I'll take it out here,' as he turned and strode out of the room, pulling the door closed behind him.

Annie leapt to her feet and went to press her ear to the door as the phone fell silent. She could hear the murmur of his voice, but couldn't make out the words. Was this the avenging fury? Did it mean she had better take off as fast as she had from Pat's earlier? Scott was fool enough to let them meet up. She stepped quickly across the carpet to the far side of the room, feeling apprehension run a shiver down her back at the thought of Scott catching her. She slipped the handset free of its rest and, praying he wouldn't hear her, she clicked the button to open the line.

It was a man's voice...unfamiliar. It said, '...get back to Lance Mailers.'

As shock prickled her skin, she heard Scott's voice say, 'OK,' and the call was cut.

SEVEN

ANNIE BUMPED HER car on to the grass verge. Up ahead was the rutted lane that led to the back entrance of the racecourse. Her phone beeped a text message. Scott. She glanced at it.

WTH was that about?

Her mouth curved to a cold smile. Well might he ask, she thought, noting that a wife and young family had moderated his language. In the old days it would have been WTF. And what had it been about? Had she acted precipitously in running out on him; simply slipping out of the door when his back was turned? On balance probably yes, but after that snatch of overheard conversation she'd had no intention of taking a risk she would later regret.

Up ahead, the lane that had been all but deserted on every previous visit now bustled with people and vehicles. Trailers bounced behind cars as they swung off the road on to the track. A horsebox followed, silver lettering on its side glinting in the afternoon sun. Even to her untutored eye Annie could see these were not racehorses arriving for a race meeting. This must be the camp Jean had told her about; the camp where drugs would be dealt, the job she'd supposedly been brought all this way to do.

Her gaze lost its focus; her mind on other things. Pat had made some reference to the horsey job that had raised no flicker of recognition in Scott. He thought she was here about some modern-day mermaid. The cases seemed poles apart and yet Scott knew Lance Mailers, the guy who had approached Jean about drugs at the pony camp. The knowledge sat in her head, an uncomfortable anomaly. Who was this guy? What had she missed?

And could she trust Jean? The only sensible answer was no. Her plan had been to leave the car here and cut across the fields on foot, so as to approach unobserved but, with the volume of people going in, she might risk driving closer. Decision not quite made, she reached for the ignition, but didn't turn the key.

She remembered her first reaction on hearing about the Hull job; her certainty that it was a ploy to get her away from London, rather than that anyone needed her help in Hull. Did the events of the last few days support her initial theory or blow it out of the water? Someone was out to trash her and Pieternel's reputation. It wouldn't be the first time. They were a success story now; they'd trodden on a lot of toes. Whatever the truth of it, Vince Sleeman was the absurd cover story. Someone, knowing he was out of action, had used him to explain her presence. Well, Vince was out of hospital now, and the someone, whoever it was, would be quaking in their boots.

A brand new Hyundai four-by-four slid past her, its trailer rattling behind it on up the lane. She picked up her phone and rang the hospital. 'I'm ringing about Mrs Barbara Caldwell…to see how she is…no, not family… just a friend, a colleague…wondering about visiting…'

'No change…no visitors…only family…'

No help to be had there. Annie must work it out

on her own. Jean was expecting Lance Mailers and Annie was determined to listen in on their meeting. She started the car.

KEEPING OUT OF Jean's way wasn't difficult. The ill-at-ease, unconfident woman Annie had come to know was unrecognizable in the granite-faced, megaphone-voiced personification of power and authority who strode back and forth waving her arms, issuing orders, cutting a path through the chaos.

With her car discreetly tucked in amongst the trailers, Annie threaded her way round the edges of the action to the building that housed the tiny bedrooms. At one end, next to the small kitchen, a space was set out as an office. It was the obvious place for Jean to hold a meeting that she wouldn't want all and sundry to know about. Annie's only fear was that the place would be awash with noisy children, but when she rounded the corner, the chaos subsided. The action seemed concentrated on the stable block.

Although clear that no children would be housed here, a rapid sweep of the building showed signs of occupancy, holdalls slung onto beds, clothes hanging over chairs. Annie's room lay undisturbed as far as she could see, but this would not remain the solitary bolt hole it had been up to now.

In one of the rooms, along with a battered suitcase containing clothes, Annie found a clipboard and sheaf of papers labelled with Jean's name. The loose pages documented the attendees at the camp, giving names and addresses, details of teams, an opaque points system. Nothing of interest. But at the bottom of the heap was an appointments diary. Quickly she flicked through the pages and felt a glow of satisfaction as she read:

2.30 p.m. Lance Malers.

She noted the spelling. Malers with no i. Unusual.

Somewhere behind her, a door creaked open on laughing voices. Annie pushed the book back in amongst the papers and shot across the corridor to her own room, where she listened intently. Neither of the voices was Jean's. Two people clattered about in the small kitchen for a few minutes and then left the way they'd come in. Annie watched from her window as they strode away, steaming mugs in their hands. She stepped closer to the window, trying to see where Jean was, unsure now that she'd made the right call. With people coming and going at will, this no longer seemed the best place for a clandestine meeting.

But it was close to 2.30, so she waited and watched and, as the half hour struck, she saw Jean and a young man approach across the grass. He stood a head taller than Jean, the high, brown colour of his skin marking him out in this largely white middle-class world of horsey East Yorkshire. Something in his build made Annie think he was older than he'd told Jean; too old for the schoolfriends story to hold water. He reminded her of someone, a younger guy, but she couldn't catch the memory of who.

She lingered as long as she dared, to impress on her memory the features of the man Scott knew too, then shot back towards the small kitchen and eased herself into a cubbyhole of a broom cupboard. Through the flimsy interior walls she would hear everything they said whether they stayed in the kitchen or moved to the office.

A door banged open upon a sudden cacophony of voices. It took Annie a moment to realize it wasn't just Jean and her companion who had entered. Questions were showered on Jean about who belonged where; about some fracas over a suitcase. Annie listened to Jean's voice and heard the strain of her trying to get rid of these people and their problems; to get them out of the way.

'OK, OK. I'll be across in a minute. Go and check with…'

Jean hustled them out. As she came back Annie heard her say, 'We can't talk here. Go across to my box. Over there. Yellow trim. It's open.'

Hell, thought Annie, what box? Two sets of footsteps retreated and she had yet to hear Lance Malers's voice.

She leapt to the door, opening it a crack to peer through. The man who must be Lance Malers had wandered off to one side, clearly wanting to keep away from the crowds that had immediately engulfed Jean, who tried with flailing hands to shoo them away. Annie risked opening the door wider, her gaze raking the area, frantically looking for a horsebox with a yellow trim.

There! At the far side of the gravelled area hemmed in by dozens of vehicles. Lance Malers hung back waiting for Jean.

Without time to think out a sophisticated plan of action, Annie dived back towards the nearest of the small bedrooms, grabbed the outsize jockey's helmet that lay on the bed and rammed it on. It was a tighter fit than she expected for its outlandish size and felt heavy on her head.

Pausing only to be sure that neither Jean nor Lance Malers was looking her way, she slipped out of the building and sprinted down the side of the gravel track. She could only hope her headgear would be adequate to disguise her as just another in the mêlée of people racing about. Her route took her in a wide arc, round the back of all the vehicles, in amongst the noise of ramps being lowered and lifted, the clatter of ironclad hoofs as ponies were unloaded.

She threaded her way through to the horsebox with the yellow trim, then stopped, momentarily fazed by the number of doors. Where would they go? Surely not the cab where anyone could see them. The enclosed space where they put the horses seemed a good bet, but Annie could find no easy way to get in from the rear other than lowering the huge ramp. Running out of options and not knowing how far behind Jean would be, she climbed up to pull open a side door behind the driver's cab and was surprised to enter a self-contained living area, complete with sink and cooker.

Desperately she spun round looking for somewhere to hide before they arrived. The one cupboard that might have held her was crammed to bursting. As she pushed its door shut again she glanced up. There was some kind of storage space stretching over the driver's cab, footholds were built into a metal pillar to give access.

A voice she recognized as Jean's murmured something from just outside. Annie threw herself at the makeshift ladder and scrambled up. Forgetting the height of the bulky helmet, she heard the crack of it hitting the metal roof. At once she flattened herself into the gap, fighting against a bundle of sleeping bags and bedding that tangled her arms and legs. She kicked them free and tore off the helmet. It had saved her from hurt but that bang on the roof sounded like it had reverberated around the lorry park. Pressing herself to the back of the space, she struggled to hold her breathing steady and quiet as the door clicked open.

'...got someone, right?' The voice, mid-sentence, held a trace of the flattened vowels of a Hull accent.

'I'm doing what I need to do.' Jean's voice was firm with a hint of admonition, but at the same time she sounded flustered.

'Yeah, but you got them in like I said?'

'I told you I'm taking it seriously, but I spoke to a Sergeant Greaves and he said—'

'What would he know? He's a copper. I told you who you need working on this.'

At first suspicious of what the exchange said about Jean's role, Annie felt reassurance as the conversation continued. Lance Malers wanted Jean to spell out what she was doing about his drugs tip off. He brushed aside Sergeant Greaves but didn't seem bothered that Jean had involved the police.

Jean was careful in her responses, acknowledging her debt for the warning, but not trusting him with information he seemed too keen to know.

Lance Malers gave in with a sigh that was half irritation, half amusement. 'Well, I hope you're doing the right thing here. But there's something you need to pass on. Tell them to look out for a horsebox that ain't.'

'What do you mean?'

'I mean a box that ought to be for horses, but ain't. All stars and glitter. A proper professional job, but no horses.'

'Are you saying that's where the drugs'll be? Have you seen it today? Is it here?'

'Nah, let's hope it ain't coming here. She's gonna have to go out and find it. But that's the one.'

'But I don't follow...' Jean's voice reflected the puzzlement that Annie felt.

'You don't need to. Just make sure you take this seriously. I don't want to see any kid come to harm.'

Annie listened as the conversation wound down. In

her head, she replayed Lance Malers saying 'she': *She's gonna have to go out and find it*, over the knowledge that Jean had been careful not to say who was working on the information she'd been given. He didn't seem to have noticed his slip, nor had Jean picked up on it, but Annie turned it over in her mind. It could be innocent, no more than a slip of the tongue, or maybe Jean had mentioned her in a previous meeting with Lance, but Annie didn't think so. Lance Malers knew who she was and that she was working for Jean.

But how could he know that?

Below her, the conversation came to a close. The lorry swayed beneath Annie as Jean and Lance climbed out and slammed the door closed. Annie twisted in her narrow bunk and peered through the tiny window high above the driver's cab. Jean strode across the uneven surface, already shouting out to someone. Lance Malers, hands in pockets, head held high, marched off at a tangent.

It was the bouncy confidence of his stride that jolted Annie's memory. Of course he reminded her of someone…of someone younger. He reminded her of himself seven years ago. She'd never met him properly, but she knew him. The recollection went right back to her first six-week stint working for Pat. His name wasn't Lance. It was… She closed her eyes and called the memory back… Carl. His name was Carl.

She thought of the words in Jean's appointments diary. Lance Malers.

And with an exasperated slap of her hand to her head, she plucked out the name Carl and saw what was left. Thoughts spun in her head. Scott knew Lance Malers, but Lance Malers didn't exist.

Vince Sleeman, out of commission, had no idea what

was going on, but Lance Malers who didn't exist knew
that she, Annie, was here working for Jean Greenhough.
And Lance Malers was Vince Sleeman's nephew, Carl.

EIGHT

LATE AFTERNOON FOUND Annie back in the building that housed Pat and Barbara's cramped office. As she climbed the stairs she could hear Pat talking to a client on the phone and slipped inside, giving Pat a nod. Pat shot her a glare, began to mouth something at her and for a moment juggled her conversation on the phone with her urge to berate Annie, before turning her attention to cutting short the former and putting down the phone.

'What's going on? Where the hell do you keep disappearing to? I've told people you've upped sticks. Are you working for me or not?'

Annie filled Pat in on the events of the day, glossing over Scott's involvement and watching closely as she mentioned Vince's nephew. 'Did you know he goes by Lance Malers these days?'

'Yeah, Vince made him do that years ago. Made him drop out of sight for a while and he came back reborn, as it were.'

'Does he toe the line these days, then? He was all out for himself seven years ago the way I remember it.'

Pat shrugged. 'Probably. More or less.'

Annie held back from voicing her theory of Barbara and Carl working against Vince. It wasn't that she thought Pat might be on the other side, but that she'd dismiss it as ludicrous and spill the beans somewhere she shouldn't. She pushed Pat for answers and discovered that yes, Carl Sleeman had been one of the people to enquire after her whereabouts.

'I'd like to get to talk to him. Do you have an address?'

'Sure, and a number. I'll ring him if you want.'

'No, I'd rather go and see him face to face.'

'Your call. He's not dealing drugs again, is he?'

'I don't think so. It might be something bigger. I think he might want my help.'

DAYLIGHT HAD BEGUN to fade as Annie made her way down a street that had once been familiar stamping ground. She headed for the pub that had been her favourite place to relax after a hard day; somewhere to gather her thoughts with the taste of good beer in her mouth. She wasn't sure it would still be there.

The route took her through an industrial landscape of high red brick walls, with occasional gaps where stout lattice fencing crowned with rolls of barbed wire showed empty sites and ramshackle sheds. A heap of classic car bodies lay abandoned in a corner plot. A huge derelict building towered over its surroundings, showing how prosperous an area this had once been. It wasn't so far from here that she had had to dive out of the way of that car, but her guard was up. She wouldn't be followed again without being aware of it. And with any luck they, whoever they were, thought she was hundreds of miles away.

At this time of night the area was quiet and deserted and it was with a small glow of satisfaction that she saw the unassuming outer façade as she rounded the corner; the word Whalebone in outsize letters above the street.

She pushed the door open onto lights and laughter,

and sniffed appreciatively at the tang of hops in the air. The pub still brewed its own beer.

A mini queue had formed, but there was no one behind the bar. Annie assumed a change of barrel and sat down to wait, allowing her mind to rerun the events of the afternoon. After leaving the lorry, she had chased after Lance Malers/Carl Sleeman and seen him disappear over a rise. By the time she'd caught up, he was gone, but a trail of dust and the receding sound of a car engine marked his path. She had noted this patch of scrubland, apparently accessible without using any of the marked entrances.

After returning the borrowed helmet she had waited in the low building. It was close on two hours before Jean, sweat-streaked and blowing out a sigh, pushed her way through the door and made for the kitchen. Annie had followed and they'd talked while Jean boiled the kettle and threw sandwiches together.

Annie allowed herself to be told about Lance Malers's appearance and strange message, then probed to see what Jean had made of it.

'It's as though he knows I'm on the case,' Annie tried at one point, but wasn't surprised at Jean's blank shrug. Carl Sleeman had had his information from Pat, who had thought nothing of his enquiries, given it was supposedly Vince who'd brought her in on this job.

But Barbara was in on something that Pat wasn't. And there was Scott. She'd heard him on the phone. He'd said the name: Lance Malers. Did he know it was really Carl Sleeman? How could he not, but then why refer to him by a pseudonym? Whom had he been talking to?

She shook the puzzle out of her head and cast her mind back to Jean, to the way she'd reacted. Her obvious mistrust of Carl Sleeman. *I couldn't make head nor tail of that stuff about a horsebox*, she'd said. *It doesn't make any sense to me.*

Nor did it to Annie, but she'd assured Jean she would follow up whatever she could.

She tried to weigh the options that lay before her. She couldn't chase after a horsebox when she knew nothing about it except that it wouldn't be at the race-course. Scott was clearly holding out on her but she was wary of falling into a trap. Scott always went by the book. It made her uneasy to see him trying to do things off record.

Maybe, above everything, she needed to figure out who was working with whom.

Seeing that the barman was back at his station, Annie approached the bar, her eyes scanning the blackboard, her mouth curving to a smile at the sight of some old favourites.

'You used to come in years ago, didn't you?' the barman greeted her. 'No, don't tell me…' He narrowed his eyes for a moment, then plucked a pint glass from the shelf. 'You used to chop and change, but…pint of Neck Oil. Am I right?'

Annie nodded with a laugh. It felt comfortable to be back where she was known but no one pushed for more than she was prepared to tell.

As she returned to her seat with her beer, she wondered if Carl Sleeman was really working with Barbara behind Vince's and Pat's backs. It was still her preferred theory and made some kind of sense with the events of the past of few days. If she was right, there was no London link, which was reassuring. Some kind of anti-Vince faction? With Vince down, was Barbara planning a coup? If so, she had more gumption than Annie had ever credited her with. When would she be in a position to talk? Would she confide in Annie? Well, why the hell not, she thought crossly, having brought her all this way and dropped her into the middle of it.

Her mind went back to the time when Pat and Barbara first set up on their own, after Vince had levered their father's firm from under them. She remembered the anger and resentment that had burnt bright, that she thought would give the three of them the drive to create a vibrant business of their own. She'd seen herself becoming a partner, but it had all evaporated in the face of the sisters' lethargy and laziness. They bickered with each other, while Vince was astute enough to keep them afloat with bits of jobs so that they became dependent on him, the more so after Annie left. But she remembered how they'd been, particularly Barbara, who had been company secretary when her father was alive, pushed aside to be a nonentity in a business going nowhere. Maybe at last the worm had turned and Barbara had decided to fight back.

If Annie stayed, she would be working with Barbara and Carl Sleeman—a lazy cow whose competence she'd never rated and a kid whose arrogance had almost undermined his uncle's business several years ago.

And she would be working against Vince Sleeman, a man she'd never liked but for whom she had learned to have a healthy respect. When she'd been too young and inexperienced to know better, she'd urged the sisters to go head to head with Sleeman, to get back what was rightfully theirs to avenge the memory of their father. But she'd seen her error as she'd come to know more about him. Vince wasn't a man to mess with. You circumvented Vince, you didn't push him aside.

Annie sighed as she gazed into the rich depths of her

beer. Where had Barbara of all people found the courage to take this stand? And surely even Barbara wouldn't have set off on this course without something behind her, something concrete with which to fight Vince.

Draining her beer, she stood up. She would follow the trail Barbara had laid for her. The decision came easily; the question was how. She couldn't trust Scott but needed a way to get information from him. She would trust Jean as far as she needed to, but Jean knew nothing. With Barbara out of commission, a face to face with Carl Sleeman was inevitable.

She didn't see him as the type to spend his evenings in, but if she found him at home, she intended asking some pointed questions.

And if he were out?

Annie disapproved the illegitimate means so readily used by others in her profession. It was no way to build respect or better standing in public perception, indeed phone and computer hacking had led to high profile gaol sentences for a handful of her peers, but her pursuit of Carl Sleeman had nothing to do with any legitimate case, and if he were out, she would not miss the opportunity to find answers by whatever means were at hand.

ANNIE LET HER gaze run over Carl Sleeman's house as she drove past. An upmarket semi, tall gateposts standing like sentries at the bottom of a substantial drive. Family money had bought this, not anything he had earned for himself. A showy alarm system winked its single red eye at her. She smiled as she pulled up a couple of doors down. Carl Sleeman had always liked a good show. It was day-to-day detail that bored him. There'd be gaps aplenty in his defences.

She walked purposefully, but without hurry, her head

down as she fiddled with her phone, her face obscured from the gaze of any nosy neighbours who might be peering through their curtains. Shadow dappled the pavement where the glow from the streetlights filtered through the trees that lined the road. Outside Carl Sleeman's house, a gash in the kerb bled crushed concrete into the road. Annie marched in between the imposing gateposts, to all the world an expected visitor. Her feet felt the change from paving slabs to smooth, solid tarmac; a quality job to go with the conservatism of the area, except that the pristine surface was cracked down one side, the edge shattered to blend with the soil. Someone, probably Carl himself, had driven in before the tarmac was set.

A path curved round to a stout front door beneath the winking eye of the alarm system. Access to the back was obscured by a high brick wall that held a panelled door. Annie avoided the main pathway and marched towards the wall. She breathed out a sigh of relief as the door clicked open. The area was too exposed to start picking locks or scrambling over high obstacles.

The high wall blocked out the glow from the streetlights and she stepped through into darkness, pulling on a pair of thin, dark gloves as the door closed behind her and her feet told her they trod on wooden decking this side.

Now hidden from prying eyes, she paused to let herself adjust to the gloom, before easing forward, edging her way, alert for hidden objects.

It was as she felt her way round the corner to the back of the house that she heard the whisper of a click high above her and light blazed, bathing her in brightness.

Her heart thudded as she froze, her eyes blinking

in the sudden glare. Security lights. She should have anticipated that.

A quick glance all around showed no sign of life. No lights flashed on inside Carl's house or in the house next door. She shielded her eyes as she strode towards a rickety conservatory that guarded the back entrance. Its door was locked, but the plain glass panel showed the key in the other side. Christa Andrew would have taped a corner of the pane to muffle the sound of breaking glass and had her hand through, which was why, thought Annie as she extracted a pair of thin tweezers from her pocket, they should avoid Christa like the plague. An old-style lock like this one never warranted criminal damage, and confirmed the carelessness she had assumed in Carl Sleeman.

It was the work of seconds to grasp the end of the key through the lock. It turned smoothly and the door swung open with no protest.

Annie stepped inside and across to the back door proper. Her hand was on the handle, just as the security light blinked out, leaving her in total darkness. She cursed under her breath as her eyes struggled to adjust back to the gloom. She felt the door give way.

Too easy! She leapt back and sideways expecting an attack out of the darkness inside. But everything remained still. After a moment, she reached out again and pushed the door, feeling it give under the pressure.

Surely this meant he was in. Even the Carl Sleeman she'd built in her mind wasn't as careless as this. She felt along the wall for a light switch and clicked it on, bracing herself for a shout of protest from within the house. A well-appointed but slightly old-fashioned kitchen met her eye. A range cooker gleamed, showroom new, its surface piled high with empty pizza boxes.

Room by room, she made her way through the house. She had no feel for hidden watchers, sensed no tension from anyone hiding from her, but she wouldn't lower her guard until she'd covered every floor. A first floor bedroom was kitted out as an office; the locks on the filing cabinet putting the house security to shame. She clocked it as her first port of call once sure she was alone. It was not until she was on the top floor in a room whose walls sloped with the curve of the roof that she saw any sign of life. A dim glow showed through the cracks of a door to a second attic and when she approached, she saw stout padlocks holding the door shut. Maybe this and not the office space was the real centre of operations in this house.

She crept closer, keeping to the edges of the room in case someone was the other side peering out through one of the cracks in the wood. When close enough, she crouched down and put her eye to the keyhole. Almost at once she was on her feet, blowing out an exasperated sigh. The other side of the door was Carl Sleeman's personal cannabis farm; the enterprise that would probably be the undoing of the business he ran for his uncle from the office a floor down.

Now sure she was alone in the house, she went quickly down to the office and looked around. A huge plasma screen dominated one wall and a stack of games consoles lay at its feet. No difficulty in guessing how Carl spent his time in here. She turned to the filing cabinet. It was modern, locked and secure. Without trying she knew it wouldn't succumb to any of the tools she carried. She would need the key. Given Carl Sleeman's track record, it was worth a search.

On a wall at an angle to the huge plasma screen was a bank of six smaller screens. Carl had his own security cameras by the look of it. But he couldn't lock his back door. Annie shook her head as she searched the desk, the cupboards, the nooks and crannies where people often kept their spare keys. Her search uncovered the CCTV console but no key, so she turned on the small screens and sat at Carl's desk to see what he valued enough to record.

Two of the small screens flickered to life. One of these was trained on the locked door in the attic. Another showed the driveway. She would keep half an eye on that as she worked.

Annie had seen no camera in the attic and tried to judge, from the angle, where it was hidden. She frowned as she worked the console, unsure whether these cameras ran continuously or only when the console was on. Playing the footage back showed the one in the attic to be triggered by movement sensors; she watched herself approach the door and lean down towards the keyhole. Would it be possible to erase that stretch? Carl Sleeman wouldn't notice it was missing. He didn't do detail.

Then another screen lit up, showing her own head bowed over the console. Instinctively she looked up, giving the camera her full face, though she couldn't see where it was hidden. If she were to remove all trace of her visit, she'd have to erase that footage, too. She gave a mental shrug. If it had to remain here as a record, so be it. What would he do, after all?

She found the manual switches for the dark screens, which crackled to life, one remaining black, the others playing static snowstorms. One of them at least must watch the back of the house, but Carl hadn't bothered to readjust them or clear the lenses when they'd become obscured. His security blind spot was truly blind.

Turning back to the ones that worked and starting

with the office camera, she ran the images back. Carl, sometimes alone, sometimes with a mate, marched staccato in and out of the office fairly regularly, mostly playing games on one of the many consoles, but occasionally heading for the desk where she sat now. He checked the cameras, but briefly and lazily. He might miss her visit, but if he didn't, she'd live with it. She hoped to see him approach the cabinet, pull a key from some cranny she hadn't discovered, but in a high-speed fly-through of days of footage, he never once went near.

She looked again at the filing cabinet, modern, four-square and secure. Carl was here to guard whatever was in there, but maybe he had no access to it. It made sense. She wouldn't trust Carl with secrets that warranted such a secure berth. With sudden misgiving, she wondered about the camera images. Were they being transmitted somewhere? Was someone watching her right now in real time?

A fingertip search of the console reassured her. No sign of any connection or transmitter. These cameras were Carl's baby. If anyone else had routine sight of the footage, they'd have repaired the dodgy ones and cleared the lenses.

She turned next to the driveway camera which should show her who came to visit. This camera looked inwards and must be set on one of the tall gateposts.

Again she watched the high-speed swoop back over the hours and days, and saw the arrival and departure of both Carl and his games-playing friends. Her attention strayed to the plaster moulding high on the wall. In her peripheral vision one of the screens showed her face staring directly out, yet she could see no trace of a lens up there. If she were to chuck some dirt about up there she could probably obscure that lens too. But that wouldn't erase the images already recorded and she couldn't see how to do that without wrecking the whole console.

A movement from the other screen diverted her. She reached out to slow the playback. Carl was there in his own drive. How long ago? A few weeks, she estimated. The images weren't labelled but she'd gone back a long way on this one whilst mulling over the possibility of hidden keys.

She leant forward to watch closely. Carl was upset, angry. She hadn't seen him like that before; had thought of him as too laid back to do real anger.

She slowed the playback to real time, watching as the top of a lorry edged into view backwards. Then Carl was there, waving his arms and shouting, all in mime. A small woman appeared, maybe from the cab of the lorry that was out of shot. Carl's demeanour changed as though she was so small and slight he couldn't hold onto his anger. His gestures and expressions became more conciliatory, but still firm. Whatever had upset him was still upsetting him. He pointed at the lorry, his mouth working overtime as the tempo of his gestures rose again. The woman's back was all Annie could see, but it was clear that Carl fell silent every time she spoke. He seemed to accord her respect, but she couldn't dampen the embers of his anger and they flared alight time and again.

Eventually, the woman waved her hands in apparent surrender. Carl seemed to slump as though exhausted by victory. The next move was so quick that it jerked Annie upright in her chair. The tiny mouse of a woman darted forward and dealt a blow from which Carl reeled back, surely just in shock; the woman was too slight to knock a matchstick aside. Annie stared at the image of Carl clutching his hand to his face.

A shudder ran down her spine. It had been madness to come here, to the heart of Vince Sleeman's operation. She'd been lulled by the laid-back persona Carl turned to the world, but he was a thug like his uncle. And Vince might be down but he was far from out. She had Carl's number. She'd ring him and arrange a meeting somewhere public.

Her ear attuned to any sound that might signal Carl's return, she reached for the console one last time, needing to know what it was that had disturbed her so suddenly. Who was the tiny woman? As the images reran, Annie stared closely. The woman walked into shot, her back to the camera. The disjointed exchange with Carl; the abrupt attack. And the woman backed off. Three strides and she was gone, never once turning to give the camera even a part view of her face. Whoever she was, she knew the camera was behind her.

Annie hesitated as she studied Carl's reaction. Why so extreme? He couldn't really be hurt. His hand still to his cheek, he watched sullenly as the lorry eased out of shot, leaving his driveway. As he turned, he glanced down and kicked something away, then spun back and pointed, shouting again in another burst of anger. Annie froze the picture and took a closer look. There was the source of the damage to the neat drive. It wasn't that the tarmac was newly laid; it was that the vehicle had been too heavy and crushed the edges.

Had she just wasted twenty minutes over a strip of crushed tarmac? Was that what had riled Carl Sleeman to white heat? She ran her hands over the console, closing it down. Her gaze darted about the room. She'd left a clear record of her presence that she didn't know how to erase, but she had hopes Carl's lack of attention to detail might allow her to get away with it.

As she retraced her steps back down the stairs and outside, using the thin tweezers to relock the garden door, the images she'd watched played in her head. Carl turning and glancing down; kicking out at the debris as part of his sulk. He didn't care about the damage. It was an afterthought that made him spin round to shout about it.

She remembered the solid feel of the surface under her feet as she'd marched up the driveway; remembered, too, the crushed kerb that she'd noted only incidentally. She would check as she left, but memory told her it matched the line of damage up the drive. That lorry was too heavy for a residential road. Even packed with the sturdiest of Jean Greenhough's horses, it wouldn't be heavy enough to inflict that level of devastation. Not much had been visible to the camera, not enough to say for certain what face the vehicle presented to the world, but Annie would lay bets it had arrived in the livery of a horse box.

NINE

BACK AT THE OFFICE, Annie pushed the chairs together into a makeshift bed. In the old days, this had been a regular occurrence. She hadn't expected to be doing it again, but the racecourse was packed with children and their adult guardians. If she'd wanted more privacy, Jean had told her, she could use an overflow room. And she'd shown Annie into a tiny corridor divided into two miniature compartments and a cubbyhole that housed a kettle. 'The overcrowding has to be terminal before anyone'll use these,' Jean had said. 'The lads would rather sleep in the lorries. You have to trek right round to get at the kitchen and the bathroom.' But Jean hadn't considered her creeping back in the small hours. She'd have to traipse through the centre of the children's camp to reach the overflow rooms.

She had her overnight bag with her and had tucked the car out of sight in an adjacent street. Easing the window open allowed in a cool breeze, but she didn't bother with lights. The gloom was restful. Glancing across towards Pat's desk, she remembered the scrap of conversation she'd overheard before Pat marched out of the office. A woman's voice at the other end of the phone. The fear on Pat's face. She'd assumed it was the caller who'd had that effect on Pat, but maybe it had been the message. The news that Vince was out of hospital. And was it fanciful to make a match with the alarm on Carl

Sleeman's face when that tiny slip of a woman had hit out at him? Was it the same woman?

Annie had no idea what had been going on these past few years. But if she was right in what she'd surmised, then something had triggered a seismic change. Barbara working with Vince Sleeman's nephew…and desperate enough to connive at bringing Annie back to work against Vince. She couldn't fit the pieces together. Without being able to talk to Barbara, she didn't know enough. As for Carl, she wouldn't risk another close encounter on her own. She'd been seduced into thinking he was no threat by the memory of the lad she'd come across years ago, but he was Vince Sleeman's nephew, and should be treated as equally dangerous. Yet where else could she go? Carl Sleeman might already have sussed that she'd been in his house. He might be on his way to find her, so she should get in first. She took out her phone, scrolled through to find the numbers Pat had given her, and clicked out a text.

Carl, let's meet and talk through the case. Annie.

She gave him a couple of minutes but there was no immediate response so she turned off her phone and settled down in the chair.

A DOOR SLAMMED, bringing Annie abruptly out of a deep sleep. She sat up, momentarily blinded by a shaft of early morning sun. Shading her eyes, she swivelled sideways off the makeshift bed as she listened. Voices from downstairs. Not Pat. Too early for Pat. It was the downstairs office opening for business. She waited long enough to be sure no one was on their way upstairs then pulled her phone towards her, turned it on and watched for incoming messages. Nothing from Carl Sleeman. Nothing from anyone. She clicked in Pieternel's number as she stretched and yawned. Pieternel was upbeat. 'Everything's fine. Christa's behaving now the job's all but finished.'

Annie decided it was simpler to take this at face value and save probing questions for later. After a sketchy wash in the tiny kitchen, she used Pat's PC to check her emails, then studied Google maps of the area close to the racecourse to find the spot where Carl Sleeman had parked his car. The satellite view showed a rough track leading from a narrow lane. She traced the line of it back to the main road. Still too early to ring Pat and hurry her along so she reached across to Pat's heap of magazines and began to flick through. At five to nine her phone beeped an incoming text. Annie smiled. Carl Sleeman.

No need. Case wrapped up. Go back to London. Contract terminated as of now.

Cradling the phone, she ran her gaze over the words. Case wrapped up? She'd lay bets Jean wouldn't think so. Carl had been one of the people keen to have her around. Now he too wanted her gone. Contract terminated said no more money, but he couldn't take back the advance payment, which meant she was free to stick around for a while longer if she chose to. She thought of the exchange between him and Jean. He'd been quite unsubtle then in his need to know that she was on the case and pursuing it to his agenda.

The office phone rang. 'Annie.' Jean's voice sounded relaxed and upbeat. 'So glad to catch you personally. I rang to say thank you. Thank you so much. I've just heard about the lad who's been arrested. I wanted you to know that no one got near the camp with any drugs. All the kids are fine. We can get on with things properly now. It's such a relief.'

'Oh…yes, good. Uh…who told you? When did you hear this?'

'That lad Lance called up. He told me you'd been in touch.'

Annie resisted the urge to question Jean further. She didn't trust the office phone and anyway, Jean knew nothing; had never known anything. They exchanged pleasantries and Annie put down the phone with mixed emotions. Carl had set up the situation at the pony camp and now he'd resolved it. End of story. Or was it? Loose ends flapped all around her. There'd been an arrest, had there? She could get Pat to check on that. As she formed the thought the downstairs door slammed and footsteps sounded on the stairs. Recognizing Pat's heavy tread, Annie moved towards the kettle and clicked it on.

'Hi. Coffee?' she greeted her.

'You been here all night? I thought Vince had arranged a hotel.'

'Uh… I was late getting finished. I need you to do something. It's about the case.'

'No point. The case is closed. You're off the books.'

Annie looked over to where Pat had wedged herself behind the desk and pulled her keyboard towards her. 'Vince has terminated your contract. Pity really, I could have done with you a bit longer.'

'When did you speak to Vince?'

'Oh, I haven't spoken to him in months. He just gives out orders from his sickbed.'

'Who did you speak to?'

'Carl… Lance. He's the trusted lieutenant these days. Anyway, the woman's called it off. They've sorted it themselves, whatever it was.'

Annie tipped boiling water into the cups. So someone had told Jean there'd been an arrest, and Carl had told Pat that Jean had called it off. She handed Pat her coffee. 'How's Barbara? Any change?' What she really wanted to ask was: how soon will she be able to answer questions?

Pat gave a shrug and glanced up to meet Annie's eye. 'She's pulling through much faster than they expected. It looks like she'll make a full recovery, but too early to be sure.'

Pat's tone more than her words pulled Annie up. She'd forgotten the reality as she'd pursued her own theories. Barbara was Pat's sister; the sister she'd worked with for years. Despite the constant bickering, they must care for each other. Pat must be horribly worried as she struggled to keep the business afloat whilst Barbara hovered between life and death. 'I can stay on a bit longer,' she blurted out. 'They paid up front.'

'Thanks, kid.' Pat gave her a lacklustre smile. 'But I don't know if it's worth it. With Babs as she is and Vince about to peg out, I ought to think about winding the business up.'

'No, don't say that. This isn't the time to make those sorts of decisions. I'll stay on as long as I can. The pony camp thing's off our backs now so I won't have to be rushing out there. I can stay and take over Barbara's stuff here.' Pat gave a half shrug. 'I need you to organize a meeting with Carl Sleeman,' Annie rushed on. 'I've got to find out what's really going on. That job was a blind just to get me on board because I did a couple of jobs with kids and ponies in the old days. Carl's up to something and we need to find out what. So can you arrange something but don't say I'll be there?'

Pat's eyebrows rose in surprise, then she gave a wintry smile. 'The same old Annie after all, wanting every last detail on everything. Well, OK, I need to see him anyway. If things don't turn a corner, the business'll wind itself up.'

Annie listened to Pat's side of the call. 'I need to meet. Babs might be out for the long term and now Vince has sent Annie packing…no, I'm not trailing all that way…oh, all right…a bite to eat? Café in North Point, OK? What? Yes, Annie's gone. Yes, it's for definite.' Pat turned to her as she ended the call. 'What have you done to rattle his cage? He wanted to be extra sure you weren't turning up again. He won't be best pleased to see you.'

'I can't help that. I need some answers. Let's go.' As she drove them across town, Annie found herself glancing sideways at Pat. She wanted to come clean about her suspicions, to tell Pat everything, but a voice in her head urged caution. Wait until there was more time. On the other hand, maybe she should do it now before they met Carl, so Pat would understand the questions she was going to ask. Her phone rang. She glanced at the handset—Jean—and clicked it off. 'Pat, listen, before we get there…'

The jingle of Pat's phone interrupted her. Pat put the handset to her ear and immediately jerked it away again. 'Bloody hell! Calm down. I can't make out a word you're…what…yes, hang on. She's driving. I'll put you on speaker phone.'

'Annie! Annie, are you there?' Jean's voice shrieked into the air.

'Yes, I can hear you. What is it?'

'Drugs! The kids! They're dying…' Jean's voice caught as she struggled to get the words out. 'I thought it'd be a few of them swapping pills. It's all of them. Oh my God! Annie, you've got to come out here.'

Annie pulled the car to a stop at the side of the road.

She and Pat exchanged bewildered glances. Behind Jean's voice they could hear screams, sobs, a whine of sirens and the plaintive wail of a child's voice crying, 'Help me. Someone help me…'

TEN

FOR A MOMENT, Annie floundered as she struggled to pull her thoughts to a coherent focus. She felt Pat's worried gaze; Jean's expectation of help. *Why me?* she wanted to ask. *Who am I to know what to do?* Instead, she fired questions at Jean. 'The emergency services are there, yes? Ambulance...police?'

Jean's words tripped over themselves as she answered. 'Yes, they're sending for more...there's too many...they're treating them out in the open. I hadn't thought about the police... I rang you...what shall I do? Shall I ring now?'

'No, leave it. One of the ambulance crews will have called them. Listen Jean, has anyone left the site in a horse box since it happened?'

'A box? Why would they? We've all been helping the kids.'

'Think, Jean. It's important. Have any of the boxes gone?'

'No, they can't have. They'd have to come past here. No, definitely not.'

'Keep watch. If anyone takes a box out, get every detail you can. I'm on my way.'

Perturbed, Annie turned to Pat. Again the hidden hand hovered behind the scenes, orchestrating her every move. 'I don't know what's going on, but this isn't co-incidence. I'm called off the case, then this happens. I'll drop you at North Point. Go ahead with the meeting. Don't tell Carl I'm still around.' Annie paused, realizing she was barking orders at Pat. But Pat didn't seem to mind, so she went on, 'Arrange to meet later. I'll come with you then. It'd be useful if we have time to talk first. There's some stuff I need to run past you.'

After she'd left Pat at the shopping centre Annie headed out of Hull and towards the racecourse. She found the lane she'd seen on the map earlier, and drove up, looking for the track. With misgivings she turned the car off the tarmac and on to the rutted pathway. It was well worn but the tyre tracks were from motorbikes and four-by-fours, not ordinary cars. She inched up towards the dusty patch where there was space to park, feeling some apprehension that she'd find a horse box already there, but knowing that was absurd. A conventional box couldn't get up here, never mind the heavyweight monster she'd seen in Carl's drive. Once out of the car she crept forward to peer over the rise and down at the lorry park. One by one, she set her sights on the vehicles, dismissing the cars and small trailers, but scrutinizing every box and lorry. Did it match the shape she'd seen? None of them seemed big enough, but then she'd only seen a fraction of it. It was hard to judge. When satisfied there was nothing useful to be seen from this vantage point she scrambled down the bank and went to look for Jean.

As she rounded the corner from the lorry park Annie saw half a dozen people in a cluster, dishevelled and sweat-streaked. She recognized Jean and a couple of the women she'd seen yesterday. A man and a woman clung on each other's arms, whilst a tall blond man drooped miserably beside them. As she watched, a brown pony clattered up the track towards them, saddle askew, reins trailing. The tall man stepped towards it and reached out but it sidestepped and put on a burst of speed to avoid him. The rest of them glanced up as it galloped past, then turned away. The hairs stood up at the back of Annie's neck. All she knew about ponies came from the couple of cases she'd worked on for Pat and Barbara years ago, but one thing she'd learnt was that people like Jean never shrugged and ignored a loose pony. She found herself shouting and flapping her hands to head it off. Her sudden movement brought the group to life. They jerked into action and cornered the animal, which gave up the fight as soon as it felt a hand at its neck.

'Thank God you're here, Annie,' said Jean, her voice weary, all hysteria gone. 'Come on,' she said to her companions. 'We mustn't leave the job half done. We've two ponies unaccounted for.'

'We'll find them,' said the blond man. 'You go and get things sorted out.'

'Can we talk somewhere?' said Annie. 'Get a coffee maybe? Is it safe?'

Jean nodded and they walked together towards the small kitchen where they'd spoken only the day before. Annie stationed herself by the window where she could see any movement from the lorry park, but she didn't expect anything. It was too late.

'It couldn't have been worse timed,' Jean began. 'The kids were bringing their ponies out. The first group was in the far paddock, just getting warmed up. It was a lad called Lee who started giggling. I went over. We've a new instructor. I thought he was playing her up. By the time I got there he was babbling and shrieking with laughter, shouting out about...well, I won't name names, but about his friend's father. It's semi common knowledge the man's having an affair with a teacher at the school but there was little Lee shouting out the details for everyone to hear.'

Annie could see that Jean was operating from another planet, shocked by the morning's events into a semblance of calm. She eased Jean aside and reached for the kettle herself. Opening the cupboard, she took out a fresh jar of coffee and checked its seal before opening it and preparing two cups.

'I was set to give him a real dressing down,' Jean was saying, 'but before I reached him I could see the pony getting agitated. Lee was…he was twitching around in the saddle, babbling nonsense. Then he just sort of threw himself backwards, banged on to the pony's rump and fell to the ground. The pony took off like a cork from a bottle, straight through the open gate. Another pony got loose in the mêlée and two more kids fell off.

'I shouted for people. To get the ponies caught… and for a first-aider. I rushed over to Lee. He was having some kind of fit, frothing at the mouth, eyes rolling. We were trying to clear things…the instructor, the new one…we were trying to push the jump stand out of the way. And there was Catherine…right beside me. She's one of the older ones, a sensible girl. I told her, "Go and call an ambulance. Get Lee's mum". But she… she just stood there…just looking at him. It was like… I can't describe it…like she was paralysed by shock. I shouted at her to get going. She burst into tears. She was saying, "It was me. It was us. We did it." Over and over.' Jean pulled in a breath and took the coffee cup that Annie offered.

'Take your time,' Annie said, glancing out through the window where the parked vehicles sat in an eerie silence.

Jean took a gulp of coffee, flinched at the heat of it,

and went on, 'I was shouting over for one of the girls to get an ambulance. Shouting at Catherine to tell me what they'd done to Lee. Next thing, she's gabbling about sweets and crisps. I realized it was about a theft from the shop back at the stables. Two years ago. She was confessing to it…sobbing…tears streaming. Lee might have been dying right beside us…and she was hysterical over something that happened two years ago. I… I almost went to slap her, but… But then she starting shrieking and babbling, and she was on the ground jerking around just like Lee.'

Annie watched Jean's hand shake as she relived the events. Jean described her rising panic, trying to call for help for Lee and Catherine; seeing a pony bolt down the road, its reins swinging down by its front legs; and realizing that all she could see were loose ponies and children writhing in the dust. 'I didn't have my mobile with me.' Jean looked up at Annie, the panic she'd felt visible in her eyes. 'It was in my jacket. Only about twenty yards away. For a terrible moment I thought there was only me. But I still had that young instructor with me. She was shocked but still standing. I remember shouting to her to look after them while I went for help. Then… I don't know… I heard her say, "He's stopped breathing"… I saw the blue light…the first ambulance. I don't know who called it.'

Annie questioned her carefully, and it became clear that it must have been a good hour after the initial wave of panic that Jean had called her. Exhausted, pushed to the periphery, Jean still wasn't thinking straight. This was her event, her responsibility. Annie understood the turmoil she must be going through, but wished now they'd stayed outside with the other group. She might have learnt more from them. 'How are the children?'

Annie felt she had to ask, but tensed in anticipation of an answer she didn't want to hear.

Jean shook her head. 'I don't know. I just don't know.'

'You said one of them had stopped breathing.'

'We gave him mouth to mouth. It was awful. All the time wondering what was happening to the rest of them.' Gentle questioning got out of Jean how she and the young instructor had kept the two children alive until medics arrived. Annie imagined Jean surfacing from her focus on just two of the children to a sea of chaos; probably trying to get back to the centre of it to direct operations, but not being able to. In the midst of the turmoil, she'd called Annie in a panic, but someone had restored some order by the time Annie arrived.

'Have you any idea what it was or how it was administered?'

'Not what, but we know how. Everyone had a drink before getting the ponies out. The kids had cola, warm cola. It's a thing they've got going. Ordinary cola with boiling water, only it wasn't boiling water this time. They'd boiled something in it. Whatever it was it had them gabbling out their secrets like it was some kind of truth drug. Then they keeled over.'

Annie nodded. 'And those who weren't affected?'

'Three of the kids who don't like cola. And the instructors. We had tea.'

The door clicked open and the blond man walked in, holding out a phone, which Jean grabbed. 'That policeman rang back,' the man said. 'He's not on now. I took a message. The kids are OK.'

Jean let out a sigh as she cradled the phone in her hand. 'Wouldn't you think I'd keep it with me after this morning? I don't know what's the matter with me.'

'You're in shock,' Annie said. 'And what policeman?'

'I rang him after I rang you. The one who was rude to me. He was OK. He said he'd keep an eye on things and let me know.' She turned to the blond man. 'What else did he say?'

'He said a couple of the kids'll be kept in overnight but they're going to pull through. They're treating it like a childish prank gone wrong. Not drugs, something herbal, but they haven't isolated it yet.'

'Herbs couldn't have that effect.'

'Oh, they could,' Annie put in. 'Foxgloves, crocus, deadly nightshade... Well, no, none of those,' she amended. 'They probably wouldn't have pulled through. Bay, maybe. Harmless in small quantities but pretty deadly when it's concentrated, say in a strong brew.'

Annie watched as the two of them swapped theories on who had been the ringleader, where the idea might have come from, and it occurred to her that all the talk of drugs, all the precautions that had been taken might have planted the seed of the idea in the children's heads. Mass poisoning with some sort of herbal concoction was a blunt instrument and a dangerously unpredictable one. She'd said to Pat that it couldn't be coincidence, but maybe it was just that. The door swung open and the couple who'd been in the drive came in, looking dishevelled. 'All ponies caught and stabled,' the man said to Jean.

The woman looked at Annie. 'You're Annie, aren't you?' she said. 'You've had a call on the main phone. Your mate Pat Thompson. She couldn't get through on your mobile.'

'Orange Pippin gave us a real run around,' the man interrupted.

'Huh, he would.'

Annie pulled out her phone. No missed calls. The

woman leant on a chair back, exhausted, diverted by the talk of the runaway ponies. Annie clicked in Pat's number. The call went straight to voice mail. 'Signal's dodgy at the best of times round here,' the man said, eyeing Annie's phone. 'Here, let me have a go.' Annie passed the phone across and watched as he moved to the far corner and held it up high. 'Up here, you can sometimes get away from—'

'Oh my God!'

Everyone turned to stare at Jean, whose face had drained of all colour.

'What?' The woman and Annie spoke together.

'His tendon wasn't right. If he's damaged it again, it's the end. How will I tell them? They'll never forgive me.' Jean slumped over the table, a picture of despair.

'No!' The woman rushed to Jean and grasped both her wrists, giving her a shake. 'This is not your fault.'

'He'll be OK,' the man said. 'He seemed sound when we brought him in.'

Annie cleared her throat. 'I'm sorry, but what was the message from Pat Thompson?'

'What?' The woman turned to Annie, her face blank. 'Oh yes, the message… What did she say? Um…bigger reception than she'd bargained on at North Point and… uh…could you go…no, could you get back there pronto.' For the second time in half an hour, Annie felt the hairs rise at the back of her neck. The woman tossed out the words as though of minor importance compared to the real agenda here at the pony camp. But for Pat to have gone to the trouble of chasing up the landline meant something bad had happened. A bigger reception than she'd bargained on. The words too held menace. What had Pat walked into? Had someone laid a trap for them both that Annie had shimmied away from by chance?

'There's nothing I can do here, Jean,' she said, aware that no one listened. 'I must go.' She ran across the lorry park and up the grassy bank, scrambling over the ridge to her car. This was a more frequently used route than she'd realized. Already, there were fresh bike tracks. She fired up the engine and eased the car forward, resisting the urge to rush that might get her stuck in the soft earth. As the car bumped on to the dirt track she reached round to pull on her seat belt, making herself concentrate on the ruts ahead, forcing herself to take it slowly. The last thing she needed just now was a cracked axle. As she made it to the lane and approached the main road, she clicked on her right-hand indicator, relieved to see an empty carriageway ahead.

'No you don't,' said a voice in her ear. 'Turn left.'

Annie gasped as cold metal pressed into her neck.

'Drive!' the voice barked out.

Annie spun the wheel to take the car out on to the main road. Something hard and sharp jabbed into her flesh. A blade or a firearm…she couldn't tell.

'Get a move on.'

As she pushed down on the accelerator, the car surged forward, heading the wrong way, taking her further from Hull. Her glance shot to the mirror, but it had been twisted out of line.

'Stupid cow,' the voice went on. 'What d'you go and break into my house for? You've really messed up now.'

It was not being able to see him that freaked her out. Back to basics, she told herself. Don't antagonize him.

Get a clearer picture.

'How did you know where to wait for me?' she ...

Silence, '...' She bit the dry... 'And he told he...

had understood about it of here.

ELEVEN

SHOCK RUSHED THROUGH ANNIE. She felt both fear of the cold metal pressed hard to her neck and impotent anger that she'd dived so willingly into the trap. The wheel felt clammy under her hands. She eased her foot back, knowing she was in no state to drive this fast.

'Put your foot down!' Carl Sleeman's voice barked in her ear, too close, making her jump all over again.

She wanted to say, don't make me, I can't concentrate. Again and again her gaze flicked to the mirror, her hand itching to reach up and straighten it. Her wing mirrors showed one small car receding as she sped away from it. Her eyes returned their focus to the road ahead and at once she gasped and stamped on the brake as a traffic island loomed in her face. An angry cry signalled that Carl Sleeman had been knocked off balance, and with it came the jolt of something solid and metallic rammed painfully into the side of her head. 'D'you want to do the rest of the journey asleep in the boot?'

Annie fought back a wave of nausea as she negotiated the island. He'd no idea what his threat meant. It was less than a year since she'd been discharged from the Glasgow Royal Infirmary. Too soon to take another knock to her head. And now she'd inadvertently alerted him to the one weapon in her armoury. She was in control of the car and might have faked a skid or a crash; had him off balance long enough to disarm him. He was on his guard now.

It was not being able to see him that freaked her. Go back to basics, she told herself. Don't antagonize him. Get a dialogue going.

'How did you know I'd been in your house?'

'Stupid cow,' he muttered. 'Pissing about with Vince Sleeman's cash. Shut up and drive.' Another traffic island appeared ahead. 'Left here.'

Annie slotted the turn into her mental log of the route and completed the manoeuvre before she spoke again. 'If you want me—'

'I said drive!' Carl snarled in her ear. 'Try anything and you know what you'll get.'

Cold metal pushed against her neck. Annie sensed no outrage that she'd violated his space by breaking into his house, but anger that she'd wasted Vince's money on pursuing the wrong target. If he were siphoning off a pot of money Vince knew nothing about, he'd want her on the job he'd brought her here to do. But couldn't he see he'd left her with few options for finding out what that was, since he wouldn't come clean with her? Perhaps he thought Barbara had told her. That was worth a punt. 'I was on my way to talk to Barbara when—'

It wasn't his voice that cut her off this time, but the deliberate twisting of the object at her neck. Up to this point it might have been the flat edge of a blade, but now she felt a gun barrel push into her flesh for a fraction of a second before he whipped it round so the grip brushed her ear. 'Last chance,' he said, voice low, breath hot on her neck.

Annie's mouth dried as she felt the butt of the gun tap against her head. This wasn't the dozy kid she remembered from years ago. This was Vince Sleeman's crazy nephew. She fell silent. All she could do now was memorize every twist and turn of the route.

Twenty minutes later Annie had almost relaxed into the rhythm of obeying the curt orders that were barked into her ear every time they approached a junction. She didn't know where they were but had impressed the detail of his instructions on her mind so she could reproduce the route on Google maps. She deliberately pushed away all thoughts of the chasm that lay between her and her next opportunity to sit at a PC.

The sound of a phone jangled discordantly. Not hers. Wrong tone. An awful thought struck her. She'd handed her phone to the guy at the racecourse, but had no recollection of taking it back. Her phone was her lifeline. Surely, it was in her pocket and the shock of events had chased away the memory of putting it there? She sensed Crazy Carl's irritation as the pressure of the gun on her neck eased and she heard him answer the call. 'Yeah? Uh… Of course. No problem.' Annie listened intently to the abrupt change in his tone. Something had snapped him to attention. 'Yes, I'm in Hull, just by the station.' Annie couldn't make out any words, but she heard an angry outburst at his lie. 'OK, OK, only joking,' he said, with forced joviality.

Annie weighed in her mind whether or not to shout out. But it could be anyone. It could be Vince. 'Yeah, yeah. I'm on my way. I was all set to surprise you, that's why. Nah, you can stop worrying. Disposed of her myself not half an hour ago. Annie Raymond ain't gonna be back unless she's a ghost doing a bit of haunting.' His voice was relaxed. His tone confident. Annie felt a chill run through her. Then he clicked off the phone and swore. 'Shit!'

'Right at these lights. Here,' he snapped suddenly. With a squeal of tyres, Annie pulled the car round into a narrow street, slowing instinctively as she saw it was a dead end and squinting as the sun bounced back from the shiny road surface ahead.

'Keep going.' The road ended in the wasteland of a recently cleared site with a rough track snaking across the dirt. Annie bumped the car up on to it, making herself resent every jolt that tore rubber from the tyres and threatened the suspension; telling herself he wouldn't go this fast if it were his car. Forced resentment kept a lid on her fear. The terrain dipped between a number of industrial-sized skips. She gulped, her mouth dry. Was this where he intended to dump her? The car slewed down a steep slope. Annie saw the depth of the potholes ahead and instinctively pressed her foot to the brake just as Carl said, 'Stop here.'

'Lean forward.' The gun barrel grazed her ear to match the order. She leant forward.

'Hands behind your back.' She felt the solid grip of a pair of handcuffs followed by Carl's hands reaching round her, delving into her pockets. 'Where's your frigging phone?'

She cursed the catch in her voice as she told him she'd left it at the racecourse. Why should he believe her? What would he do? Her glance strayed sideways trying to see outside. They'd driven past houses. There must be people about somewhere. His phone clicked again and she heard him talking, his tone subtly muted. 'Yeah, Annie asked me to call you.'

Jean! He was ringing Jean to check her story. She drew in a breath. How much could she shout before he silenced her? *Call Pat Thompson.* She could scream those three words loud and clear before he could do anything. But what if Pat, too, had walked into a trap? And what would Carl do to shut her up? It would be a swift blow to the head with the butt of the gun. It might crack down on the site of the barely healed injury. Sweat oozed down her neck at the image of the fracture re-opening, her skull caving in beneath the blow. There was nothing she could shout that was worth the risk. It wouldn't take much to stop her, kill her probably. And it would leave Carl with all the time in the world to explain away the interruption. She listened to him tell Jean to turn off her phone and leave it in a drawer, not to let anyone know it was there. 'She'll come back for it when she can.' The call was over; the chance gone if it was ever there. His hands were at her head. A cloth engulfed her face cutting out the light. She felt it tied tight and flinched as her hair caught in the knot. 'Get out.'

With her hands immobile behind her back and her vision gone, it was almost impossible to stay upright on the bumpy terrain. Without Carl's hand clasped round her upper arm, she would have fallen. He dragged her a metre or so. She wasn't sure where until she heard the click of the car boot and he ordered her to climb in. Sensing his agitation, she clambered awkwardly into the small space, feeling his hands pushing her so that her face was pressed up against her holdall. She kept tools in here. There must be something she could use to get out of these restraints, to force open the boot lid. The blindfold was insecure, but the handcuffs were proper ones, and with her arms behind her, and his hands shoving her further in, it was all she could do to keep her face clear enough to breathe. Then his hands were gone; there was a moment of quiet, then the slam of the boot lid cut out all light.

The car jolted suddenly. Her ears filled with the whine of it reversing up the slope, turning on the bumpy terrain. The stench of unburnt fuel pressed into her face. Helpless, she was thrown about the small space as the car bounced back over the waste ground. Struggling against the battering, the rising nausea and the fight to keep her face clear of the spongy side of her case, Annie tried to concentrate. Back on to tarmac, they were heading out of the cul-de-sac, back towards the traffic lights. She expected him to continue the route he'd interrupted when he took that call, and was taken unawares when the car swung abruptly the other way, tyres screaming, the blare of a car horn orchestrating his manoeuvre.

Thoughts of finding a useful weapon or tool were swept away. Desperately she tried to find a hand hold, somewhere to brace her feet. Nothing in the boot was anchored down. The toolbox banged painfully into her legs. It was as though the car fishtailed down a long road at speed. There was nothing she could do. She gave up any attempt to memorize the turns. When the momentum slowed, she felt only relief that the battering had diminished. The car turned sharply, but smoothly, then she was pressed back as it accelerated. If she'd thought the fishtailing was bad, this was a hundred times worse. The car banged and leapt over whatever surface Crazy Carl was racing it down. Annie heard herself cry out as she fought to keep her head from banging down on the hard edges.

The torture ended with a scream of tyres that pushed her face hard up against the holdall as the car jolted to a stop. Before she could react she heard the boot lid wrenched open and light flooded through her blindfold. She could hear Carl Sleeman panting as though he'd been running. She sensed his panic. She fought against the pictures in her head. His gun pointing at her. His finger squeezing the trigger. No! Push the image away.

Back to basics. What did she know? Where were

they? Outdoors. The air was still, quiet. His feet crunched on a soft surface, not concrete. The only other sounds were birdsong and the gentle rustle of leaves. She flinched as she felt his hands behind her back. Cloth was wound around her wrists and instinctively she tensed her muscles as he tied it. Why would he do that when he'd handcuffed her? She lay very still, willing him to be in enough of a panic to get things wrong. He cleared his throat. She recognized the sound people make when they're about to speak but feel awkward. What would he say?

The words and the way he said them were unexpected. He tried for a light, conversational tone. 'So, you came back to work for Vince?'

'Don't give me that crap,' Annie shot back at him and could have bitten her tongue. Dialogue was what she needed. The battering she'd taken on the journey had dulled her senses. 'I know who I'm working for,' she added quietly. 'If you and Barbara want me to…'

He talked over her, betraying no interest in what she said. 'You heard about a girl who walked out of the sea?'

'What?' His question threw her. She saw Scott in his neat living room:….*she just appeared…out of the sea…like she'd expected me…didn't try to run….* She'd overheard a man's voice when she listened to Scott's call. He'd used Carl Sleeman's other name. They were all tied up in this together.

An exasperated sigh and the sound of his feet fidgeting told her he'd waited long enough for an answer. 'Yeah, well, she's in worse trouble than you are.'

A sudden yank on her arms freed her of the handcuffs. Now she was tied only by the cloth restraint. It wasn't tight enough. She fought an urge to pull against it. He mustn't know he hadn't done the job properly. The boot slammed and the darkness engulfed her.

Annie held herself immobile, sudden hope rushing through her body, making her skin tingle. She listened to Sleeman junior's footsteps scrunch away. He was in a hurry. Would he really leave her here with the means to escape? She strained to hear every sound, whilst praying she was right about the jolt she'd felt as the boot lid banged down. A discordant scrunch, but no click. She hadn't heard the catch click home.

TWELVE

THE PHONE CALL had forced him to hurry, to panic. He didn't do detail. A car door slammed and made her flinch. Hot on its heels came the roar of an engine, then wheels spinning, spitting gravel as a vehicle sped away. Crazy Carl had left. She was on her own. Cloying darkness wrapped itself around her. He wouldn't stay away a second longer than he had to. She twisted in the small space, pulling at the material around her wrists, feeling it give bit by bit. The moment she had enough play to pull one hand free, she yanked the blindfold from her eyes, then kicked out with her legs. They met no resistance. The boot lid flew open with such force that it bounced back and she had to brace her feet against the rebound or she might have locked herself back in. She scrambled out, looking all around, staggering as her cramped muscles protested. As far as she could see she was alone. No immediate threats, but the knot of fear in her gut screamed at her to hurry.

Her car sat on a patch of bare earth in a small copse. Carl had pulled off a long driveway that curved away between the trees. The air was still. She could hear traffic in the distance. Looking through the trees the other way, she made out the shape of a large square farmhouse. It showed no obvious signs of habitation. She tensed, her gaze drawn to the dwelling, half expecting someone to come running down to investigate the sound of the car boot bursting open, but if the sound had carried that far, then the noise of Carl taking off in the other vehicle would have brought them out.

She dragged her attention away. She knew nothing about the place except that Carl Sleeman had not intended to bring her here.

If she only had her phone the police could trace her from the phone signal, and would be out pronto when they knew there'd been a gun involved. And a Sleeman. Officialdom would slice through the hidden agendas, glad of the chance to collar Vince Sleeman's nephew if not the man himself.

But if she'd had her phone, he'd have taken it. No time for regrets. She had to get away before he came back.

For the first time ever she felt a pang of nostalgia for one of the old bangers she used to drive when she first worked for Barbara and Pat. She could have hotwired one of those in an instant, but not this one.

The boot still gaped open. She had to shut it. There was a chance Carl would race back, jump in without checking and drive off, thinking she was still trussed up inside. A wad of something had stuck in the catch, preventing it from clicking home. She had nothing that would level the playing field against his firearm but, before closing the boot, she grabbed a sturdy screwdriver as better than nothing.

For form's sake, as turned to set off, she pulled on the handle of the driver's door. It opened, knocking her off balance. She had to fight to stay on her feet. And then a gasp escaped her as she stared inside. How much of a panic had Carl been in? How careless was this guy? The keys swung in the ignition. If he hadn't been certain she couldn't escape, it was as though he'd wanted her to get away.

At once, she jumped behind the wheel, started the engine, skidded the car round in an arc on the bare earth and bumped up on to the driveway, heading for the road.

Instinctively she straightened the mirror and saw the square building recede behind her. Ahead, the drive took another curve and she could see tall stone gateposts in the distance.

Again a glance at the mirror. Now it showed only the trees, waving her goodbye. The farmhouse had disappeared.

She slowed and then stopped the car, took in a deep breath and felt her heart thud rapidly in her chest. Was she facing an opportunity not to be missed, or a really terrible idea?

It was no legitimate case that had brought her here. This was personal. Herself and the Thompson sisters against Vince Sleeman, just like she'd wanted it all those years ago. And Crazy Carl? Whose side was he on? Everyone's probably, for as long as he could get away with it. She thought back to how he'd been summoned by someone he daren't say no to; someone who apparently accepted his casual assertion that he'd killed her.

There was no time to think through every detail. Either she did this or she put her foot to the floor and made her escape.

Carl would be back as soon as he could. How long would that be?

The car's clock showed 2.05 p.m. He couldn't have been gone more than two or three minutes. This remote spot must be half an hour from civilization, so she could hope for an hour, plus whatever time he had to spend at his destination. She knew the rules. In this type of situation, if you knew you had an hour, you counted on ten minutes, stretched it to fifteen if you had to, with twenty-five as your absolute limit. Except that the rule didn't say that at all. It said get out as fast and far as you can and then call for help.

She twisted in her seat and reversed the car to where she'd driven it out of the copse. Alert for any sound beyond the distant hum of traffic, she climbed out to look. Her tracks were obvious and fresh until they joined the driveway where they vanished on the hard, worn surface. Carl would come back and see the car gone. The churned soil told its own story about which way she'd headed. She turned her gaze the other way towards the farmhouse, invisible from this angle, hidden by a tangle of bushes.

The trees the other side of the drive grew from dense undergrowth. She clambered into the brambles, stamping them down, gauging the solidity of the ground beneath.

With care, she backed the car off the track, bumping it down into the scrub, urging it to force a path between the trees until it was well off the driveway. Then she yanked up swaths of brambles and fallen branches, that raked painfully across the barely healed scratches on her arms, and piled them at the front of the car until it was invisible to all but a determined searcher. And Carl Sleeman wouldn't even think to look. Before she left the car, she reopened the boot and equipped herself with a torch and set of picklocks.

Keeping to the cover of the trees, she set off towards the farmhouse.

Shafts of sunlight speared through the trees, flashes of white light blinding her momentarily as the branches bent lazily overhead. A few feathery clouds hung in the sky. No hint of rain.

What was he so keen to keep hidden? Maybe nothing.

Maybe this was just a convenient place to stash a car. All she intended was a quick look. And if she saw anything that warranted a second visit, she'd be back better equipped and maybe not alone.

Logically, she knew he couldn't be on his way back yet, but once she had left the security of the car and her only access to a clock, she couldn't fight off the tingle at the back of her neck, the feel of someone watching, creeping up behind her.

She kept to the cover of the trees as she approached the house, dropping to a crouch to avoid putting herself in direct line with any of the windows. Using the trees and bushes as cover, she crept closer.

The driveway widened as it neared the building, spreading an arm each way to embrace the farmhouse leaving room, Annie supposed, for things like combine harvesters to drive right round. It was a substantial, square dwelling. Up close, bits of straggly gardens hugged the front walls, unkempt, weeds choking out anything that had been intended to flower there. The house itself looked abandoned but in reasonable condition. The windows were uncurtained. The rooms looked empty.

Some kind of alarm system was attached above the front door. It too looked abandoned and old, but that might be deliberate, to be in keeping with the neglected air of the place. The approach to the house was too open to risk drawing any nearer, so she began to pick her way round the side when a sound stopped her. She froze, then sank lower into the bushes.

Someone was outside, round the back of the house, and they were humming.

Pushing twigs and branches aside, stepping awkwardly to avoid the open spaces, Annie crept in a wide

arc, circling the house. The scene changed as she moved
away from the façade that faced the drive. A Dutch barn
lay to one side, fringed by tall conifers. Annie gave it a
quick glance, took in the huge locked doors, then turned
her attention to the yard where a youngish woman stood
with her back to her, hanging washing on a line. The
basket of clothes was almost empty. Annie remained
still. She wouldn't risk the house as there was someone there, but she could try for a peep inside that barn.

The humming continued. The woman didn't hurry
as she pegged out each item carefully, making sure it
hung straight. Her hair was tied up in a scarf. The angle
of the sun made it hard for Annie to pick out detail. The
woman moved easily, light on her feet, but her age was
hard to judge.

She remembered the question Carl Sleeman had
thrown at her before he left. If she had her phone she
would risk a photograph and look for a way to get it
in front of Scott. Is this the woman who walked out of
the sea? But this didn't look like a woman in any sort
of trouble. When done with the clothes she gave an ex-
travagant yawn and picked up the empty basket, carrying it towards the house and out of Annie's line of sight.

At once Annie eased herself a little further forward,
but then had to duck down as the woman reappeared
with a steaming cup in one hand and a tabloid newspaper under her arm. She settled herself at a small cast-
iron table, setting the paper in front of her and raising
the cup to her lips. Chores done, she clearly wanted to
enjoy the fine weather.

The woman's hand reached forward to trace along
the headlines on the page. Annie watched the woman's lips mouthing the words as she read. She gave her
a couple of minutes to relax properly, then began to

ease herself back, further into the undergrowth. If the woman remained where she was Annie could risk crossing the small stretch of open ground to reach the big barn.

She hesitated. The woman didn't quite have her back to her and might see the movement in her peripheral vision.

'Hey!'

Annie froze. But the woman's sudden exclamation wasn't aimed her way. A large black cat had stalked out of the house, tail vertical, ignoring the woman, who jumped out of her chair to flap her paper and chase it away.

The second she was on her feet, Annie leapt up and sprinted the short stretch to the barn, tucking herself down at the foot of its wall. Holding her breath, she peered towards the house. The cat had jumped on to a tall planter and, disconcertingly, seemed to stare right at her, but the woman was back in her seat.

Once round the side of the barn and out of sight, Annie gave the building further scrutiny. The walls were metal sheets bolted to concrete pillars; the sort of structure that housed farm machinery and big bales of straw.

She wondered if the woman who read with difficulty was some sort of caretaker, like Carl at the house in Hull. And if so, what secret did she guard?

Alert for any sound from the direction of the house, and keeping close to the wall, Annie edged her way round the perimeter of the high building, aiming for those big doors at the front. At the far side, with nothing but fields and straggly trees to watch her, she tried to peer between the metal plates, but even using her torch there were no gaps big enough to show her what was inside. She paused at one of the corners. An animal had burrowed out a wide hole beside one of the concrete pillars, under the lowest of the panels. If she lay flat, she might see underneath. But there could be an easier way in so she carried on.

The front of the barn wasn't quite in line with the back of the house, but she would have to be careful. If she stepped out of the shade of the tall structure the sun would throw her shadow out beyond the cover of the walls, betraying her position. Pressed to the side wall, conscious of the sunlight through the trees waiting to magnify her presence, she leant round to look.

One glance, a second's triumph as she saw a person-sized door built into the huge locked gates, and then a horrified intake of breath and she threw herself back round the side of the barn and crushed herself flat against the wall.

A diamond sparkle had played down at her from high above the doors. A lens. They had a camera up there. Her heart thumped as she twisted her head to look up at the wall that rose behind her. She remembered how well-hidden some of the cameras at Crazy Carl's house had been.

After a moment she let out the breath she'd been holding. Industrial metal sheeting wasn't a good place for hidden cameras. There was nothing this side that resembled the wooden mount above the big doors. It was just the entrance that was guarded.

It might mean nothing. Farm equipment was valuable and targeted often enough to warrant extra security. The sensible thing would be to get away, to come back at a better time and check the place out properly. But by then Carl Sleeman would know he'd given away the location and would expect her back, might even alert others to the risk.

The building was well secured but it had started life as a Dutch barn, designed with plenty of gaps. She retraced her steps, away from the camera, away from the woman by the house, and returned to the fresh earth at the back corner. Gingerly, she knelt by the hole and reached in, feeling under the barn wall, cringing inwardly at the thought of a set of teeth snapping at her fingers. The concrete pillars were bedded deep in the earth, but the panels weren't and the one above the animal's incursions wasn't secure. She might be able to prise it open enough to see in.

She longed for a means to check the time. The sun didn't seem much lower in the sky but she must be over her first ten minutes by now.

Suppressing audible grunts of effort, she grasped the edges of the panel and forced it away from the ground, using her foot to shove in half a brick to hold it open. Lying face to the ground in uncomfortable proximity to the animal hole, she peered through the gap.

She could just make out the shape of a wheel but didn't try to examine it. She was too vulnerable out in the open. If Carl came back and didn't fly straight off again in pursuit, he might come up here. For all she knew the woman at the house would have some business to bring her round the back of the barn.

The shadowy shape of a wheel. A large wheel. Not a tractor wheel.

She looked again at the hole and at the bent panel. The animal's excavations had loosened one of the bolts from the concrete pillar. If she could free it altogether, there would just be room to slip through.

The bolt itself wouldn't budge, but the concrete

crumbled and she eased it away from its mooring, looking with some trepidation at the recently disturbed soil. She must use the depth of the hole to wriggle her way in.

The rough earth stung her arms where the brambles had left their mark, and she caught a painful new scratch from the jagged edge of the panel. Cursing silently, she twisted the edge of her T-shirt round the cut on her finger. It wouldn't do to leave a trail of blood behind her. Sweat and dust felt gritty on her skin. It was a tight fit but she squeezed through, knowing this was beyond just looking, beyond reasonable risk, but she had the feeling that it was now or never.

A heavy gloom hung inside.

She used her pencil torch and played it up the walls, looking for cameras, wires, anything to suggest hidden surveillance, but knowing it could be hidden well enough that she'd never find it. Just as long as there was no live feed, no one watching her right now, she might get away with it. And in case there was a mob on its way to stop her, she must be quick.

She ran her torch over the single huge vehicle, walking up and down its length. It was a massive trailer. Looking up at the sides, she half-expected to see the words *Breast Screening* or *Radiography*.

Patches of glitter twinkled at her from the bottom edges of the panels, the pattern rising haphazardly up the tall sides. *All stars and glitter*; Carl's words to Jean. She played the torch across the metal where giant letters spelt out the single word HORSES.

There was no tractor unit. The trailer's huge towing bar thrust forward towards the barn doors through which it had been backed in and parked.

The door was high off the ground. There must be a ladder or mobile staircase to allow access, but the place was bare apart from some empty wall racks and huge coils of electrical wire, too heavy to drag across to use as a makeshift support to stand on. If the door were open, she might leap up, get a hold and haul herself in, but she had nothing long enough to reach up as high as the door handle and assumed it would be locked. Even if she could get up there, there was no window, nothing to look through.

The only breaks in the blank sides were small slatted windows high up near the roof, three on each side. As she circled the huge trailer, she spotted something at last. The far back corner sported a rail. If she could get up to it, she could haul herself up on to the roof and lean across to see in through the high windows.

Bracing herself, measuring the distance, the slant and shape of the rail, she took a leap from the floor and grasped the shiny metal with one hand and then the other, flinching as her feet banged noisily on the side of the vehicle. Once she had a grip, it was an easy climb to the roof, where she lay flat and eased herself along until she could peer over the side into the first of the windows.

It was blacked out. Playing the torch through the slats showed her nothing. Frustrated and without much hope, she moved to the next. This one was not covered. Through the slats, she saw the inside of a small cubicle with a locker and a seat. Pulling back, she slid further along to the third one. An identical space showed through this one, too. She eased herself across the expanse of the roof to the other side and leant over to the corresponding window there. This, too, showed a similar space, but when she moved to the middle section she stared transfixed.

Even in the gloom, the surfaces glinted back at her.

Some kind of minimal showroom kitchen in gleaming stainless steel, walls, units, surfaces. A weird-shaped table sat in the middle of the space, reminding her of something she'd seen before, someone's fantastically expensive experimental kitchen maybe. She was certain no horse had ever seen the inside of this place, and she inched out over the edge to see further in. Two huge gas bottles attached to gauges and tubes came into view along with tantalizing edges of things she couldn't quite see. And that table. It wasn't a table at all, it was a sink. It had a drain hole. And so did the floor. What was it, some kind of wet room?

She looked again at the central fixture, the focus of the strange space. Not a sink. Her first instinct had been right. It was a table. And she knew exactly where she'd been the last time she'd seen one like it. In a mortuary.

THIRTEEN

ANNIE SAT AT the desk in Pat's office. The monitor in front of her showed the satellite view of an isolated farmhouse that she might never have had the chance to look up. After a few moments, it flipped to its screen saver picture of two swans gliding across a lake. The only sounds were the steady drip of the tap from the small kitchen down the corridor and the whisper of her own breathing. The area around the office, busy enough during the day, had nothing to bring evening visitors and now settled itself for night. If any legitimate keyholder came on a late mission they would find the outer door jammed. Annie was determined no one would catch her unawares tonight. The day had held hijack, incarceration in a stuffy car boot and the threat of fatal injury; it had led to a farmhouse that exuded tranquillity whilst housing a mobile morgue. She had see-sawed between extremes of fear and bewilderment, been battered both mentally and physically.

Her first act after putting distance between herself and the place where Carl had left her was to contact Pieternel from a pay phone in a pub. Pieternel had grumbled at Annie's demand for a fast car swap, but only because calling in the necessary favour would make a serious hole in the firm's fat profit from the Hull job. She'd told Pieternel everything and they'd tried to work their way to a plausible theory, but there were too many pieces missing. And Annie knew she was too hyped to think clearly when she heard herself saying, 'Send me Christa. I need someone lighter on her feet than Pat. You've finished with her for now, haven't you?'

Pieternel laughed. 'That's just what you need. A loose cannon like Christa.'

Annie smiled. Pieternel was right. The quickest way to an early grave in this situation would be to bring in someone as impetuous as Christa.

'Just watch your back, Annie, and keep your wits about you. They've had two pops at you in a few days. That's bordering on careless.'

That was true, too. Irritated, Annie half-heartedly waved the rag at Pieternel for her lack of concern about insurance cover.

'Not a legit case, Annie. No business risk. Get yourself shot and we might wangle a nice wad of compo.'

On her way to an industrial park on the western outskirts of Hull where Pieternel's influence would have a car ready for collection no questions asked, Annie stopped at a phone shop to renew a years-old contact who provided her with a new handset with a live battery and an untraceable SIM. With the change of car and a phone in her pocket, Annie clawed her way back towards being in control. She picked up her new handset, watched her fingers reach to the keypad to call Jean, but the number wasn't there. Not in her phone…not in her head. Very deliberately she put down the handset, drew in a breath and relaxed, allowing the tension to drain and give her memory the space to retrieve what she needed. After a moment, she picked it up again and punched in the number.

After a couple of rings, Jean Greenhough's voice was in her ear saying, 'Hello.'

'Are you at the racecourse?'

'Yes, I've to stay on till all the ponies are collected. Someone must, and...' Annie let Jean unload her worries for her aborted pony camp, listening to the way the woman's relief that everyone was all right had become tempered by budding annoyance at the trouble the perpetrators had caused. 'We know who the ringleaders were, but they've made sure to be the ones kept in overnight. Oh, I know I should just be grateful they're all OK, but really...'

'Go and see them at the hospital,' Annie suggested. 'If they're still under the influence, they'll tell you everything. Jean, has anyone been for my phone? No? OK, then I'd like you to do something for me. Can you go and get it now?'

Annie talked Jean through removal of the SIM card, told her to put the handset back in the drawer and listened to her flush the SIM down the toilet. If Jean felt surprise at the request, it was drowned in her more immediate worries. Throughout the process, she chuntered on about the children who had initiated the drugged cola and wrecked her camp.

She left the car on a street parallel with Pat's office, thinking it probably unnecessary but reflecting she'd rather overdo the paranoia than have a gun shoved in her neck as she drove. The pain in her left foot, from some sharp edge in that graveyard, made itself felt and she flinched at every other step as she made her way through the tenfoots of Hull's industrial wasteland, letting herself into the building when there was no one to watch and treading softly on the stairs to avoid notice from anyone working late in the downstairs office.

Once sure she was alone inside, she did a thorough sweep for bugs and was amazed to find a crude device inside each of the telephone handsets. It was less the presence of the phone taps than the low level technology of them that surprised her. She'd assumed remote listening devices, nothing so crude as this, and kicked herself for not checking the handsets when she'd first suspected a tap. As she put the gadgets back into the phones-no need to alert anyone just yet-she thought of the way the sisters had fallen into sloth. They probably hadn't swept their own office in years. There was no need for sophisticated technology to keep an eye on them. She took the time to do a thorough job and found nothing else.

It would be a long night. She set the alarm on her new phone to wake her in time to unblock the outside door and tried to settle down to sleep. She'd been a fool to judge Carl Sleeman by the memory of someone she'd barely known eight years ago. And he'd been a fool, too, in his misjudgement of her. It didn't matter. None of it mattered. Whatever she'd felt earlier in the day, the fear, the bewilderment, the panic of losing control, it had all hardened into a knot of anger deep inside. She had no intention of letting this go.

THE DAWN BROUGHT a text message that beeped from her phone as Annie lay half-awake. She sat up, grimacing at the crick in her neck from where she'd curled up in the pushed-together chairs. With a yawn, she reached into her jacket pocket and pulled out her phone. Two messages. Pieternel and a number that was familiar but not yet known to her new handset. She clicked on Pieternel's message.

RU sure re Christa? U can change yr mind b4 6am, after that I'm offline rest of day.

Annie glanced at the time. Ten to six. Pieternel was more worried than she'd realized. It would cost money

to send Christa, but Pieternel was saying she was prepared to do it if Annie wanted. Annie smiled as she
thought of the chaos Christa would bring. She'd floated
the idea because her mind had been in a spin. And great
though it would be to have someone as light on her
feet as Christa, Annie had never been serious. Christa
would be the worst sort of loose cannon to bring in to
this situation. She texted back.

100% sure. Thanks. Speak later.

She yawned again as she turned to the second message, but as she glanced at the number, realization ran
a shiver down her spine. It was Carl Sleeman. But he
shouldn't even know this number. He should be leaving
messages on the dead SIM of her old phone.

Keep yer hed down. Play dead or you will be.

What the hell? She was on her feet, pulling her things
together, certain she'd missed a tracking device. Cursing silently, she grabbed her shoes and jacket, wondering if there would be a reception party waiting outside
the office. She'd thought all along he'd been too careless for credibility in allowing her to escape from that
car boot. He'd planted something on her.

Then she stopped and made herself sit back down.
Think this through. He knew she'd left her phone at
the racecourse. He might even have been back for it.
Or maybe he'd rung Jean. Jean's concerns were all for
her pony camp. She wouldn't have thought twice about
giving out Annie's new number. There was no tracking
device. Carl was a slapdash operator. Maybe he'd let her
escape because he couldn't be bothered with her any
more. She chided herself for overreacting and looked
again at his message.

Keep yer hed down. Play dead or you will be.

It made some kind of sense with the events of

yesterday, but what was his agenda? Pat must arrange another meeting, and this time both Annie and Carl would be there. Annie rearranged the furniture and sat down to wait.

Pat arrived early, just after eight, acknowledged Annie with a nod, and said, 'Better news on Babs. She's getting better by the hour.'

'That's good. Can we go and see her?'

Pat gave a huff of exasperation and snapped, 'No, not yet.'

Annie held up her hand in a gesture of apology. No good came of firing questions at Pat at this time in the morning. 'I'll make coffee, but we really need to speak to her as soon as we can. How long will it be?'

Pat's gaze tracked Annie's progress towards the kettle, the mugs, the coffee jar, but she waited until Annie went out of the office towards the kitchen to get milk, before calling after her, 'I've been thinking about it. You're wrong. Babs had nothing to do with you being brought here.' She waited until Annie re-entered before adding, 'I know you don't think it was Vince, but things have changed since you were here before.'

'Pat, you know full well it wasn't Vince.'

'I know nothing of the sort. We were hard-pressed and he brought you in to help out. Whatever Vince is, he's not small-minded. He's never liked you, but he knows you can do the work. He offered you a job once, remember?'

Annie's mind raced across several angry retorts: I turned him down...you weren't hard-pressed at all... but she swallowed them. There was no time to argue. She pulled forward the computer monitor and brought up the satellite view of the house. Pat leant forward to see. 'What's this?'

'I'm hoping you're going to tell me.' Annie zoomed in on the square building. Close up, the resolution was poor, but Pat nodded.

'Oh, yeah, it's Vince's place, but that's somewhere you definitely want to steer clear of, whether Vince brought you here or not. It's their home. Nothing to do with the business. It was going to be our home once, but Mum died and Dad had to have us in town where he could keep an eye. We used to go there at Christmas when we were little.' Momentarily, Pat's face took on a wistful look of fond memories revived.

'Who lives there now?'

'Just Vince and Leah. But it's sacrosanct. Vince sailed a bit close to the wind a time or two and Leah put her foot down, said she wasn't risking her home. What's your interest?'

'I was there yesterday.'

'Bloody hell, Annie! Why? You keep your distance. If anyone gets to know, they'll think it was us; me and Babs. We'll get no more support if he thinks we've led you there. I told you. It's sacrosanct, that place. How did you find it?'

'Carl took me.'

Annie watched Pat's face drain of blood as she said, 'Whoa,' her voice a whisper. 'He's had it then.'

Not wanting to waste time on details, Annie raced through an abbreviated account of what had happened to her. 'He told someone he'd killed me,' she ended. 'And then he left me in the car by that house.'

'He must have been in a panic,' Pat said. 'I know you can be a bloody Houdini when you're cornered, but he doesn't.'

'Come on, no one's that stupid. He must have known

I'd get free. He didn't tie my wrists properly. He didn't make sure the boot was shut. He left the keys in the car.'

'You said he tied your wrists on top of the handcuffs. If he was in a panic, he won't have realized they weren't tight enough. He wouldn't have risked uncuffing you first. And he was planning to be back, that's why he left the keys in. The boot was a lucky break.'

Annie pulled a face. 'It's stretching it to believe he could have been that careless.'

'Careless is Carl's trademark. He's had an uncle to pick him up out of the holes he's got himself in. He's never learnt better. It sounds improbable, I'll give you that, but there's one thing I'm sure of: Carl Sleeman would no more lead you to that house on purpose than he'd jump off the Humber Bridge. Suicide either way.'

This was family stuff: history. Annie wanted hard facts. 'Have you any idea who it might have been who called him? Who would have put him in a panic like that?'

'The obvious one's Vince.'

'If Vince was happy to hear I was dead, how does that fit with him bringing me here?'

Pat opened her mouth to reply, then closed it. There was a silence. It doesn't fit, thought Annie. None of it fits. She knows it as well as I do. Annie changed tack and described the woman she'd seen hanging out washing. Pat shook her head. 'Too young for Leah. An au pair or something. They have people in, especially since Vince got ill.'

'Would Vince have been there yesterday?'

'Oh yeah, that's where he's been for weeks when he hasn't been in hospital. He rules the roost from a bed upstairs.'

Annie thought about the barn and the huge trailer,

but decided to get everything else straight in her head first. She asked Pat, 'What happened at North Point yesterday?'

'Carl rang me, said he couldn't make it. He was on at me for ages wanting chapter and verse on what it was about. I didn't tell him anything.'

Annie reconstructed this in her mind. Carl had rung the racecourse and left the so-called message from Pat. It wouldn't have taken much to disguise his voice enough to fool the guy who'd taken the call; they'd all been wrapped up in the aftermath of the poisoning. Then Carl had called Pat to keep her phone busy in case Annie managed to ring back. 'We're going to need to catch up with him at some point.'

'I'll ring him now.'

Annie held up her hand to stop Pat as she reached for the handset. Instead, she pulled the phone towards her and opened it up to show Pat what was inside.

Pat frowned at the device and looked up at Annie. 'Have you done that? What for?'

Annie shook her head. She told Pat of the suspicions she'd nursed since her call to Barbara had led to both of them being the targets of hit-and-run drivers. 'I hadn't had the chance to check it out properly before last night. It's pretty basic but I don't want to shift it till we know who put it there and what they're after. There's one in the other phone as well.'

Pat stared round the office, indignation clear in every move. You've become too cosy in here, Annie wanted to say. You talk about Carl being careless, but it's a family failing.

'Who? Why?' Pat swung round on Annie with a flare of anger. 'That blasted copper of yours!'

'No, he'd have used better kit than this. Anyway,

they were there before he came poking about. And he's not mine.' She paused and watched Pat carefully, before asking, 'Has Carl Sleeman been here much lately?'

The answer was obvious without Pat saying a word. She looked up at Annie. 'But why? Why us? What are we doing that he couldn't find out just by asking?'

'Could it be to do with one of the jobs they passed on to you? Not the pony camp, that was the ploy to get me here. What else have you done recently that came from Sleeman?'

'Not much. Not since Vince was ill. There was the Egyptian guy. That was all very hush-hush. But I can't see why he'd have bugged the phones. He called in a time or two, though, wanting every last detail. Babs dealt with it. It was a nothing of a case in the end.'

Annie drummed her fingers on the doctored handset as thoughts chased through her head. Was this relevant or just one of Vince's iffy cases? 'What was it about?'

'Someone wanted the guy out the way. Now, what was his name? Carl was jumpy, now I think about it, too interested, round here too often. That wasn't like Carl. They wanted the evidence to get the guy deported. I think he had something to do with that hospital scandal in the Midlands; some doctor with dodgy qualifications. It made the national press.'

'It rings a vague bell,' said Annie. 'And did you get the evidence?'

'No. Well, yes, we did the job. Well, Babs did. She got the evidence that the guy was legit. He wasn't an illegal; had nothing to do with that other business.'

It sounded like nothing but Annie wanted to be sure. 'Can I see the file?' she said, adding, 'There's something else, but first I want to get face to face with the little toerag. How can we be sure he's not going to pull something stupid?'

'Make it somewhere public,' Pat said.

'OK, but will he turn up?'

Pat shrugged. 'We can try. What's the other thing?'

'I want to go back out to Vince's place.'

Immediately, Pat held up both her hands. 'No way. And no point. Nothing goes on out there that's anything to do with any of this.'

Annie fought back a wave of impatience. Pat had always had a blind spot where Vince was concerned. 'I wouldn't be so sure.' She told her about the huge trailer.

'A mobile morgue? What on earth would anyone want with a mobile morgue?'

'I don't like to think, but that's what it looked like. And I'm certain I've seen it before on some CCTV footage.' She told Pat about the lorry that had backed into Carl's drive in Hull, the lorry that had been too heavy even for the properly laid kerbstones. Before Pat could think to ask about where and how she'd seen the images, she added, 'And if you remember, he told Jean that I should look out for a horse box that wasn't. That trailer had horse logos on the sides. We need to get back out there, but we need to be careful.'

'Huh, careful! I'll say. This is one suicide mission you're not going to talk me into.'

Annie sat back and reached for the keyboard where she played the cursor over the satellite view of the farmhouse. She wouldn't entrench Pat's opposition by arguing. She'd sown the seed and would wait, but not too long because a knot in her gut told her they were on a deadline. Barbara lay in a hospital bed and someone had wanted Annie there, too. She felt the dull ache in her arm. It would be a multicoloured reminder for weeks.

From the corner of her eye she watched Pat, deep in thought, lever herself upright and go across to the filing cabinets. As Pat flicked through files, Annie listened to the sounds of the building, the footsteps back and forth between the downstairs offices, the occasional slam of the front door as a smoker went out into the street or came back in. When the buzzer sounded, she said, 'Expecting anyone? I'll disappear to the back office.' She was still no closer to Carl Sleeman's real agenda, but his advice about keeping below the radar was good.

Pat shook her head and turned to Annie, her face troubled. 'It's gone. 'The file for that guy Vince wanted deported. I can't remember his name, but I've looked all through.'

'Computer file?'

'No, Vince wanted it kept offline.'

As their eyes met, they both registered the sound of someone running lightly up the stairs. With no time to get out of the way, Annie leapt from her chair so she would be behind the door as it opened. Pat could take the visitor to the back office and she could slip out.

After a cursory knock, the door swung open and from behind it, Annie heard Pat say, 'Yes? Can I help you?'

'No, but I can help you,' said a voice that made Annie's heart thud hard in her chest. 'I'm here to track down a morgue or something. Where's Annie?'

Annie stepped out from behind the door. 'Christa? What the hell are you doing here?'

FOURTEEN

ANNIE WATCHED AGHAST. Christa, undaunted by her reception, leant forward to peer at the computer screen, ran her gaze across the papers on the desk and darted across to the filing cabinet, ostensibly to shake Pat's hand—'Pat Thompson, yeah? I'm Christa'—whilst taking a good look into the open drawer.

Without a pause, Christa pointed back towards the image of the farmhouse. 'That the place we're targeting? D'you want me off out there now?'

Too late, Annie clicked off the monitor, knowing Christa had already hoovered up far too much information, including enough to get that image back on to the screen or even to find her way out there. How could this have happened? Quite apart from what she'd picked up in her first ten seconds in the office, Christa had walked through the door with information in her head that shouldn't have been there. What was Pieternel playing at?

Nothing she'd said could have been misunderstood to this extent.

It was Pat who asked the question. 'Who are you and what are you doing here?'

'Hasn't Annie told you? Pieternel sent me down to help her out on this job? And I know how to hit the ground running; it's why people employ me, so you need to get me something to do. I'm costing you money while I'm standing here.'

Annie pulled in a deep breath, preparatory to telling Christa to turn right round and go back where she'd come from, but she stopped herself. She daren't do that. Christa was already a ticking bomb. The first thing to do was to call Pieternel, but not in Christa's hearing.

'Yes, you're right,' she rapped out, ignoring the outraged stare Pat turned on her. 'OK, first thing, we've mislaid a file, and it's important to the case.' Annie nodded her head towards the open filing cabinet and, as Christa turned to look, gave Pat the ghost of a wink.

'No, it's not in there. It should be, but it's been misfiled and we need to find it. It'll be in one of the cabinets in there.' She pointed to the door of the back office. 'I want you to get looking for it.'

Christa shrugged and gave a resigned, 'OK,' looking at Pat to ask, 'name, date...?'

Pat thinned her lips and stared at Annie. 'I can't have her in there messing everything up.'

'Don't worry,' Annie said. 'She's good. She can go through an office with a fine-tooth comb and not leave a trace.'

'But it won't be—'

Annie made a fierce gesture at Pat to shut her up, as Christa gave a self-satisfied smile and said, 'Well, yes I could, but I don't need to be careful, do I? This is your office, right?'

'Oh yes, you do.' Annie dropped her voice, throwing Christa a glance that crackled with insinuations. 'No one must know we had to search for it. It's...well, it's complicated...details don't matter now. I'll fill you in later. The important thing is to get our hands on it.'

Christa perked up now that the routine task had an interesting undertone. Annie heaved an inward sigh of relief. She'd given Christa a goal and it would keep her searching all the longer. 'We can't give you a name. You see, it wasn't one of Pat's cases. An Egyptian guy, wasn't it, Pat? What else can we give Christa to help her track him down?'

'He's the surveillance, is he?' Christa broke in.

'That's right,' Annie said, as Pat's gaze bored into her in a way that said she would play along but only so far. 'We're to find evidence to get him deported. What else do we know?'

Again, Annie stared hard at Pat to stop her saying they'd found the guy to be legit. Christa needed to think it was a live case. It might keep her from meddling elsewhere.

Pat cleared her throat. 'He's a doctor. He worked at one of the private hospitals. I last saw the file about two or three weeks ago.'

Annie stood up and ushered Christa through to the small back office. 'Be thorough,' she told her. 'We have to have that file, but Pat's not the only partner in this firm so make sure no one can tell you've been looking.'

If Christa felt dismayed at the junk room that was the back office, she didn't show it, just gave Annie a cheerful, 'Sure thing. And then we'll get out on the road, yeah?'

'Depends what you find.'

Annie closed the door on Christa and beckoned Pat to the far side of the room.

'Who is she?' Pat hissed.

'She's someone we've used on a freelance basis. She's good, and me and Pieternel sort of mentioned maybe using her here, but we agreed not to. Honestly Pat, I have no idea how this happened but we really don't want her around just now. She'll be straight in feet first unless we can get rid of her or keep her occupied on something else.'

'Well, just tell her to piss off.'

'I would, but I don't think she'd be here unless she's been paid something up front. She's rash enough to stay and do a bit of freelance work on the job.'

'What harm can that do?'

'She saw Vince's house on the screen, complete with postcode and map reference.'

'What? And you think she'll remember that sort of detail?'

'I know she will. I know how she works. I told you she's good, but she's also a five-star liability when she goes off on her own. I don't want to antagonize her unless we have to. She has a temper on her if she thinks she's being messed about. I'll spin her a line about money, but let me get on to Pieternel first.'

The call went through to voice-mail. 'Pieternel,' Annie hissed into the handset, whilst keeping a wary eye on the door at the other side of the room. 'What the hell are you doing sending Christa? I'm sending her back. She'll be lethal on a job like this. Ring me, first chance you get.' She turned to Pat. 'Pieternel said she'd be off line most of the day. I'll email. She might get that faster. In the meantime, let's get shot of Christa before she absorbs too much from your file archive.'

She called Christa out from the small room. 'I'm really sorry, Christa, there's been a cock-up over money. We can't pay you beyond this morning. I can't get Pieternel at the moment but we'll give you out-of-pocket expenses and enough to get back, and I'll make sure Pieternel—'

'Oh, don't worry about that. I've had a stash up front

and I'm being paid direct from London. I'll have that file for you soon.'

Pat and Annie exchanged a glance as Christa disappeared again. After a short silence, Annie said, 'That complicates things a bit. Looks like we'll need Pieternel to tell her. Heaven knows what she's playing at. She can't have thought I really wanted her here.'

Annie's mind ran through the things she'd told Pieternel in her last few calls. An attempted hit-and-run, a gun in her neck, kidnap, incarceration. Maybe Pieternel genuinely thought she needed help.

'If, for any reason, we can't get her to go straight back, we'll have to find something to keep her out of mischief.'

'Well, I need someone to get to grips with Babs's cases, but could she do that?'

Annie let out a sigh. There'd been a few occasions on which she'd worked with Christa when Christa was free of chemical cocktails diluting her blood. 'She can be inspired, work miracles even. But she's volatile; goes off on her own.'

'There's one thing. Unless that boss of yours has changed, she won't have shelled out a cent more than she had to.'

'That's true, probably a day or two at worst,' Annie agreed, then burst out, 'Hell, we can do without this. We need to be getting at Carl, not dealing with bloody personnel cock-ups. Let's hear the worst. Let's see how long we're stuck with her.' Raising her voice, she shouted, 'Christa!'

'Gimme a chance,' came the muffled reply. 'Who am I, sodding Wonder Woman?'

'No, not that. Just come out here a moment... How long are you expecting to be here?'

'Five weeks max, I was told.'

'What exactly did Pieternel tell you when she sent you here?'

'Nothing much. She mentioned the morgue thing.' Christa shrugged as though to say, does it matter?

'What do you mean, nothing much? She must have told you something or you wouldn't have known anything about it.'

'She rang me, told me you needed a hand and to get my ass over to this little place near King's Cross. The guy there gave me the gen. And here I am. Now can I get back and get this file found so I can get on with something useful? I hate wasting time.'

Annie held her expression neutral as she felt the shock prickle the hairs on her neck. Barely registering the answers, she shot a couple more questions at Christa: how much of her time had been bought in advance and how much had Pieternel given her in hard cash. Christa gabbled out impatient replies and Annie watched Pat's face. Had she cottoned on yet?

'OK, get back to it. Let's have that file found.'

As the door closed again behind Christa, Annie murmured, half to herself, 'I wonder if that cuts Barbara out of the loop.'

'What are you on about?'

Annie thought about an agency near Kings Cross and about someone paying for six weeks of her time. She'd been here a week now. Christa's time had been paid for five weeks. She could feel bewilderment etch itself on to her face; she and Christa were both here to do the same job.

But why? Had she not been working fast enough?

Pieternel's text made sense now. The request for Christa had come from someone else, the same some-

one else who had originally called in Annie. No doubt
Pieternel had been told that Annie knew all about it.
Her text had been to make sure. She became aware of
Pat, who crossed the room and slumped down in one
of the chairs. She must be impatient for answers. Annie
hardly knew where to begin.

'The agency she mentioned, it's…' Annie stopped.
Pat wasn't looking at her. She had her head in her hands;
her breathing exaggerated, as though she were about
to cry. Pat? Cry?

Annie sprang forward and reached out, but then drew
her hand back, not knowing what to do or say.

It was Pat who spoke, without raising her head.
'What the hell's happening, Annie? What are we playing at? The business is done. I can't pick up Babs's
cases. I don't even know what they are…don't know if
she'll be back. And if we've the Sleemans against us
now as well…'

Awkwardly, Annie placed her hand on Pat's shoulder. 'Barbara's going to be OK,' she said. 'She'll be
back before you know it, and she won't thank you for
letting things slide. And I've been paid upfront, remember? I'm going to stick around and help to get through
this. As to—'

She stopped as the door to the back office swung
open. Pat's head shot up and she heaved herself to her
feet, brushing Annie aside, as Christa marched over
and waved a sheaf of papers under her nose. 'Is this the
one, Aker Hassan?'

Annie watched Pat form a contemptuous 'No' and
watched it deflate like a pricked balloon. Their eyes
met. Annie knew her own bewilderment was reflected
in Pat's face. Only Christa, between them, retained
her bounce.

'Yes,' Pat murmured. 'That's the one.'

The anomalies crowded in, making Annie's brain spin.

'Good work,' she barked at Christa, a little more harshly than she intended. 'Now we have it, we can find what we need to get this job rolling.'

'I can get straight out after him now. Every second we stand about, he gets that much start on us.'

'No, no.' Annie held up her hand. 'It's not that kind of job. The guy's not going anywhere.' She pulled in a deep breath. For the time being she had to take charge, shield Pat until she was ready to pick up the reins again. The first thing was to get Christa defused and walled off somewhere she could do no harm. 'Now listen carefully, Christa. This office has been bugged. It's OK at the moment but any time you come back in, do a new sweep. It isn't quite clear who's getting access.'

She told Christa about the phones. 'If you need to make a call about the case or any call that mentions me, remove the thing, then put it back afterwards. It's very basic.'

'I'll say,' said Christa, taking the device from Annie and turning it into the light. 'This isn't for real, right? This is someone taking the piss.'

Annie shrugged. 'Maybe, maybe not. But leave them both in place for ordinary calls. OK, first things first, did you drive straight down here? Have you had anything to eat this morning?'

'I grabbed some crisps on the train.' Christa gave another amazed stare at the device as she handed it back to Annie, then shook her head. 'Oh, and I got up here by cab. I don't know the buses yet. Can I get the fare on expenses and when can I get a car?'

'Yeah, note it down.' Annie felt a surge of relief.

Christa wasn't dangerously mobile. And whatever she'd been paid up front, she wouldn't shell out to hire a vehicle from her own money.

'Like I said,' Annie told her. 'Glitch with the finance. We can't run to a car for you, but don't worry, the business end of this job's right here in town. Did you see that coffee bar at the far end of the street, the one with all the posters in the windows?' When Christa nodded, Annie pulled a note from her pocket and handed it across. 'Go and get us a decent coffee each and some sort of snack. By the time you get back, me and Pat'll have dug out all we need.'

Annie watched Christa clatter down the stairs and let herself out of the building before she returned to the office. Pat squared her shoulders as Annie swung open the door.

'What now?' she said.

'First thing, we need to set her on to something that'll keep her quiet while we get on with things. And what's with that file?' She pointed to the folder still clutched in Pat's hand. 'Why was it in there and not in the filing cabinet?'

Pat's expression was troubled. 'This isn't the original. It looks to me like Babs made a copy. I don't know why. We wouldn't normally, but maybe with Vince saying not to enter it on the system... I don't know.'

Annie held out her hand. 'Can I see?'

She flicked through the few pages and read through the notes.

'Is he a Dr or a Mr?' she asked.

Pat shrugged a *don't know.*

An email from Barbara, subject line 'Latest case', sent to a generic address at Sleeman's firm, said simply, *The guy's 100% legit.*

On the bottom of the page was a handwritten scrawl:

When I said keep this off the bloody computer I meant no emails stupid cow. And I don't give a damn if he's legit, I said find me something.

The page was a copy of what had been a well-folded sheet of paper, no hint as to how the written reply had been delivered. Annie held it out to Pat. 'Did Barbara tell you about this?'

Pat shook her head. 'I knew she was furious with Vince over something. I'll bet that's when she took copies for the archive.'

'But is this anything to do with what's been happening this last week?'

'I don't see how. As far as I know, Vince lost interest in the guy, or maybe he set someone else on to him.'

'Well, I suppose it'd be something to keep Christa out of our hair. She's good if you can keep her focused and stop her running away with things. Look how she ferreted this out. Let's see how the land lies, then we'll get her to find out all Barbara's live cases. For now, if we can make out that this guy's at the heart of the case, she'll be happy chasing him while we go out and about. She can check up online, then go and follow him. In fact, she can find out why Vince was after him; that'll be a reason not to blab to any of the Sleemans if they catch up with her.'

'And what are we going to do? Shall I get on to Carl again and set up a meeting?'

Their stares locked for a second as though Pat dared Annie to say any more about a trip to the farmhouse. Annie noted the bait but ignored it. She wasn't ready to have that battle with Pat just yet, and there were other things that had begun to bug her. 'There's another line of enquiry I'd like us to try first. I want to chase up that stuff Scott Kerridge told me. He was pulled into something dodgy with a guy called Greaves.'

'That thing about them picking up some woman off the beach?'

'Yeah, but I can't see Scott overstepping the line voluntarily and he seems convinced this Greaves guy is straight, too. How do you fancy taking a trip out to talk to Scott's wife? It has to be you. She sure as hell won't talk to me.'

'OK, but what am I after?'

Annie shrugged. 'Whatever you can get out of her; her views on Greaves; whether she knows about it at all.'

'I suppose she might let slip exactly where this so-called woman was picked up from. That's if she'll talk to me at all.'

'I don't see why not. It was me she had the problem with.'

'So what will you do?'

'See if I can follow it up from another angle, and then...'

Annie paused at the sound of footsteps on the stairs. She raised her hand to quash further discussion as Pat said, 'She's never been all the way down there and back by now.'

Christa marched through the door, coffee shop carriers swinging from her hand, bringing the tang of fresh coffee and the aroma of warm pastry. Pat sniffed appreciatively as Christa handed round the polystyrene cups.

'I told you she's good,' Annie murmured to Pat. 'And quick. Too bloody quick sometimes.'

But not this time, she added to herself as she smiled at Christa preparatory to explaining her surveillance role on the unwitting Aker Hassan. Christa's reappearance had been perfectly timed. Annie hadn't wanted to

go into the detail of her own intended part in checking
Scott's story. Far better that everyone, including Pat,
should assume she had no idea where Scott's strange
tale had played out.

FIFTEEN

FORTY MINUTES LATER, Annie drove along a thick tarmac ribbon of a road that had passing places every few metres. It was wide enough for two cars to pass, but only just. The frequent passing places and the extra thick surface were for the lorries and heavier vehicles that plied their trade along it. This Friday afternoon, with barely a hint of dusk in the sky, it was quiet. Acres of fields stretched out either side, boundary ditches invisible from the road, their course marked by changes in the colour of the crop and an occasional ragged stretch of hedgerow. The breeze held the sharp tang of salt, though the gentle rise of the landscape blocked the sea from view. She clicked the button to close the window, seeing a combine harvester cough a cloud of dust in the field beside her, just as an orange-and-red striped police Range Rover swept past in the other direction. Annie glimpsed a man and a woman in uniform, the woman flapping her hand at a cloud of harvest flies and throwing an irritated glance at the field. Annie caught a glimpse of an automatic weapon, the sight of which gave her a jolt. She knew the plant was heavily guarded, that they had no interest in her, but it pulled her up to see them, made her feel guilty, as though her errand was blazoned on the sides of her car.

The forty-minute journey, a familiar route from years ago, should have been long enough for her to relax. Hedon Road had taken her east out of the city, where less of an industrial wasteland than she remembered bordered the docks along the Humber. Changes on the inland side of the road had been more marked. Where memory told her there would be a run-down terrace, she'd driven past a row of smartly renovated dwellings, and further along, where she recalled large square houses standing back from the road alongside bustling factories, she'd seen only derelict shells.

Christa had seemed happy enough to go after Hassan. Vince's apparent malice towards the guy might have meant he'd had a hand in the treatment of Vince's recent illness. Pat didn't know. She'd pulled herself out of that moment of despair, but Annie wondered how long she would be able to function normally if Barbara took a turn for the worse or they couldn't find any answers. Annie herself felt dazed by the events of the past week. For Pat it was all so much closer to home.

Vince's condition was long-standing and had recently become worse. Pat had muttered that Vince wouldn't buy or threaten his way out of this one, but Annie wondered if that was exactly what he'd tried, and the legit Dr Hassan had earned his wrath by giving him the wrong answer.

After she'd passed the familiar skyline of the Salt End chemical works that marked the transition from urban to rural, Annie found her mind turning to Jean and her gang at the racecourse. She had toyed with the idea that they were in on things with Carl Sleeman. After all, it was the job set up by Crazy Carl and one of them had taken her phone, maybe not by accident. But she couldn't make the theory stick. Her gut instinct was rarely quite so wrong. Those people were wrapped up in their own world of ponies and the plethora of trouble and vexation that world seemed to carry with it, even when amateur poisoners weren't involved. They had no time for pacts with people like the Sleemans.

Following the twists of the road through the villages and hamlets towards the seaside town of Withernsea, she'd fought back a wave of frustration. From being an irrelevant nuisance at the edge of her thoughts, Scott's intervention had begun to stand out as more significant. The link with Carl Sleeman via his pseudonym, Lance Malers…his going to the trouble of warning her off… then breaking into Pat's office.

Get back to the source or as close as you can: a prime rule of the job. She wondered how Pat was getting on with Scott's wife.

Withernsea had been quiet as she'd bounced through the speed bumps of the main street and out beyond the town, heading south down a road that ended with Spurn Point at the tip of the Humber, except she wasn't going that far.

She'd driven towards Hollym, past the neat grasslands of an air strip, incongruous here at the edge of the sea, its orange windsock flapping, on through the village itself and out to a landscape of ploughed earth, the sea occasionally visible over the undulations of the fields to her left, until an abrupt turn brought the ocean head on, its crashing waves surprisingly close. The blades of a single wind turbine reached up ahead of her, becoming one in a cluster of half a dozen or so spinning lazily as she drew nearer. She passed the road to RAF Holmpton with a feeling of officialdom closing in. Ahead lay the vast acreage of the gas plant at Easington, with its high wire fences and ever-circling armed guards. The road drew her closer and closer to the heart of it until she drove with well-maintained double fences either side, electric wires standing ready to catch anyone who made it across the rolled barbed wire of the outer defence. The shiny eyes of multiple CCTV cameras watched her and she heard the low rumble of the rotor blades of a helicopter overhead.

The bright silver of the armoured boundaries turned abruptly into an ordinary street; a village with a picture-postcard pub, village store and red telephone box, overseen by a tall church. With a single sharp twist, the road whipped away all sign of the vast complex from her rear-view mirror.

Barely a stone's throw from here lay a small cove that must have been a haven for smugglers long before officialdom and big business laid down roots across the area. That it had continued to run a low-level operation almost under the noses of the tight security at Easington seemed to Annie to mirror the tiny flies that plagued the area at harvest time-ever-present, a universal source of annoyance and no respecter of heavy weaponry.

She'd never heard of anything more lethal than skunk weed changing hands, but then she'd made sure not to enquire too deeply. It was a hazard of the job that people confided more than they should, more than they would have given to an investigator with a warrant card rather than a licence. It was all about perception. The PI was the slightly shady character who dealt in matters not entirely legal. She wondered how it was in the States, where private investigation had a far higher standing. Maybe it was the uniformed police who heard the impromptu confessions.

What she knew of the cove was that it was a low-volume concern, dealing only in resin and skunk. But trafficking people? If it were the same crew that she'd known before, and Scott's descriptions had fitted, then it just wasn't credible.

But here was the source of Scott's strange tale and Annie intended to rekindle some old contacts.

SIXTEEN

ANNIE PULLED THE car off the road well before her destination and tucked it as close as she could under a stubby hedge, flinching as the hawthorn screeched on the paintwork. Easington's security would already have matched her identity with the vehicle and stashed it in a database somewhere, but she had to hope these were not sources that Sleeman could access. As far as anyone connected with the case was concerned, she intended to keep her identity unconnected with this car for as long as possible.

The headland was uneven, the ground stony; her feet tipped this way and that on the large clods of earth. She squeezed through the thin remnants of a hedgerow that bordered the seaward end and used the tough dune grasses as handholds as she slithered down the drop, letting go and taking the final metre in one jump, careful to land on her good leg on a smooth patch of shale. The mini cliff behind her cut off the rest of the world. She was alone on the beach, a stiff breeze ruffling her hair, the steady swish of the waves sucking the shale up the beach and dragging it back out. Ignoring the track to the cottage that was her goal, she walked down to the edge of the sea and along towards the rise over which Scott and Greaves would have come.

She passed by a well-blackened patch above the reach of all but the spring tides and kicked out at the remains of burnt driftwood. This was where the guys

lit their barbecue. Scott had talked about a man and a
woman, woollen caps, well-wrapped against the night
air. It fitted her memories, but maybe it was a new firm,
a new operation. It had been a long time. Far out to sea
was the indistinct outline of some sort of vessel, possibly a passenger ferry. At night, it would only be visible
by its lights. A boat could come in close without being
seen if it kept itself dark. Scott had described a string
of lanterns that Annie had recognized as the signal for
don't land. Someone either hadn't understood or hadn't
cared when they'd dropped the woman in the shallows...
if that was what had happened. Just beyond the reach of
the waves, looking out to sea, she tried to imagine the
beach on a dark night four weeks ago. Maybe it wasn't
a landing at all. Had the woman waded into the water
that night to get into a boat, not out of one? Had she seen
the vessel turn away as the lanterns flared to life, and
then had no choice but to wade ashore? She glanced towards the cottage, knowing that anyone up there would
be able to see her, expecting someone to wander down
as though by accident. That was how meetings used to
happen. But no one came and after almost ten minutes
of walking up and down on the shale, she headed for
the path that would take her up there.

As she pushed open the garden gate she could see
a shadow through the frosted glass. Someone sat in
the kitchen where the window overlooked the shore,
and must have seen her. The door swung wide at her
knock and she walked inside, to be met by the sweet
tang of cannabis although the windows gaped open and
a draught blew through. The man at the table looked
at her. She took in his tattered jumper, the frayed tar-
tan collar of an old shirt, the woollen hat pulled tight

over his head. He looked thinner than she remembered, and frailer.

'Hi. Do you remember me?'

His shrug was noncommittal. 'What do you want?'

'Just to talk.'

'I've nothing for you, whatever you're after.' He lifted a cracked cup to his lips.

'I'm not here to buy.'

He shot her a glare. 'Good job, because I've nothing to sell.'

Abruptly, he stood up. Annie moved aside as he pushed past her and peered out through the door as though to check she was alone. 'Where's your car?'

She told him.

Coming back in, he stopped close to her and stared into her eyes; close enough that she could smell the mustiness from the old jumper. It was hard to tell if his skin was grimy or if the shadows were healing bruises. If the latter, he'd taken quite a beating not too long ago.

'Yeah, I do know you, don't I?' He turned away, eyes screwed up in thought and went to sit down again. 'Were you the private eye or the one who came to score for—'

'The private eye. I didn't come to score for anyone. And I'm not here for that now.'

'Just as well, because we've nothing to sell,' he repeated. 'I've not seen you in years. What are you after?' The suspicion in his voice had ebbed, but not altogether.

'I've been working down south. How's things?'

'You'll get nothing here just now.'

'Why not?'

'We're taking things easy. Letting things settle.' These statements were made with more weary resignation than suspicion, so Annie risked getting to the heart of the matter.

'You mean after that woman was picked up by those two coppers?'

'What do you know about that?'

'Nothing. I'm trying to find out. Can you show me where?'

He tipped his half empty cup towards him, stared into its depths for a moment, then drained it and stood up, wiping his mouth on his sleeve.

As they left the cottage and made for the path down to the shore, Annie felt the buzz of her phone in her pocket and slid it half out to snatch a look. She remembered these guys of old. Whether it was a background level of chemicals in their blood or something else, they acted on the whim of the moment. He'd decided to walk with her to the beach, to show her where the strange events had played out. This was not the moment to break his mood. She clicked off the phone, noting that it was a number on the screen and not a name. If it were someone she didn't know, they could wait. The man took the steep slope with the sure steps of someone who could walk this path in his sleep. Annie scrambled behind him, grabbing at the roots and grasses to avoid tumbling down on top of him. Back at the sea's edge with the shale crunching beneath her shoes, Annie felt a fresh breeze ruffle her hair and watched the man kick out at the remains of the barbecue, just as she had done.

'Everyone knows we don't do that sort of stuff. But you run the risk in a game like this that someone'll come along and make you say yes to something.'

'Someone threatened you to deal with the woman. Who?'

He gave her what she read as an old-fashioned look, so she prompted, 'Sleeman?'

He nodded.

'Which Sleeman?'

'Oh, they sent the runner with the orders first time round, but we said, "no way". Then next thing they've brought in the big guns. We stood our ground. We know what'll happen if we push the boundaries. We've a good thing going here. Why would we wreck it? They weren't even offering good money. We told them to piss off, and they did.' He paused, looking out to sea, then bent to pick up a flat stone which he skimmed out across the incoming waves with an expert flick of his wrist. Annie watched as it bounced over the water's surface and thought back to the heavies who'd leapt out of that car in pursuit of her when they failed to run her down. Had they been here, too? She'd never know for sure. She turned back to the man beside her. He'd never been this talkative before, but she sensed his need to get this off his chest.

'Then we learnt they weren't going to take no for an answer. They...well, let's just say they got in touch with someone else, so it wasn't us they were threatening. They're a dirty lot. They'd target a kid just to get their own way.'

'D'you want to give me any detail? It might be something I can help with.'

'No.'

'So what was supposed to happen? The woman was with you and there was a boat coming in to collect her?'

'Hell, no. She was to be dropped and we were to keep her up there,' he nodded back towards the cottage, 'until she was picked up. We had a call to say she'd be ashore in minutes. We watched the road like we always do and the signal came that a cop car's pulled up so we light the lanterns and get the old barbie going. I never saw any boat, big or small, but she was only wet from the legs down so they'd got her in close. Couldn't see a thing that night.'

'But who was she?'

'Don't know. Don't want to know.'

Annie looked into the man's face. She saw residual fear and frustration but nothing to make her think he was hiding much, though he'd clearly kept back some personal details. Here was yet another story that didn't add up. She felt her own frustration well up again.

'So what happened next?'

'We cancelled everything. We burnt stuff. We thought about going on the run, but where would we go? And anyway, Sleeman was there before we had a chance, wanting every detail. It was the lad who came, the one who goes by Lance. It was odd…'

'What? What was odd?'

'We thought he'd come to have a go, not that we were going to take it from a lad like that, but he just said it was all OK. Then he wanted every last detail. Things he shouldn't need to know if everything was OK. That's when we talked about packing up and taking our chances, but in the end we sat tight.'

'What's happened since?'

'Nothing. Nothing from Sleemans. No visit from the boys in blue. It's like that calm you get when you can feel the pressure rising.'

'Tell me about the woman, what did she look like?'

The man blew out his cheeks and let out a sigh. 'Youngish. Dark hair. It was night; hard to see anything and the coppers took her straight off with them. Slim, I'd say, but you could see she was wearing a stack of clothes.'

'OK, tell me about the hired heavies?'

'Two guys built like brick shit-houses, hands like

meat plates, snap you in two soon as look at you. They were there to tell us we were going to do the job whether we wanted to or not. We weren't asking questions. All we were doing was making clear to them that we had boundaries. There's stuff we'll ship and stuff we won't. And we don't land people.'

Annie looked at him and saw he was hoping for answers she couldn't give. If nothing else, she thought, Sleemans had cut off a minor supplier. He'd confirmed Scott's story but left her with more questions than answers. 'Tell me again,' she said. 'The woman, what she looked like. Every detail you can remember.'

She was on the way back to where she'd left the car when Annie suddenly realized who had called her. With an annoyed exclamation, she snatched her phone from her pocket. Brand-new SIM. Everyone who rang would show up as a number not a name. It had been Christa, and it was always a bad idea to leave Christa to make her own decisions once she'd made up her mind to call in. Christa's phone was off. Annie left a message telling her to ring and then turned to her voice mail. Christa's voice was there, bright and chirpy.

'Guess what? I've found a link between Hassan and the guy who hired me. I wanted to clear it with you first, but I'll take the chance while I've got it. Don't worry if you can't get me. I'll be somewhere where my phone has to be off.'

Annie could only shrug and hope for the best as she climbed back into the car. She and Pat had agreed a rendezvous with Christa later, but before that she and Pat had arranged to meet. As she set off, Annie wondered what, if anything Pat would have prised out of Scott's wife.

'MORE THAN I EXPECTED,' Pat said, as they sat over coffee and sandwiches in a pub at the eastern edge of the city. 'She's worried and she wants to know what's going on. I had the impression she knew full well you were on the scene but she didn't mention you, so I didn't.'

'What did you get?'

'Story of the woman on the beach. Same as Scott told you. Only she claimed she didn't know where. Of course, she must have, but she wasn't telling me.'

'Uh…that doesn't matter for now. How did you get her to talk?'

'I was all ready with a line about her and the kids being in danger, but I didn't need it. The minute I started on my opening pitch, she said, "Cut the crap. We both know what you're here for," and she made coffee. Said Scott was out with the boys but I'd to be gone before he came back. It was like she was glad to see me.'

'She hates private detectives. And not just me; because of Scott. Really hates the whole profession. She's not changed that much in a few years. Are they just spinning us a line? Is it all an act?'

Pat took a large bite out of her sandwich and chewed on it. Then her eyes lost focus for a moment and the movement of her jaw lost tempo, as though she chewed in rhythm with her thoughts. When she spoke, it was with a shake of her head. 'Was he spinning you a line when he came looking for you…when he took that key and came back to the office…when he risked his whole career? I don't think so. The way I see it, they've met up with something they've never had to deal with before. Something dodgy that they can't take through official channels. That Kate'll be giving her head a mental slap and saying, so that's what private eyes are for. I'm sure she still thinks we're scum, but now she knows we're here for a reason. I'll tell you what, though, I'll lay odds you're right about Greaves.'

'Greaves? What, that he's bent, mixed up in it?'

Pat nodded. 'My guess is he's got himself into bother. Drugs, gambling, who knows? And someone's got their claws into him. I tried to hint at it, but she wasn't having it. Far as she's concerned, he's as straight as the day's long. Probably was till the going got tough. It's surprising how easily some of them crack.'

'Yes, I could buy that, but what I don't get is why he involved Scott. I know you've never thought much of him, but—'

'No, no, I know what you mean. He's a good copper. Straight. He might look like a wet weekend, but money would never buy him.'

Annie thought back to Scott carrying out a clandestine search of Pat and Barbara's office; of stealing a key so he could come back at night. 'It doesn't have to be money to corrupt a copper, does it? Maybe it's just a case of dragging Scott into something until he thinks he's in too deep and then threatening his family. He's already worrying about that.'

'What are you saying?'

Annie looked at the half-eaten sandwich on her plate and pushed it aside. 'This whole thing can't be an elaborate hoax to get Scott Kerridge drawn on to someone's payroll, can it?'

Pat's gaze snapped up to meet Annie's. 'That's a thought. And it fits with Greaves being in on it.'

Annie thought about how the events of that night had put the frighteners on a couple of small-time drug-runners. Two birds with one stone, almost. But no, that made no sense. Why would Vince suddenly care about their operation? 'Let's just think this through,' she said. 'Scott was in Withernsea taking a witness statement and some kids had a go at his car so he couldn't get back. I guess that's easy enough to arrange.'

'Then Rob Greaves is on the spot to give him a lift. He gets involved in grabbing the woman off the shore and Greaves spins him a line about it all going pear-shaped and they have to keep quiet.'

Annie's gaze locked with Pat's for a moment. 'It was a hell of a risk,' said Pat.

'Or maybe it wasn't a set up; maybe his car got trashed and he spotted Greaves. Why would Greaves be down that way at all? Suppose he got lumbered with Scott at the last minute and had to busk it. Scott was off on leave the next day.'

'Yeah, she told me all about it. Holiday to Whitby with the kids. So he'd be happy to keep his head down, not risk anything that was going to stop him going.'

'Then Greaves has time to think up a line to keep him quiet after he gets back.'

For a moment they sat in silence, then Annie glanced up at the clock. 'We should get going soon to meet up with Christa, see what she's found on this Hassan guy.'

'You said she reckons to have found a link with Vince?'

'She didn't say Vince, she said the guy who hired her. But I'm guessing she was told Vince Sleeman, just like I was.'

Pat shrugged. 'He could have been one of the ones who saw Vince in the early days. Vince kept sacking them. It was all Leah could do to keep him from dumping every doctor in the country. He's been thrown off several GPs' lists over the years.'

'Why? What does he do?'

'He hates them. Reckons they know nothing. He only went to hospital in the first place because he collapsed in a pub. Discharged himself as soon as he could get on his feet. Leah really kicked off, but he got his own way.'

'He usually does,' Annie pointed out coldly.

'Oh, not with Leah. She keeps him on the leash when he's under her roof, and of course he's had to be under her roof a fair bit since he got ill.'

'This is all very recent, isn't it?' Annie asked, thinking back to the call Pat had received three days ago telling her Vince had discharged himself from hospital. She glanced at the clock again, but couldn't summon the energy to rise. The battering she'd taken over the last few days had sucked the energy out of her.

'No,' said Pat. 'It's been a few months. He's been in and out of hospital. He's getting used to it now.'

'I'm surprised they put up with it.'

'Yeah, he's a crabby old sod. I know for a fact Leah got him back in once by knocking him out with something she shouldn't. Claimed he'd taken it himself. She had to tell them because if they'd treated him not knowing what was in his system they'd have killed him.'

'What did she do?' Annie asked idly, thinking that if she'd been in Leah's position, she'd have let Vince take his chances.

'Injected him with that same stuff that killed Michael Jackson, I think.'

'Christ! Where would she get that from?'

Pat shrugged. 'In that family, everything's on tap. She said he'd have to get used to hospitals because he was going in for an op and you can't discharge yourself in the middle of that. They had a real row right there in the clinic when they told him he'd just about cashed in his chips. She had us all down there getting tested.

There was me, Babs and Carl with a gaggle of kids, Barbara's and a stack of Carl's cousins.' Pat laughed. 'I said to Babs, "Drop a bomb on this waiting room and you've wiped out everyone in our family under sixty".'

'What were you being tested for?'

'To see if we matched to give Vince a kidney.'

'I thought it was his liver that was packing up.'

'I dunno. Not my thing, medicine, doctors, all that. I've some sympathy with Vince on that one. Liver, kidney…same difference. I suppose we should make a move.' She gripped the chair arms preparatory to rising.

'No, it's not.' Annie put out her hand to stop Pat from standing up. 'Just hang about. If we're late for Christa, she'll have to wait.' She paused to tap the table top for luck on Christa waiting, but noted it was plastic, not wood. 'You can donate a kidney because you have two of them. You can't donate a liver. Liver transplants come from people who've died.'

'Maybe they can take a bit. You've seen liver in the butchers, all in lobes. It's all the same stuff. These days, can't they just take a section?'

'No… I don't know… I don't think human liver's the same.'

'And anyway, they said kidney. They were testing us to see if we could give Vince a kidney.'

'And were any of you a match?'

Pat shook her head and laughed. 'Nope, not one of us. Family like ours, you shouldn't go into who's a blood relation and who isn't. I'll never forget the look on Leah's face. If the doctor who did the tests had been there at the time, she'd have had a knife in him for sure.'

'Was it Hassan?'

'I'm pretty sure not.'

Reluctantly, Annie stood up, glancing out at the darkening sky. 'We ought to get going, but just before we do, there's something I need to ask you. I don't want an answer right now, but the answer has to be yes. I know where the woman is, the woman who came out of the sea. I had an inkling earlier, but now I'm sure. We're going to go and find her, you and me.'

'So what the big deal? Where is she?'

'She's at the house Carl Sleeman took me to. Vince's house. And we're going back there.'

'Whoa! Not a—'

Putting her hand up again, Annie cut across Pat, annoyed at her diving right in with a negative. 'I said I don't want an answer right now. I just want it crystal clear that the answer's going to be yes, so get used to it.'

Hearing the words out of her own mouth, Annie tensed. That hadn't come out right at all. Who was she to keep shelling out the orders? It wasn't so long ago that Pat had been her boss; still was on paper for the duration of this assignment. She gritted her teeth for Pat's retaliation, but Pat just curled her lip with a contemptuous, 'Huh!' and grumbled her way out of the door, turning back towards Annie as she pulled out her car keys, muttering, 'All right, do your bloody act. I haven't forgotten.'

Annie patted her pockets and with an irritable gesture, turned back to the pub as Pat climbed into her car. The act was that Pat would sit behind the wheel as though waiting for Annie to come out with whatever it was she'd forgotten, giving Annie time to go out the back way and get to her own car. If they were being tailed, Annie wouldn't keep the car a secret for ever, but she hoped to retain its anonymity for a while longer. She skipped across the waste ground behind the pub,

seeing no one as she made her way down one of Hull's
many tenfoots to the back street where she'd parked.

Whilst keeping an eye out for clandestine watchers, her thoughts were with Barbara still lying comatose after the hit-and-run. Had Barbara been a match, a
possible donor for Vince? Annie's medical knowledge
was sketchy. For all she knew, liver disease and kidney
disease might go hand in hand, but she was as sure she
could be that a kidney transplant couldn't cure liver
failure. And for all the speed of medical advances, she
didn't think liver transplants came from live donors.

Again, she knew the pieces didn't mesh, but Barbara
was in hospital after a hit-and-run, and there was a mobile morgue hidden at Vince's house.

SEVENTEEN

CHRISTA LOOKED MORE RELAXED, happy to have been brought properly on board, and either oblivious to Pat's simmering hostility or uncaring about it. 'You know, I swore you were playing me along 'smorning,' she said, sinking her teeth into a fat cheese-and-ham panini. 'Giving me a makeweight job. I was gonna give the guy the once over and get myself off out to that place you were recce-ing.' Her words were muffled, breadcrumbs and specks of tomato sauce clustering around her mouth.

Annie gave Pat a hard stare to stop her saying the wrong thing, and murmured, 'Oh, Hassan's at the heart of it.' Behind her words played the image of Barbara in a hospital bed, of Carl Sleeman shrieking at an oversized trailer in his drive, of a car almost mowing her down in a secluded street. Annie felt the thud of her heart and swallowed against a hollow sensation in her gut. She was beginning to think that Hassan could genuinely be at the heart of it. Or if not him, one of his colleagues. But Christa's gaze was too twitchy as it darted about the room, resting on each of the few dozen customers, the hurrying waiters, the late shoppers meandering past the windows. Christa was high on something; speed probably. Annie wouldn't let her out of her sight until she'd fallen off the peak of invincibility and into the paranoid fantasy about hidden watchers that was already building in her addled brain.

Pat lifted her own sandwich to her mouth as she returned Annie's look. Annie sat in silence while her two companions tucked in. She'd suggested this coffee bar just across from the station because she remembered it for its large portions of freshly cooked food that would meet both Pat's and Christa's approval. Christa's appetite was a symptom of the chemicals swirling through her system; Pat's simply a love of food. Christa let out bits of information in between mouthfuls. She thought Hassan had been blackmailed but wasn't sure. She was going back this evening to check it out. Annie told her, 'That's good. That's interesting. We need to get more on that.'

Annie watched as a crowd of people, all smiles and bonhomie, swarmed in through the door and threaded their way between the tables to the counter. Once they were firmly in place as a substantial queue, she pulled a note from her pocket and leant across to Christa, saying, 'D'you want some cake? They do a really good toffee muffin here.' Seeing Pat's eyes light up, Annie blew out a sigh and added, 'Get one for Pat, too, and three more coffees.'

With Christa at the back of the queue avidly listening to the conversations around her, Annie turned back to Pat. 'We have to get out to Vince's place. They've got that woman there. I want a proper look round and I need you to help me.'

'No way. You've no idea what you're asking.'

'But why? What's the problem? Vince is in no state to make a fuss.'

'Yeah, but Leah… It's different out there. Leah doesn't fuss about what goes on in town, but no one treads on her toes.'

'I don't see what the big deal is with…' Annie

stopped as she remembered the fragment of the call she'd overheard that day when Scott had been in the office. 'Pat, you remember when someone called you to tell you that Vince had discharged himself? Was it Leah?'

'Yes, why?'

'Nothing.' Annie shrugged. So Pat was genuinely frightened of Vince's wife, but why? 'Uh...does she... did she have much to do with the firm years ago? I don't remember anything about her from when I was here before. I didn't even know Vince was married.'

Pat shook her head. 'No, she never had anything to do with Dad's business or Vince's. Dad couldn't abide her, but he respected her. And he taught us to do the same.'

So it was a childhood thing, without rationale or reason behind it. Annie glanced up to check on Christa's progress and said, 'Ignore any reference she makes to Vince's place. Don't try and tell her it isn't important or anything like that. It'll only focus her on it.'

'She's wasted on something, isn't she?'

Annie nodded. 'And I don't want to let her out of my sight until she's off the high and desperate to hide herself away in a dark corner; shouldn't be long. But I don't see why you shouldn't call in to see how Vince is getting on. Hell, you might not get on with the guy, but he was your dad's best mate. Would that be such a difficult thing to do?'

Pat pulled a face and let out a sigh. 'Well, all right. But if we're going to go through with this, it's on my terms, not yours. I'd never go out there asking after Vince, but I'd go if something was going on that I didn't understand, and if I was worried about it. Something like you turning up on the doorstep out of the blue, apparently called in by Vince, then disappearing again, and I want to know what's going on. How does that sound?'

Annie nodded slowly. 'Yes, good. That gets right to the heart of it. And of course, I won't come right to the house with you. I'll come as far as—'

'I was getting to that,' Pat interrupted. 'You won't come as far as anything. If I'm going out there with that cock-and-bull story, I'm going on my own.' She held up her hand. 'No buts. I can't talk to them knowing you're skulking about outside. I'd give the game away, I know I would. Anyone but Leah, maybe. Sorry, but that's how it is. And it might at least bring out who's behind what. Don't tell me you don't want to know. I do.'

'Yes, OK, but suppose Vince is behind it-well, some of it-giving orders through Carl. Maybe his wife knows nothing about it. If you go there with that line, she'll get to know. What happens then?'

'On the whole, she leaves him be. As long as he doesn't interfere with anything she's doing, he can be as obnoxious as he likes. And if it's something Leah doesn't want him to do, I guess she'll stop him. She wants him well again, and he's not doing himself any favours getting mixed up in stuff. If he wasn't as ill as he is and she tried to interfere, they'd fight, but with him being on his deathbed he'll have to do as he's told. I've Babs's washing to do in the morning. I'll go in the afternoon. And I need to be off soon anyway to get to the hospital.'

Annie opened her mouth to query Pat on her exact timing, but quickly shifted gear as Christa came back, slumped in her seat and reached forward to plant a large plastic '27' on a stalk in the middle of the table. If Pat were going out there on her own, Annie intended to be close behind, but she knew Pat would suspect exactly that, so maybe her real intention was to go out in the morning and Barbara's washing was an excuse to put Annie off the scent.

'I ordered chocolate fudge cake,' Christa said. 'Looked better.'

Pat nodded her approval, and Annie said, 'We've not met Hassan. He was Pat's sister's case. What does he look like?'

Christa shrugged. 'Dunno. Haven't seen him.'

Pat glared at Christa. 'You said he told you he was being blackmailed.'

'I didn't say it was him. It was one of the medical secretaries thought he might be being blackmailed. She said as much to her mate at the time. She's going to look me out some stuff tonight if she can.' Christa gave a short laugh. 'D'you think some stuck-up consultant's going to talk to me about stuff like that. Get real.'

Annie shot Christa a hard look. 'Emailed her mate about it, did she?'

Christa replied with a knowing wink. A kaleidoscope of emotions crossed Pat's features; gobsmacked at Christa getting so much so quickly; annoyance at her tone; a need for a cutting comment to cut the cocky newcomer down to size. Annie was relieved to see a waiter arrive bearing a tray with a trio of steaming coffee cups and two plates of chocolaty goo with long spoons. Christa, stick thin, and Pat, three times her size, dived in with equal enthusiasm as Annie raised her cup to her lips and shot another narrow-eyed glare at Christa. One of these days, she'd land herself in trouble too deep to find a way out. Gaining unauthorized access to emails was a trick Christa prided herself on. And it had had its uses. Pieternel had piled on too much praise when she'd needed the party trick performing. But it was legal quicksand on which to build a case. She sat back with a sigh. This wasn't a case. The real cases—the ones Pat was worrying over, the ones Barbara had been in the middle of—were piling up in the office while she and Pat chased the shadows that closed in around them.

'Your sister's in Hull Royal, yeah?' Christa said, wiping her mouth on her sleeve.

Pat acknowledged her with a tiny nod.

'You gonna see her tonight?'

'I go every night.'

'You can give me a lift, then. I'm due to meet my contact later.'

'Oh, I can, can I?' Pat snapped, clearly nettled at Christa's tone.

'Uh…no, don't worry,' Annie broke in. 'Come with me, Christa. I'll drop you off.' She flashed a quick look towards Pat to remind her of her intention not to let Christa out of her sight just yet. 'Remind me, where is it from here? Oh, it's OK. I can see your car over there. Mine's just round the corner. Don't set off too fast and I can track you in.'

'God, what a fuss!' Pat slammed down her spoon, making them both jump. 'Down to the traffic lights, turn right, keep going.'

Annie looked at Pat in surprise. She thought she'd relaxed a bit since this morning, but maybe Christa had got further under her skin than she'd realized.

As Annie pulled into the hospital car park, she saw Pat stomping down the pavement towards the crossing at the front of the main building, annoyance still radiating from her. She wasn't sure whether Pat spotted her, but didn't try to catch her attention. Christa, beside her, yawned extravagantly and pulled out her phone. Annie snaked around the lines of parked cars looking for a space, hearing the click-click-click of Christa tapping out a text. She would stay close to Christa when she met her contact, but as soon as she could manufacture the opportunity she intended to attach a crude tracker to Pat's car. Pat was not going to sneak off to Vince's place without her. 'Where to?' she asked Christa as they walked together towards the main entrance.

'We'll have to wait a bit, but she'll nip out when she can. If she asks, you're undercover Special Branch.'

Annie rolled her eyes heavenwards but said only, 'How long will she be?'

'Fifteen, twenty minutes.'

Annie smiled. Fifteen minutes were plenty to see to Pat's car.

'Just a sec,' Christa said suddenly, taking Annie unawares as she darted off between the vehicles and made for a gang of youths clustered round a motorbike. Annie glared after her, but kept her distance. She didn't want to be on CCTV with that crowd. Nor should Christa, but too late for that. These would be Christa's latest dealers. She'd probably found them on her first trip before going into the hospital and delving into unattended computers. As soon as Christa came back, Annie took her arm and hurried her towards the hospital. 'Look, you know what's going to happen if—'

'Yeah, yeah, yada yada. You can bollock me later, OK? Let's get to my contact first.'

Annie pursed her lips but said nothing. The number of people around them grew as they neared the bottleneck of the entrance doors. When they reached the corner where Christa said they must wait, Annie let Christa sit down before she said, 'If we've fifteen minutes to wait, I'll nip up and see how Barbara's doing.'

Christa shot her a suspicious glance. 'You want me to come?'

'Hell, no.' Annie laughed. 'Pat'd have you thrown out. I won't be long.'

She turned and walked towards the lift bay, cursing under her breath. Christa might be in the process of frying her mind but she hadn't lost her wits and had sensed an undercurrent. Now Annie would have to go all the way to the ward in case Christa followed. She marched along the corridors, not allowing herself to turn until within sight of the door of Barbara's room. No obvious sign of Christa behind her. About to turn back, she was stopped by a voice saying, 'Hello, it's Annie, isn't it?'

'Yes. Hi.' She reached out to shake hands with Barbara's son. 'How's your mother? I was dropping someone off so I thought I'd just call up and enquire. Is Pat here?'

'Yeah, she's doing well. But Aunt Pat couldn't make it tonight. She rang me not ten minutes ago. She'll be round in the morning instead. D'you want to come and see Mum?'

'Uh...no, thanks. I... I have to be off. I only had a minute.'

Giving him a beaming smile and hoping he wouldn't think her too rude, Annie turned and sprinted back down the corridor. Damn it! No wonder Pat had been annoyed to learn they would follow her to the hospital. She'd had no intention of visiting tonight. She was heading off for Vince's right now. How much of a start would she have? She'd made for the main doors in full view of Annie and Christa as they'd arrived, but then what? Had she concealed herself in the concrete jungle that was the entrance to the big hospital, let them walk in past her and then doubled back? As she ran, her phone began to vibrate an incoming call. She snatched it out. Christa. Still running, she jammed the handset to her ear.

'What's up?'

'My contact nipped out as soon as you were gone. I'd have called, but she only had a minute. What are you doing? Are you running?'

'Uh…no. No, it's noisy here, that's all. What did she say?'

'She's gonna come back down later,' Christa rattled the words out as though on a timer. 'But she said you'd be able to look out the case 'cos there was police involvement. You know, you being Special Branch—'

'Yeah, yeah, but what else did she say?'

'There was a complaint. She mentioned the name Greaves.'

'What? Hassan complained about Greaves?'

'No, I don't think it was that.'

'Christa, where are you?' Annie barked out the question, in agonies of indecision. Did she tell Christa to head out and look for Pat? Or did she try to get out of the hospital unobserved and leave Christa to wait for her contact?

'Just gone to get a coke from the machine.'

That put Christa the wrong side of the hospital for the car park entrance and made up Annie's mind. She was within a spit of the exit herself now.

'Sit and wait, Christa. See what you can get. I'd better keep out of the way now.'

'Why?'

'Well, if I'm supposed to be Special Branch, I know it all, so it'll look suspicious if I'm asking. You spin her a line. You don't need me telling you what to do. OK?'

'OK.'

She cut the call as she sprinted out across the narrow street towards the car park, taking a leap to teeter on top of one of the small posts that held the chain-link fence. Her gaze scanned the expanse of cars and she suppressed a crow of triumph. There was the unmistakable bulk of Pat's form hurrying to the far end. *Should have parked nearer*, thought Annie, *and you might have lost me.* Then she gasped as a gang of youths emerged from the dusk and looked about to ambush Pat. On the point of leaping down from her vantage point to go to help, she saw Pat swing round angrily and shoo them away with fierce hand-gestures.

'Hey, missus!' A boy of about fourteen materialized at Annie's elbow. 'Spare us a few quid, missus. I've lost me bus fare.'

'Sod off.' She gave him a glare and he darted off, looking for easier prey.

Annie hurried to her car and eased it forward out of its space, hanging back to let Pat be first to thread her way through the maze to the exit. As she waited, she glanced at her phone. Christa's contact had mentioned Greaves. This was a link they hadn't begun to figure out. Christa shouldn't be left alone with this. Reluctantly, Annie punched in Scott's number, not sure whether this would prove to be a bad move or a sensible one. She had to find more, to get a handle on what Christa might walk into. As Pat's car bumped its way to the exit, Annie clicked her handset to speakerphone and positioned herself in the queue a few cars back. Pat might just be going home, of course, in which case she would get back here pronto. The ringtone morphed into Scott's voice telling her he was unable to take her call and inviting her to leave a message. There didn't seem much option, but what was she to say? 'Scott, it's…uh… hello.' She wouldn't leave her name. He ought to recognize her voice. 'It's about what we were talking about. I've come across some stuff. A doctor called Hassan. A complaint. I need to know about it. Will you ring me?'

Annie watched Pat's car cross the junction and head towards the big roundabout. If Pat were on her way home, she would turn left ahead and Annie could be back with Christa in minutes. The traffic slowed, an industrial vehicle of some sort was manoeuvring up ahead, holding up the line of cars. The handset rattled on the dashboard as it vibrated an incoming call. Annie peered over at it. Scott. That was quick. She clicked to accept the call and turned up the speaker.

'Annie, there's a lot I want to say to you.' Scott's voice was low and hurried but held angry undertones. 'But I don't have the time. I need to know what you've found out about Hassan's complaint about Sleeman. And don't piss me about.'

Complaint about Sleeman? Annie was pleased they weren't face to face. She didn't want Scott to see her surprise. The large vehicle ahead was out of the way. The cars began to move forward. With time short, she took a chance. 'I...uh...heard about Rob Greaves's involvement.'

'What do you know about it?' His voice was hard, or at least she felt he tried to make it hard, but there was something else there, too.

'I don't know anything for sure, Scott. That's why I rang you. Is there anything you can tell me?'

There was a pause, then he said, 'All I know is that there was a complaint. I don't know the detail. It wasn't taken anywhere. It was clear it was malicious. There was history between Hassan and Sleeman.'

'History between them? What kind of history?' Annie let her surprise show this time.

'All I know,' Scott repeated, 'is that there was a complaint and it was dropped. Rob had something to do with getting it dropped.'

For the first time, Annie heard unease in his tone as he mentioned his colleague's name. She felt a sinking sensation in the pit of her stomach. Christa needed her at the hospital, but Pat's car was signalling a right turn. She wasn't going home. And if Annie were to get there first, she had no option but to carry on. She knew what she wanted to ask, but wasn't sure what words would do the trick. In the end she simply said, 'Please, Scott, don't say anything to Rob. We don't know what he might have been threatened with to keep Sleeman up to date. If we're to help him out of it, we can't give him even the glimmer of a chance to leak.'

EIGHTEEN

SCOTT'S VOICE RERAN in Annie's head as she tried to pin down the emotions she'd heard behind it. His hurried call could have been down to all sorts of things. He was probably working somewhere he shouldn't use his phone. But the wobble when he spoken about Greaves; the way he hadn't contradicted her about Greaves being in Sleeman's pocket; the very fact he'd called back so quickly all confirmed what she already knew. He had been dragged into something that he had to keep below the official radar.

Annie watched Pat's car glide through a gap in the traffic and sweep round under the concrete legs of the Daltry Street flyover. She'd be out of sight before Annie worked her way to the head of the queue, but it didn't matter. Once on the dual carriageway, she couldn't get away. Pat had only ever seen the new car at a distance and would think she'd left Annie at the hospital, so Annie wasn't worried about being spotted. She had an old woollen cap to pull down over her hair for when she made her move and overtook.

Once out on to the wide Clive Sullivan Way, she had Pat in sight again in minutes, but lost several opportunities to get ahead in another bout of indecision. What if Pat weren't on her way to Vince's? But where else could she be heading? If Annie didn't follow, it would be a lost opportunity. And Pat would come to no harm with Vince, unlike Christa back at the hospital, digging for information on someone who had made a complaint about Vince that had been buried with Greaves's help. She knew she should go back, but Pat had the power to walk into the heart of the operation out there and Annie might not get another chance to be on her tail as she did so.

What she really wanted was to flag Pat down, tell her to leave it until tomorrow like they'd arranged, to tell her about Hassan, the complaint and Greaves and to beg for her help to go back and protect Christa. She might have done it, tried to persuade Pat to turn back, but no one had been straight with her since this job began. She couldn't even be quite sure of Pat.

If she left it much longer she'd leave herself in limbo. Decision made, she slipped down a gear and waited her chance to surge past with the next group of fast-moving cars.

She put her foot down and sent up a silent prayer for a problem-free route. When the road was clear enough to juggle with her phone, she put in a call to Christa. After a couple of rings, it went to voice mail—not long enough to have clicked through automatically. Christa had red-buttoned her. Maybe she was with her contact again.

She fought to keep her voice light, no trace of tension, 'I've found something more about your guy. It's really important you don't make another move until I can debrief you. It's good. You'll like it. Ring me. If my phone's off, either keep trying or wait for me to ring. I won't be long.'

With luck, that would intrigue Christa enough to get her to ring. She'd seen Annie's number on her phone and she was sure to check her voicemail the moment she could. Annie was confident there would be a call back within minutes, long before she'd reached Vince's hideaway.

As she settled back to navigate the unfamiliar route, Annie rehearsed a story in her head that would persuade Christa to go back to her lodgings and do nothing until morning. Her fingers drummed impatiently on the steering wheel as she drove. Come on, Christa, ring me back.

At the same time, she struggled for a mental image of the terrain around the farmhouse. When she'd been there, she'd thought more about getting away unobserved than of memorizing the surrounding countryside. And back in the office with the place revealed on Google Maps, it hadn't occurred to her that she'd find herself heading out there without the chance for a thorough examination of the information.

She smiled to herself as she remembered Christa's explosive entry into the office. When the woman rang back, if she ever did, and if Annie could think up a plausible line to spin, Christa would give her a clear and detailed picture of the map she had only glimpsed.

Ten minutes later, with no incoming call, Annie phoned her boss in London.

Pieternel answered promptly. 'Ah, Annie, at last. Did you get my email?'

'I haven't been online. Haven't had chance to set up the phone yet. But listen, I'll have to cut you off if another call comes through.' Briefly, she outlined the situation with Christa.

Pieternel tutted. 'Should have trusted my instinct. I knew you couldn't really want her there, but I couldn't raise you and you sent that text. If I'm honest, Annie, I was only too pleased to send her away. I've sussed out that job, the dodgy one. They're trying to get our licence revoked.'

'I knew it! But why? How?' Annie felt both shock and anger. Loss of the licence to operate would effectively close them down, would drive away their big clients. But she hadn't needed to ask how. The how was simple-by showing them up as dodgy operators; an outfit that employed illegal tactics; employed functioning addicts like Christa who didn't give a damn about phone hacking, email mining, using young kids to do her dirty work.

The road ahead was dark, just the moonlight shining a thin strip of silver on to the snaking ribbon of tarmac. She'd turned off the main road some time ago, but it would be the work of a moment to swing back round, to head out of Hull, to leave Christa and Pat to their fate.

'Is this to do with why I've ended up two hundred miles away?' she asked.

'I wondered at first, but no, I don't think so. I can see why they might want you out of the way, but why get rid of Christa? If it was deliberate, they'd keep Christa right here where she'd do most damage.'

'Do you want me back? I can be there in a few hours.'

'No need. In fact, best if you can keep Christa walled off with you where she can't do any harm.'

Annie felt her eyebrows rise, but she said nothing and Pieternel went on. 'This is personal. It's to do with me more than you. Do you remember a case where we uncovered a motorbike scam, saved our client a lot of money? Well, we trod on some toes when we did that.'

'I'll say,' murmured Annie. 'Didn't you doctor the evidence? You came pretty close to shooting us in the foot as I remember it.'

'Desperate times call for desperate measures, Annie,'

said Pieternel, unabashed. 'And we pulled it out of the fire in the end.'

Annie thought back. It had been a spectacular result against the odds. One of the early cases that had taught her the value of researching the detail. Hardly their fault if some other outfit had done a shoddy job and lost business because of it, but clearly someone had held on to a grudge.

'Are you sure you don't need me there? I'll just leave this lot to rot.' Though not quite, Annie thought, as she made the offer. She would have to extricate Christa. It wouldn't be fair on Pat to leave her to create havoc. Pat had enough on her plate.

'No, no. It's all in hand. People who hold grudges are inveterately dense. If they weren't, they'd live their own lives, not waste time hankering after things they're too thick to accomplish under their own steam. By the time you get back, they'll be history. Game, set and match. They won't pull another trick like this. On anyone.'

'OK, best of luck, and try not to enjoy it too much. I've got to go. I want to try Christa again. I've to find somewhere to stash the car, too, and it'll be pitch bloody dark soon.' She glanced up at the sky as she spoke. Not quite pitch dark. The moon was on the wane but the sky was clear.

'Just one more thing, Annie. I don't know if you've been checking voicemail on your old phone.'

'Not for hours,' said Annie. 'Every villain in the place already has the new number.'

'Well, I did, in case you hadn't, and you've a message from Mike. He's flying in from Zurich a week on Sunday, he'll be back for a few days. He says do you want to meet up?'

Annie felt her mouth curve to a smile. Mike had been part of her life for years; an intermittent part since he'd followed his job to Switzerland. He was one of the few people who understood her work and didn't get huffy over missed dates and ignored calls. A few days with him was exactly the break she would need after all this. She resisted the urge to reach out and touch the fake wood fascia on the car's radio. Of course she'd be around and able to meet him. She asked Pieternel to ring him back, give him her new number and let him know she'd call him sometime in the next few days.

As she approached the lane that led to the farmhouse gates she slowed. The waning moon outlined a straggly row of trees that seemed to mark some kind of track. She found the access point and bumped the car along until it was well hidden. Pat should be at least ten minutes behind her and it was vital that the car was out of sight.

Christa's phone went straight to voicemail this time. Annie wasn't sure what to make of that. It could be that Christa had come looking for her, got spooked by her disappearance and gone back to sleep off whatever was in her system—or maybe gone to top it up. If she considered herself still on duty in the job it was unusual for her not to have returned the call.

From where she watched the moonlight picked out the field edges and silhouettes of trees. In the distance she could see the copse where Carl had parked with her tied up in the boot. She had two choices: to go back down the lane and along the road, or to cut across the fields and hope the way wouldn't be barred by deep dykes or impenetrable hedgerows. The route across the fields was the obvious choice and she could always double back to the road if it proved impassable.

She tucked a few bits of kit into her pocket along with a torch and had just set off when her phone vibrated an incoming call. Shielding the screen so it didn't flash an anomalous light out across the landscape, she saw it was Pieternel.

'What is it?' She lowered her voice to a whisper although the rustle of the nearby trees would swallow any sound.

'Don't know if you need this right now,' said Pieternel, 'but I had a thought. I just checked the voice mail on your old phone. Your really old phone, I mean. The one you had when you first came to work for me.'

A shiver ran up Annie neck. That was the phone she'd had when she worked in Hull years ago. Old contacts would still have that number, and Pieternel hadn't rung for nothing.

'What did you get?'

'There's a message, a recent one, from a couple of hours ago. It's from a guy called Stills. Wants you to ring him. Mean anything to you?'

Surprise silenced Annie for a moment. She'd never known his real name. Stills was short for Still Waters, as in still waters run deep, a youngish guy in bulky oilskins and a woollen cap. They'd only met once on a sunny afternoon down at the cove. He'd been peripheral to the action, as she had been, or that's how she remembered it. A boat, the size of a small trawler, had moored a few hundred metres out. Stills had come ashore from it in a dinghy. They'd talked for quite a while beside the barbecue on the beach. If he'd taken the trouble to look

out her contact details from years ago, then she needed
to hear what he had to say.

'Text me the number,' she said. 'I'll get back to him.'

IT TOOK LONGER than Annie anticipated to cross the expanse from the small track to the edge of Vince's property. She kept to the field edges to have the cover of
the stubby hedgerows, but had to take a detour round a
reed-filled dyke, being unable to judge the depth of the
water in the dark. Along a straight stretch with a hedge
to guide her, she took out her phone and rang Stills.

It took a while to convince him it was really her, that
she had a good reason to ring him back from a different number. A detailed description of their meeting all
those years ago seemed to relax him.

'I won't speak on the record,' he told her. 'And I'm
not talking specifics. People I rate have told me you're
OK, but that doesn't mean I trust you. Twenty-first cen-
tury now, isn't it? Slavery should be a thing of the past
if we want to call ourselves civilized.'

'Slavery?' she queried, feeling her way along the
hedgerow, peering ahead to try to pick out obstacles
in the dark.

'Yeah, there are thousands of slaves hidden behind
the veneer of what we call civilization. It was Sleeman
who paid for bringing that woman in.'

'I already knew that, Stills.'

'Yeah, but you didn't know he'd paid me twice.'

'What do you mean?' She slowed her pace, concentrating on what he said.

'There was the usual payment for the landing. You've
seen the drill. Single lamp, everything's above board.

String of lamps, abort the landing. This time, right at the last minute, there's new payment. It's a whopper.'

'New payment for what?'

'Compo for if I get picked up. I've to go ahead with the landing, make sure she gets ashore whatever's happening on the beach. And I've to keep my mouth shut.'

'And both payments came from Sleeman?'

'Yup. And that's what I'm telling you. There's a civil war going on. I've no idea who's on which side, but don't be shackled by thinking it's a united front against you. Get that woman out. It's not right. And sorry, but that's me done.'

With that, he cut the call.

For a moment, she stood still looking at the silent handset. Civil war within the Sleemans. An almost inevitable outcome given the way they operated. She wasn't sure the information would be as useful as Stills thought, not until she'd figured out who was fighting who and why, but she would tuck it away for later consideration. For now, she must get across that dark expanse on foot before Pat completed her journey by car.

When she was finally at the boundary of the meadow that stretched almost to the side of the house, she was no longer sure whether or not she'd made it before Pat. She hadn't seen car lights, but then the undulations of the landscape had disoriented her. Not only that, but intermittent bursts of sound—hammering and screeching—had orchestrated her clamber over the rough terrain, each burst a little louder.

Once she could see the place, she expected to find building works in full swing, but the side of the house that faced her showed only a single window high on the wall, the light from it spilling out to the grounds below.

It made her wary of continuing the straight path across the meadow. She would have to skirt round in a wide circle to get to the far side where the barn lay.

Again the noise of hammering cut through the night air. Annie tried to home in on where it came from, but she couldn't tell if it were from the back of the house or further away. She scraped her boots on a fallen log to remove the heavy clods of mud that clung from her trek across the fields. Other than the occasional clattering bursts of sound, everything lay quiet, but close to the house, security lights blinked on and off, apparently randomly but maybe triggered by animals.

Gradually, she edged her way round the house in a wide circle, listening for the sound of a vehicle crunching up the driveway, and at the same time scanning the hard—standing close to the building for any sign of Pat's car.

The front of the house was as desolate as she remembered it, not a light showing from inside. Again, that sudden burst of sound had her ducking lower into the scrub, but she saw no movement to match it, and continued on. Once she could see down the side of the building, clear signs of life showed themselves. Lights leaking round from the back, but no sign of Pat's car.

The gravel stretch at this side of the house was too exposed to risk crossing it. She decided to retrace the footsteps of her earlier visit and go right round the barn. There was CCTV at the front to worry about, but the building would shield her from the house and give her a path to the vegetation at the back from where she could get a look in through those big French windows, where she'd seen the woman from the sea coming and going with her washing.

Up by the wall at the back of the barn, Annie found

herself in inky blackness and felt her way with care along the uneven panels. Then at last came the unmistakable crunch of wheels on gravel and she spun round to peer through the darkness.

Security lights clicked on at the front of the house, bathing the approaching vehicle in light. She experienced a momentary worry that the car's headlights would pick her out as they swung round the corner, but it sank to the back of her mind as she saw Pat's face. Just a glimpse as the angle of the light lit the inside of the car. Pat looked scared; surely too scared for some nebulous childhood trauma. In the last moment before the corner of the barn obscured it from view, as the light clicked off leaving only silhouettes, and as the car bumped across the uneven ground towards the back of the house, Annie saw what had frightened Pat.

There was someone in the back. Now it was clear what had delayed Pat's arrival. Pat had been hijacked, just as Annie had but, unlike Annie, had been allowed to stay behind the wheel.

Speed was essential now. She must get right round the barn as quickly as she could.

As she plunged back into the undergrowth, she was almost knocked off her feet by the sudden burst of sound; hammering so loud she felt the ground vibrate beneath her. It turned to a high pitched screech, and with it came a weird pattern of light on the ground in front of her, as though a miniature firework display was played out in the grasses by the barn wall.

It took a moment to interpret. This was the hole under the back wall, the panel she'd bent back to be able to creep underneath. As the noise died away and the darkness engulfed her again, she tried to make sense of the shapes now dancing in front of her eyes.

It wasn't a trap, not one laid for her anyway. That blinding burst of light had glared out at her through the gap like a searchlight. And the noise was coming from inside. As it died away, a voice came through the gap, a hollow echo. '...stability...the electrics...'

She scrambled to her feet, fighting and wading her way through the bushes and a sea of brambles whose long tendrils reached out to tug at her clothes and snap their tiny teeth at her face. Taking this detour round the barn had become the worst possible idea when there was something major going on inside, but she carried on because there was no other way to get unobserved to the back of the house.

Towards the front of the barn the going was easier, but the cover more sparse. The big doors stood open, throwing light on to the gravel yard and into the wood-land beyond. She would have to take an enormously wide circuit to remain hidden beyond it, and if she wasn't quick about it, she wouldn't see where Pat was taken.

She glanced briefly towards the open barn doors as she fought her way through the undergrowth. The huge entrance was covered in some sort of giant white cur-tain, glowing with light from within. She turned away before it etched patterns in front of her eyes, and set her sights on the house. It was an awkward angle from deep inside the copse, but the back of the building was now visible. Pat's car sat empty to one side, but the big win-dows were uncurtained and she could see Pat at a table inside with two other people; one was the woman she'd seen before, the other a small, stolid woman, maybe Leah. At least one other person lounged in the shadows at the back of the room, but the angle was too acute to make out detail. Annie could only assume it was Carl.

Her gaze raked the back aspect of the dwelling. There was one point where she might conceal herself close to the house, but no obvious way to get to it. There was another door. If she could make it that far and ease her way inside…? But it might be locked and again, there was no obvious way to reach it. She measured the distance with her eye between Pat's parked car and a straggly patch of bushes to the side of the door. If she could get to Pat's car, could she cross from there unobserved and try the door? Unlikely. It would have to be a move of last resort.

Gradually, she fought her way closer to the edge of the gravel expanse, all time keeping a wary eye on the figures inside the house, lit like actors on a stage. Pat sat at the central table. Annie thought she held herself stiffly, but wondered if she could really tell from this distance. Was she just extrapolating from the knowledge that Pat had been stopped somewhere along the way? Should she have followed and not rushed on ahead? Where had it happened? What could she have done?

It wasn't all her imagination, she realized. There was a heaped plate of biscuits on the table. The small woman had reached forward twice to pick one out since Annie had been watching; Pat not once. She glanced back towards the barn as the hammering noise rang out again, and she fingered the phone in her pocket. If she called Scott and had him mobilize officialdom, what would they find? The Sleemans had decades of experience of keeping below the radar, of covering their tracks. This wasn't the moment to make a wrong move.

She had to know if Pat were in trouble and if so, how much. Taking in a deep breath and hoping it wasn't a bad decision, she pulled out her phone and tapped in Pat's number. Inside the house, Pat leant sideways to pull her phone from her pocket. Annie was aware of the stumpy woman's gaze on Pat as she took the call.

'Hi, is everything OK?' said Pat's voice in her ear, then she saw Pat look across the table and heard her say, 'It's Babs's lad from the hospital.'

Keeping her voice low and rattling the words out, Annie said, 'Pat, are you in trouble?'

There was a pause before Pat responded. 'Hmm, I'm not sure. I don't think so. I'll be round mid-morning. I'll have her laundry. Don't worry. Bye.' She cut the call.

Annie ducked down in the bushes, watching closely, and wondering how to interpret this. *Not sure...don't think so...* Had Pat cottoned on that Annie was nearby?

Pat pushed herself up from the table. Annie tensed, wondering if Pat would come outside looking for her. Surely not, she couldn't even know she was here. Pat lumbered off at an angle and out of Annie's line of sight. She looked again at the thin corridor of shadow that she might use to get into the house if she could get that far unobserved, and wondered if she could use the bulk of Pat's car to get partway across the gravel yard.

Too many unknowns. Was the door locked? Did it lead anywhere useful? Would there be cover once inside? If she had to get away again, could the route be reversed?

After a couple of minutes, Pat returned to the room and took her seat at the table, her hand reaching to her mouth to mask a yawn. She looked relaxed enough, but Annie wasn't convinced. Something had changed.

Her thoughts were interrupted by the vibration of an incoming call. She stared across into the lighted window, suddenly convinced it was Pat using the call-back button without taking out her phone. Turning the handset away from the buildings, not to give away her position by a flash of light from under the trees, Annie looked at the screen. It wasn't Pat. It was the office land-line. It must be Christa.

She felt a load lift from her shoulders. If Christa had made it back as far as the office she had avoided walking into anything awful back at the hospital. Annie crouched down as she answered the call.

'Hi, Christa.' She kept her voice low, confident the rustling leaves would blend her words into the sounds of the night.

'Where the hell are you?' screeched Carl Sleeman's voice in her ear.

Annie felt her bottom jaw drop open and her gaze snapped back to the tableau in the window; the shadowy figure in the background; and then to Pat's car. And as her brain told her it hadn't been Carl in there after all, she saw the car's door open a fraction. Thinking her eyes deceived her, and ignoring the voice that snapped from the phone, she stared at the car door as it inched open, tensing as though watching a balloon expanding too far. Any moment the interior would light up and surely catch the eyes of the people inside the house. But the car's interior remained dark.

She clicked off her phone, cutting Carl mid-sentence, and stared as an indistinct figure slithered down on to the ground, easing the door to again before crouching at the back of the car clearly setting themselves up to have a try for the side door that Annie had looked at and discounted as too risky.

Her heart plummeted to her feet. It was Christa.

NINETEEN

ANNIE CROUCHED LOW, her mind in turmoil, the pieces spinning. Both herself and Pat hassled by youths back in the hospital car park. Youths doing Christa's bidding. Oh yes, she was quick all right. No one could touch her when she was on song. She'd sussed Annie, seen through her excuse of visiting Barbara; had probably been close behind her all along. Pat had no idea she'd brought her here. Christa must have been delayed for some minutes immobilizing the inside light in the car. The way it was parked, she couldn't have reached up to turn it off without being seen. She must have got at the fuse or the wires from under the dashboard.

Easing herself sideways around a patch of brambles, Annie stretched out her legs one by one as she watched Christa. From here she was powerless to get to her, to attract her attention or even create a diversion that might let Christa cross the expanse unseen. Pat said she didn't think she was in trouble. Well, she was now.

Inside the house the young woman yawned extravagantly, Pat said something and at last reached her hand forward for the biscuits. The older woman, who must be Leah, rose to her feet and marched out of Annie's line of sight.

Christa kept close to the ground and didn't try to hurry. It was the right tactic. It would be movement that caught someone's eye. Annie tried not to hold her breath as Christa crept closer and closer to the relative safety of the shadow by the house. A movement from inside showed Pat rising to her feet, a smile on her face, nodding as she spoke, apparently to Leah. Was Pat taking her leave? If so, something changed her mind. Her smile vanished and she sat down again.

Christa was at the door now, pressed against it as she twisted the handle. It didn't open. Annie watched Christa bend her head close to the lock and a moment later saw the door give way. Christa opened it just enough to slip through, then it closed, leaving Annie to stare intently and try to still the rapid beating of her heart.

What the hell should she do now? Having found her way in, Christa ought to be able to keep herself hidden, but Annie had no way of knowing the lie of the land in there. Could she risk a second call to Pat to whisper to her what had happened? Maybe Pat could provide a diversion from inside, enough to allow Annie to get Christa out.

Before she could make up her mind, her phone vibrated another incoming call. Again she had to turn away to shield the light to check the screen. She'd assumed Carl, but it was Pat's mobile. Her gaze snapped back to the window. Pat sat still at the table, no phone in sight. Leah was back in view, on her feet, talking to a man who stepped out of the shadow as Annie watched. As she clicked to open the line and put the handset to her ear, she took in the size of the man, and thought back to her conversation at the cove. *Heavies...hands like meat plates...*

Through Pat's phone, she heard the woman speak, her voice quiet, indistinct, but she caught parts of meat-plate-hand's gruff responses.

'...through the utility room...'

A second man stepped into view pushing the doubled-up form of Christa ahead of him, her arm impossibly high up her back.

'I asked you a question,' the voice said.

A sudden gasp of pain matched the sight of Christa's body as it flinched and she stammered out, '...followed her,' and pointed at Pat.

'And who the hell are you?' A crackle of sound, the material of her pocket rubbing against the phone, played over Pat's voice as she sat upright feigning indignation. Though it wouldn't have been entirely feigned, thought Annie. Christa's appearance must have come as a terrible shock to Pat. But she sounded convincing. Now it was up to Christa to play as good a role until Annie could find a way to get them both out.

'Where's Annie Raymond?' said another voice. Annie couldn't see who had spoken, but the timbre of the voice was a woman's; the tone chilling. For the first time she felt an inkling of why Pat might be frightened of Leah.

'I don't know,' Annie heard the sob in Christa's voice, but knew Christa well enough to know it was fake. That's good, she silently urged Christa on, make yourself look young, small and vulnerable.

Meat-plate-hands made a sudden move, forcing a groan from Christa, and Annie gritted her teeth in impotent fury. Young, small and vulnerable was exactly what Christa was.

'I'm looking for her,' Christa blurted out. 'I was sent to look for her. My boss in London...we've not heard for days...' Then Christa's voice changed, became accusatory and slightly hysterical. 'She knows! Look at her sitting there saying nothing. She knows what's happened.'

Annie heard Pat heave a sigh as she said, 'I wish to

God I did. I don't have a clue what's going on. I wish someone'd tell me.'

The voice that Annie took to be Leah's asked, 'When did you last see Annie Raymond?'

'I haven't,' Christa said. 'I told you, we haven't heard from her for days. I've been following her, Pat Thompson. It's Annie I'm trying to find.'

'She's lying,' another voice broke in. 'She has seen her.' It wasn't the words that shot a chill up Annie's spine, it was the identity of the speaker. 'We both saw her about an hour ago,' said Pat. Then the line went dead.

ANNIE FELT ROOTED to the spot, the tableau in the house played out in front of her in the big French windows. She had to find a way to get Christa out of there. And Pat? But Pat had just blown Christa's story right out of the water. Why?

Inside the house she could see Leah in mime firing questions at Pat; Pat shrugging as she spoke, reaching forward for another biscuit. Meat-plate-hands had relaxed his grip on Christa as he watched. Annie saw her raise her head far enough to stare dumbfounded at Pat.

Annie had one advantage but no idea how to use it. They didn't know she was out here. Or had Pat worked it out? Annie's heart dropped. Of course, she'd worked it out; she'd arrived at the right conclusion for the wrong reasons. She would assume Christa had come with Annie. How else could Christa have made it here so quickly?

Pat had taken the risk of opening the phone line, not to let Annie hear that Christa was in trouble, but to let Annie hear Pat betray her. It was a warning to get the hell away while she could; a nod to all the years they'd worked together.

What would they do to Christa? And how could she stop them? On her own she could do nothing. There were too many of them. She couldn't pluck Christa from their midst in any way that would give them a glimmer of a chance to get back to Annie's car. One strong spotlight across the fields would cut out all useful cover. She was stuck with no viable course of action, but she couldn't do nothing.

The only option was to get help, but who and how? Suppose she called the police with a tale of the kidnap of her colleague, what would they find? A household who had encountered an intruder, who would doubtless say they were on the point of turning her in. She'd seen no weapons brandished, seen no real violence used. She hesitated. It would be a way to get Christa out. Or would it? How long would it take to get someone out here? Would the Sleemans be forewarned by Greaves or someone else? What if there were no sign of Christa by the time anyone arrived? Why should anyone believe her, the intruder, over the legitimate householders?

Yes, officer, we found a young girl in the house... drug addict by the look of her...we thought about calling the police, but in the end we just took her back down to the road and told her to get on her way...

And Christa might be locked in a cellar or dumped at the bottom of a well.

She glanced towards the big barn. Would anyone see anything untoward if they ripped the sheeting from the front of that shed and delved inside? Certainly, they'd find something unusual, but would there be evidence of any crime? She had no idea. They all knew Vince Sleeman, but it seemed that everyone knew his country house was clean; his wife had seen to that over the years. And for all that there were plenty of people desperate to see Sleeman behind bars, it wouldn't just be Greaves he had in his pocket. If she were to initiate a raid, the only result might be to get herself thrown off the premises. And could she even persuade anyone to rush out here?

Sleeman? No, he's too ill to be up to anything these days...whatever's going on, it won't be out there... We'll call in and take a look when we're passing...

What she needed was someone who would break speed limits to get here, and do it without saying the wrong things to the wrong people. Pieternel was the obvious choice, but too far away. She pulled in a breath as the man holding Christa pulled her upright. She watched as he turned and dragged her out of sight.

Her heart sank as she reached for her phone. There was someone closer at hand; the only person she could think of who might be persuaded to race out here without blabbing to anyone else, but only if she spun her story just right. His role was ambiguous but his arrival would at least cause a diversion. Huddling over her phone to shield its light from view, she called Carl Sleeman.

TWENTY

TEN MINUTES LATER there had been no further sign of
Christa. Annie battled with her cramped limbs, trying
to stretch her legs without risking her shadow or silhouette betraying her. When Carl got here, if he ever did,
she must find a way into the house under cover of his arrival. She crouched low in the scrub, fighting against a
sensation that the darkening night around her was actually lighting up her hiding place. She told herself it was
a sign of the turmoil in her head; the confusion about
Pat's betrayal; worry for her idiot young colleague. If
Pat's call had been a warning, then it meant she would
give her away too, once enough time had passed for
Annie to make a break. Surely they'd ask Christa:
where had she parked the car? And Christa would tell
them she'd hitched a clandestine ride with Pat. They
wouldn't believe her, but they'd check, wouldn't they?
They'd find the car's inside light disabled and one of
the doors not properly closed. That would put Pat right
back under the spotlight, but she'd have to deal with
that on her own.

Carl had assumed she was returning his call; had
even tried to cut her short, saying he was fed up, going
out to get wasted; call back in the morning. In the end,
he'd snapped out, 'Just tell me where Pat Thompson is,'
and Annie had grabbed her chance.

'Not sure, but she's in trouble. I got someone to ring
her earlier, from the hospital.'

If this got back to the people inside the farmhouse—
and Annie had to assume it would—it backed up the lie
Pat had told about Annie's call being from Barbara's son.

'Yeah…so?'

'I rang her myself a bit later. I'm sure she meant to
cut me off, put me to voice mail, but she hit the wrong
button, left the line open. I heard some really weird
stuff.'

'What stuff?' The impatience hadn't left his voice,
but she'd detected a spark of something behind the question: wariness, worry.

'Christa Andrew. She's working for Pat. I thought I
heard her voice. And some guy said something catching
her skulking in the utility room…' She'd paused, hearing an intake of breath from Carl, but he'd said nothing
so she'd laid it on as thick as she could, repeating the
fragments she'd heard from behind the barn to make
sure he knew where Christa and Pat were. 'A voice saying something about an electricity supply; how they
couldn't get stability…'

'Where are you?' Carl had barked at her suddenly.
'Right now. Where are you?' As he'd spoken, Annie
had heard the change in timbre behind his words. He
was on the move.

'Just outside a takeaway on Bev Road,' she'd said,
giving him a location too ambiguous to check. 'I'm
starving, but as soon as I've had something to eat, I'm
going to check out everywhere I can think of, including that place you took me out in the wilds.'

'Whoa… No! No, don't do that.' He'd floundered
about, scratching at reasons why she should stay put.
Christa wouldn't be there; Annie needed to stay in
town…

Annie clenched her fist tight to drive out the images

of what might be happening to Christa and to force herself to keep her tone relaxed. 'Soon as I've eaten, I'm off out there.' As she talked, her gaze raked the lit windows of the farmhouse, and she'd tried to ignore the gnawing sensation from inside her. It was a long time since she'd eaten and she'd kill for a coffee right now. Pat sat back, relaxed, her jaw chewing rhythmically; Leah was in shadow; the woman from the sea yawned and sank lower in her chair. No sign of Christa.

'No, listen, you don't know what you're getting into.'

'Maybe so, but I'm fed up with people telling me that.'

'I'll go. If she's there, I'll get her out. You stay put. Go back to the office.'

'And why would I trust you?'

'Give me twenty…twenty-five minutes. I'll ring you. I'll find her. I'll sort it.'

Annie knew Carl would be giving himself leeway, but if he'd been in Pat's office when she first called, he was pushing it at twenty minutes, even with clear roads. She hesitated, wanting to keep him on his toes, but not wanting to panic him. 'Twenty minutes,' she told him. 'And then I'm heading out.'

And now he'd had ten of his twenty minutes and her hand itched to get at her phone and hassle him again, but it would take him the whole of that twenty minutes and then some to get out here. Her patch of scrub was safe. Even if someone came out with a torch, she felt confidence in her ability to blend with the stubby bushes, just as long as it wasn't an industrial-strength beam and they weren't specifically looking for her. But anything could be happening in that house in the areas she couldn't see.

It went against the grain to wait, but she weighed the

options and couldn't talk herself into trying to get in.
Christa had gone for a side door on a wing and a prayer
and proved it a non-starter. The only other possibility
was a small window at the far end of the house. From
this angle it looked to be ajar. It also showed a dim glow
from within that might have been from an occupied
space or not. No way to tell from here.

Where was Carl? It was less than fifteen minutes
since she'd spoken to him. Hopefully, he was racing out
here to create an unwitting diversion that would allow
her to get Christa out. Would he check her story as he
drove? And if so, how? He would want to be sure she
wasn't anywhere he didn't want her to be, but wouldn't
ring Pat in case she was out here. He was unlikely to
ring Leah, but might ring Barbara's son, who, with luck,
would say he'd spoken to Pat by phone and to Annie
face to face, and would seem to confirm her version.
Annie shook the images out of her head. It was never a
good idea to rely on others to follow a script they knew
nothing about.

Again, she eased herself sideways to allow her limbs
to stretch, to chase away the spectre of cramp, and the
irrational fear she was about to be found. Unless there
were a search party aware of her presence, she could
remain hidden here until daylight.

Carl must be on his way. She had no choice but to
wait.

The wiry undergrowth pressed its thorns into her
as though it were some fast-growing plant, engineered
by the Sleeman clan to trap intruders who tried to use
it for cover. Annie flinched as the tiny barbs scratched
across her skin. She couldn't throw off the feeling that
the moon was about to sail out from behind a cloud and
light the yard, turning her location into a stage and the

room inside into a box from where the audience would stare out and see her.

She glanced at the sky, but the moon was pale, barely visible. Her phone showed that just another two minutes had passed, making seventeen in all since she'd spoken to Carl. The night had a long way to go before any hint of daybreak could show itself. Not even the Sleemans had nature at their beck and call.

Every movement from inside the house made her strain her eyes for a glimpse of Christa. There were other people in the room outside Annie's line of sight, but she was sure Christa wasn't one of them. Christa and her gaoler had left the room. He might have come back. Christa hadn't.

There'd been no further hammering from the shed and no more voices that she could distinguish, but a new sound reached her; the muted screech of metal scraping against metal.

She glanced towards the shed but, seeing nothing new, allowed her gaze to rake the length and breadth of the house; that door Christa had chanced; the small window at the other end that might be ajar; the French door that led right into the lit room where they all sat.

Whatever happened, she knew she would be snatching at split-second half-chances; invading a building she knew nothing about. Circumstances and Pat's agenda had dragged her out here without the chance of even a cursory recce. She didn't know how many people were in there, where they were, what layout she would meet, what alarm systems they had in place.

Eighteen minutes since her call. The time crawled by. Staring through the gloom played tricks with her eyes, making her imagine details she couldn't possibly make out.

As she crouched lower, a new sound pierced the night. The distant scream of a car engine growing rapidly in volume. If this were Carl, he'd been recklessly quick.

She tracked the sound as it grew louder; heard the sliding squeal of a vehicle skidding round from tarmac on to gravel as it entered the far end of the long drive.

This had to be Carl. She tensed, ready to act. If her chance came, it would be fleeting.

The spray of gravel peppering the front of the house melded into a screech of brakes. Carl had parked round the front.

No he hadn't. He must have taken the turn too fast and had to stop. The scream of the engine revving up again competed with another harsh screech of metal on metal, swinging Annie's attention back to the big shed, where she saw a figure in silhouette wrestling with the mechanism for the huge curtain that hung down, obscuring the front. The figure struggled to pull it open. It wasn't the flimsy curtain she'd assumed. It was a heavy-duty thing that had been insufficient to block the piercing light that now speared out.

She hadn't imagined any of it. It really had been getting lighter as they struggled to open the front of the barn. Horrified, she saw that a multi-watt beam was about to spill out and light up the whole yard. And it would coincide with the arrival of Carl's car, which was skidding round the back of the house as she pushed her legs into action. At the edge of vision, she could see the people inside the house starting up in alarm at the sudden commotion. Carl's dramatic entrance would focus their attention on the yard outside at just the moment it was to be lit up, leaving her with no place to hide.

The only obstacle between her and the lit window

would be the moving car. At the speed it travelled, it wouldn't come to a rest until it was at the far side of the yard. Crouched low, running with it, she hurled herself alongside the vehicle, feeling her legs almost whisked from under her as the gravel wave hit them at close range. Fleetingly, her hand held to something, her fingers grasped for traction, she tried to hold herself off the ground before the movement sucked her under the wheels and disposed of her right there. In the final flurry of the car's parabolic skid, she pushed herself away and felt the momentum roll her body painfully across the ground. There was nothing she could do but tense every muscle, waiting for the crash.

The stop was abrupt and painful, banging her shoulder up against a stone step. For a fraction of a second she didn't know which way was up, where the house was, whether Carl had seen her clinging limpet-like to the side of his car for that last couple of metres, or whether she now lay exposed for all to see.

The stone step was the side of a raised bed. Its tiny lip provided a pretence of cover, the palest of shadows that might hide her if no one looked her way. But she'd been flung to the far side of the yard and the focus would be all on the car for the next few moments.

Holding as still as the night air, barely daring to turn her head, she saw the figure of Carl Sleeman leap from the car, stumbling in his haste, and rush round to the back to raise the boot lid.

Inside the house two heavies, including the one who had held Christa earlier, wrestled with the door, giving the impression their meat-plate hands were too elephantine to manage the handle.

From behind them, clearly fizzing with emotion, Leah pushed through, her tiny hand reaching forward to open the door, at which they all spilled out and the night air was filled with a babble of voices, joined at once by Carl who shouted from beneath the boot lid.

The small window Annie had noticed before was tantalizingly close, but too far from the ground for there to be any chance of clandestine access. But Leah and the two heavies were now clustered around the car boot where Carl still rummaged. The cacophony of voices hadn't begun to die down, though none of them could have a clue what the others were saying.

The figures by the big barn were intent on their own tasks, or so Annie had to hope.

Pat was still inside. From this angle, Annie couldn't see her. Neither could she see the woman from the sea.

This moment of chaos was her only chance, her only option, because if she stayed where she was they'd see her just as soon as they calmed down and turned back towards the house. They couldn't miss her.

She clawed her way across the gravel, frantic to reach the inadequate shadow of the wall of the farmhouse. Once there, she scrambled to her hands and knees, keeping low, every nerve at breaking point for the cry from behind that would signal discovery. She made for the open French door and pulled herself inside.

Once through the doorway her hand shot to her lips to signal Pat to keep quiet. But Pat had turned away, twisted right round in her seat and was hissing something at the woman from the sea, who lay back in her chair, eyes closed. Pat, too, had taken advantage of the sudden diversion to interrogate this woman. Annie had no time to wonder what it was about.

As fast as she could, she eased herself upright, gliding her feet across the polished floor, her eyes never leaving Pat or the sleeping woman behind her. It seemed too much to hope that she could creep right across the room and out of the other door under Pat's nose, and she was ready to shush Pat the moment she turned and spotted her. But Pat didn't turn round. Annie felt a door handle behind her. Silently, she twisted it and felt the door ease away from her. Her stare fastened on Pat, she had to trust to luck she wasn't about to step backwards into the arms of another of the heavies, as she slipped through and pushed the door to again.

She found herself in a gloomy, old-fashioned hallway. Tired wood panelling surrounded her. She smelt decay in the air as though the house had lain empty for a long time. Yet, clearly it hadn't. She stepped to the nearest door and opened it a crack. It led to one end of a long kitchen. She saw the small window she'd wondered about from outside. It looked no better as an escape route than it had been for access in the first place. She eased the door shut and crept to the foot of the stairs. Light leaked down from above, but it wasn't clear where it came from. The sturdy front door lay at the bottom of the flight. Well locked and barred, but was it alarmed?

From outside the two big rooms that faced this way looked empty, deserted, but Christa might be behind either of the closed doors. She'd taken no more than a step towards the nearer of them when a tiny sound froze her to the spot. A small whimper. It was Christa, she was sure of it, and the sound had come from upstairs.

Annie daren't leave herself without an escape route, so reached for the highest of the bolts on the front door. It was stiff, but surrendered to her and slid back quietly. The bottom bolt was easier. She slid open the heavy old-fashioned chain and looped it back on itself so it might pass a cursory glance. The door had only one lock: a large metal box of a thing with the key twisted at an angle in the hole. It, too, was stiff and semi-rusted, but turned smoothly enough.

The argument that still raged outside the back of the house was muted from here. Listening all the time for the commotion coming nearer, she examined the edges of the door. As far as she could tell, all she need do now was turn the handle and it would open. It wasn't necessarily the exit she would take, it might trigger an alarm, but it gave her options.

She looked up into the dim light on the stairs and, treading lightly, began to ascend.

TWENTY-ONE

AT THE TOP, she found a landing that held two doors and three more short staircases sprouting from it in different directions. As she stood undecided another small sound took her to the first of the doors. It was a tiny space, enclosing an old porcelain toilet without seat or lid, served by a tank high on the wall above it. Slumped on the floor, curved round the bowl, lay Christa.

'Christa!' Annie hissed the woman's name urgently and pulled at her arm.

Christa's head lolled sideways, her eyes closed. Annie threw herself down at the woman's side, pressing her fingers into her colleague's neck, feeling for a pulse. It was reassuringly steady, but Christa didn't react to her touch. Her priority was to get Christa away, but how? The upstairs lay in half-gloom, light leaking through from somewhere. It was hard to make out detail. No sounds from nearby, just the faint whiff of disinfectant mixing with the musty smell of the house, and the background hubbub from downstairs, still muted, still focused outside the back of the house.

She shifted her weight, kneeling painfully on some object which she pulled aside. It was a shoe; one of Christa's. Pushed into the space at the back of the toilet bowl was the other shoe and Christa's jacket. Annie yanked them out. If she were to get them both out of here, and she had every intention of doing just that, Christa would need her jacket or she'd freeze in the night air, and she'd need shoes as well, just as soon as Annie could bring her round, because she wouldn't be able to drag her comatose form very far.

Annie ran her hands up and down her colleague's limbs, feeling for injury or broken bones. Christa let out a tiny sigh when Annie pulled her arm from under her. A recent graze painted a pattern above her wrist. Nothing to worry about. With more care, she felt around Christa's head, her fingers easing their way through the fine mousy hair. She was pretty sure Christa's unconsciousness had come from chemicals and not from a blow to the head, but she mustn't risk moving her if she were badly injured. Satisfied that she could manhandle her without doing more damage, she shoved Christa's shoes into her jacket pockets and tied the jacket by its sleeves round the unconscious woman's waist.

She must drag Christa out of the house, dump her over the boundary fence, rush back and lay a false trail from the front door. A boundary fence was more than a physical boundary, it was a psychological barrier. An initial search would be conducted within it. It would give her time to cart her back across the fields to the car. Annie dragged Christa out of the tiny room and on to the landing, elbowing the door shut behind them, eyeing the steep staircase and door below.

By shoving Christa's limp form against the wall, Annie managed to heave the woman's leaden weight across her own shoulders so she could keep her in place by hanging on to one of her arms, leaving one of her own hands free. She couldn't carry her far like this, but it didn't have to be far. It just had to be balanced enough for a fast, no-hesitation rush down the stairs, outside, then sideways, hugging the front of the house. All activity was focused at the back and the far side near the barn. If she could get Christa beyond the perimeter fence, she was halfway home.

Annie pulled in a deep breath, braced herself against Christa's weight and made for the staircase. As though her movement had triggered it, a door slammed somewhere below and the hallway flooded with light. Voices erupted from the back of the house. She could hear Carl shouting; Pat's voice raised.

She stumbled under Christa's weight, pulling back. Too late. Her escape route was blocked. Fighting not to pant with the effort, she turned. Three small sets of stairs faced her, heading for further mini landings of their own. With no time to think anything through, she staggered towards the one that seemed to give the greater promise of cover, the one that backed up in the opposite direction from the main staircase. She hauled herself up onto the first of its seven steps, knowing at once she should have made it to the shortest, not the darkest. She'd never counted on carrying Christa uphill. Each stair seemed higher than the last as her knees began to buckle.

And all the time the furiously arguing voices rose in volume. Footsteps clattered in the downstairs hallway, becoming the creak of someone's feet on the main stairs.

With one hand clasped round a doorjamb to pull herself up the last step, and one hand gripping frantically at Christa, her fingers digging hard into the woman's flesh in an effort to prevent her body slipping back and tumbling down to the first landing, Annie made it to the top and almost threw herself through the nearest door, letting them both fall to the floor and praying that the argument would mask the sound.

On hands and knees, she rolled Christa's limp form

aside, pushed the door almost shut, and put her eye to the crack. She peered through on to a stage showing the top of the main staircase, the door to the room where Christa had been and the stairs up which she had just carried her.

Meat-plate hands stomped up first, showing Annie the back of his head, then making her heart lurch as he turned to argue with someone behind him. If he looked up instead of down, he'd be looking into her eyes. There'd be only the darkness to hide her. The few words she caught were meaningless, but she recognized Carl as the person ascending with him. She watched the huge hand reach out to yank open the door, whilst its owner's attention was still on berating the man behind him. There was a moment when his voice disappeared from the mix, shocked into silence by the empty room. Then he spun right round.

'The bitch is gone!' he yelled, cutting off the argument upstairs and down.

'Where the hell...?'

Annie saw Carl push his way past meat-plate hands to look for himself. They looked at each other and then turned to peer at the other landings.

Annie's mouth dried. They were going to search the rest of the upstairs. She couldn't get herself out, let alone Christa.

A sudden banging from downstairs turned both men's attention downstairs. Someone was knocking for admittance at the big front door.

'Hey!'

Annie heard the angry shout along with the creak of rarely used hinges. They'd found the unbarred front door.

Annie felt the pounding of her heart. The two men

clattered back down. She'd been handed a reprieve, but it might only be seconds before they realized no one had gone out through that door.

Frantically, she scoured the room with her eyes. It was tiny; an anteroom. No windows, no hope of escape. Nowhere to hide. A door at the far side showed a line of light beneath it. It was the only way to go. She crept across towards it, felt for the handle, turned it gently and pulled the door towards her. The smell of disinfectant and an underlying sour reek made her recoil. She could see a bed. There was a light on, but not the main one. A bedside light. The blank back of a huge TV obscured her view, so she couldn't see who was in the bed, but felt sure it was occupied. It wasn't rocket science to work out who it was.

As she crouched there, momentarily unsure, she became aware of a soft sound that had been smothered by the pandemonium downstairs. Gentle snores. Whoever was in that bed was asleep.

Annie eased the door open further, then reached back and dragged Christa's inert form across the lino. Stooping low, she pulled Christa into the room, then pulled the door closed again. A pause to be sure she hadn't woken the occupant, then she hunkered down behind the big TV and surveyed the room she'd brought them to.

A sharp breeze blew in from a window at the far side. It was only open a fraction but looked as though it might open wide enough to let her through. Whether or not it was a viable escape route depended on what was below and how high they were.

Keeping below the level of the tall bed, she dragged Christa further into the room. As she moved beyond the boundary of the bed, she saw a heap of bedding in a corner by the window. Pulling Christa further round brought her in sight of the bed's occupant. She caught her breath. It wasn't unexpected, but the sight of Vince Sleeman turned her insides over. He lay back on a single pillow, his face gaunt and hollow, mouth agape, breathing shallow. If she'd had any doubts about the reports she'd heard, they vanished at the sight of him. He was close to death. At the other side of the bed she saw the paraphernalia of his care. A drip stand; a cabinet stacked with medicine bottles.

Thankful it was lino and not carpet, she slid Christa to the corner, pushed her up against the heap of bedding out of which she pulled a stained duvet cover that she put over her comatose colleague. If they were convinced by the fiction that Christa had made it outside and no one came to fetch the laundry, she was well enough concealed for the moment.

But what next? To try to leave now with Christa would be suicide, but she might make it on her own and summon help. She fingered her phone but daren't use it for fear of waking the sleeping man.

Voices floated up through the open window. Annie crouched low trying to distinguish what they said. Then she became aware of another sound. Footsteps thumping up the stairs, coming closer. She heard the break in rhythm as they swapped from the main staircase to the smaller one, heard them approach the outer door. The bed creaked as its occupant moved. Annie flattened herself to the floor and slid silently under the bed.

TWENTY-TWO

It was a high bed with room enough underneath, but the bedding barely hung over the sides. Pressed to the back wall, she was out of sight unless anyone deliberately bent down to look. She felt she was being cornered bit by bit, trapped far worse now than when in that shrubbery with the light encroaching. And Vince Sleeman lay right above her. The thought was creepy enough that she had to fight an urge to scramble out and make a run for it. But the footsteps were in the anteroom now. The mattress above her creaked. She pulled dust into her nostrils with every breath. Her throat felt raw with it. After the exertion of carrying Christa up the stairs, the sour smell of the room made her want to gag. She crouched in a tight ball as she heard the door open. A voice she didn't recognize said, 'Now then, Vince. You wanted to see me,' and degenerated into a cracked laugh.

'Did I now?' came a rasped response from above her; a breathy tone that was all that was left of Vince Sleeman's voice.

Annie could see the newcomer's lower legs and feet as they tracked across the end of the bed; sturdy brown lace-up shoes emerged from under dark pinstriped trouser legs. She held her breath as he walked towards the window; towards Christa. The room lay silent but for the padding footsteps that didn't stop at the window but walked on, right to the laundry pile. Then there came a small grunt of effort and the scraping of wood. Vince's visitor pulled a chair round to the far side of the bed and sat down. Annie breathed out.

It wouldn't be a first to have to sit tight for a long time. Tense muscles would cramp. It wouldn't help to dwell on the precariousness of her position. They didn't know she was here. Sleeman was clearly left alone for long stretches. He was very ill. He'd be on his own and asleep at some point and she'd find a way out.

'What's the rush? I thought you must have pegged out,' said the newcomer.

'What do I know, stuck here?' rasped Sleeman's voice. 'Maybe the boy's come good.'

Through the open window the background sounds of the hunt for Christa continued, coming suddenly closer, as a voice shrieked, 'Reg! Reg!'

'And I've just sat down,' murmured Sleeman's visitor. 'They give you no peace.'

Annie watched the pinstriped legs haul themselves upright and stride back round the bed. She heard the scrape of the sash window open wide and felt the in-rush of cold night air.

'Bleeding hell,' rasped the voice above her. 'You'll give me frigging pneumonia.'

'It'll make no odds, you'll be dead soon enough,' came the heartless response, then a shout, 'Now, what's the fuss?'

'Where'd you park your car, Reg?' a different voice called up.

'There. Down by the blackthorn.'

'Oh, for Christ's sake, Reg. What d'you go and do that for?'

'I'll park where I frigging like. I'm not having your builders chuck bricks all over it.'

In the cacophony of voices that replied, Annie couldn't identify the speakers, but she caught the sense of what they said. And in amongst it all was a furious reference to 'that stupid fat cow' and her carelessness. They'd found Christa's tampering and knew she'd hitched a ride with Pat. Hope eddied inside her, because that wasn't all they'd said.

'Oh, to hell with you,' shouted the man at the window, crashing it shut and turning back to the bed. Sleeman rasped out a question, but Annie wasn't listening to the exchange above her. This guy, Reg, had parked his car somewhere round the front of the house. And it had gone. She couldn't believe her luck. The old guy's car had been stolen and they all assumed it was Christa. They were still trapped, but the pressure of the search was off.

Now how long would this old guy stay? Wouldn't he want to get off and sort out his car? He'd closed the window and the atmosphere in the room was already thickening. Once she was alone again with Sleeman she'd give him a minute or so to drop off to sleep, and if he didn't she was prepared to smother him to get Christa out. The front of the house was unused, unwatched. She'd heard them open the big front door and there'd been no alarm. Not only was the search for Christa focused on the old guy's car, they now knew she'd arrived with Pat. They were looking for Christa on her own. Her escape route was ready.

For a few minutes, as the noises from outside died away, the room remained silent but for a background whisper of gentle snores. Vince's visitor sat still in his chair. Surely he wouldn't stay much longer in the growing stagnation of the atmosphere. Annie risked moving her arm slowly to her face so she could rub at her nose and take away the constant tickle from the dust-laden air. She'd settled herself to face the direction of the door, though could see only a corner of it round the stand that held the huge TV, but she was aware of the inky blackness outside. If the old guy would just go, she would have great cover under the darkness of the night.

As though responding to her thoughts, the feet in their brown lace-ups shuffled and planted themselves for standing. She listened hard for a break in the rhythm of gentle snores, but they whispered on uninterrupted. Then, as Reg got to his feet, a door banged downstairs, the clatter of heavy footsteps ran down the hallway and up the stairs. Seconds later the door burst open. A groan from above her signalled that Vince had been pulled rudely out of sleep.

A second pair of feet came into view. She recognized the trainers as Carl's even before he spoke.

'What?' his voice said, as though responding to a question she hadn't heard.

Above her the bed seemed to rock, and it took a moment for her to interpret this as almost silent laughter. The sounds strangled themselves into a coughing fit that Annie thought might carry Vince off to the next world.

It didn't appear to worry either of Vince's visitors. Reg said, 'You'd best take me home, nipper.'

Carl gave a grunt that might have meant anything.

'And what about my sodding car?' Reg went on. 'Arse end up in a dyke somewhere, I suppose.'

Again, Carl just grunted.

'Well, let's get off. I'll see you, Vince, if you last out.'

'Not so bloody fast!' Annie heard something of the old Vince Sleeman, though a racking cough cut through his speech. 'You owe me a favour. And Reg here knows it.'

'OK… OK.' Carl sounded sulky.

'So what's with the Scots lass?' Vince went on. 'I've heard that many tales this last hour I don't know if she's on this earth or Fuller's.'

It took Annie a second to realize he was talking about her.

As Carl started a reply, Vince cut across him. 'Take my laundry with you. It's stinking the place out. Go on, and we'll call it quits.'

'You what?'

'You heard. Laundry. Over there.'

No, thought Annie, as panic boiled up inside her. Don't take the laundry. Open the window. Carl wouldn't want to touch Vince's soiled bedding. He'd open the window to freshen the room. She tried to will him to think of it as she watched the trainers cross the floor with his characteristic bouncy walk.

If it were just the two old men, she'd be out from under the bed and silence them in a moment. But Carl was another matter. Could she find a weapon? Catch him from behind quickly enough to incapacitate him and give her time to stop Reg from calling for help. Vince was negligible. Already she detected the whispering snores. He could barely keep himself conscious. A pillow would shut him up.

Could she distract Carl? Her phone. He was overdue in his call to her. He'd expect her to ring. But even if she could slip it out of her pocket without a sound, what if he answered? The room was too quiet. His voice would echo through her handset. Too late anyway. She saw his knees come into view as he crouched down. Clearly he'd kept his body very upright, his distaste clear in the hesitant way his hand reached forward.

'Call it quits?' he asked, pausing.

'You heard,' came the growl from the bed.

Immobilized by the helplessness of her position, Annie could only watch as Carl's hands reached again for the heap of laundry and made as though to gather it together.

At once, he started back as though burnt. She heard him smother a gasp; watched as his hand reached forward again, his fingers just nipping the outer layer of cloth and pulling it up. She glimpsed Christa's hair as the cloth was thrown back, covering her over again.

Carl was on his feet. The room was silent but for the laboured breathing from the bed above her. Carl started to speak, but had to swallow and try a second time before any words came out.

'Reg, take these.'

Annie heard the jingle of keys.

'Go out the back, get in my car, and drive it round the front.'

It wasn't clear whether a response would have come, but Vince's voice rasped out. 'Do as the boy says. And don't hang about.'

Reg's footsteps left the room, tracked across the anteroom and receded down the stairs. Annie hardly dared to breathe as the silence hung over the room, just the breath of gentle snores at the edge of hearing. Then Carl turned towards the window and yanked it open, allowing in a welcome blast of fresh air.

A car engine started up. At once, Carl bent over the heap of bedding, pulling and tugging at the sheets, wrapping them tightly round the unconscious form hidden within, and lifted the bundle.

For a second, Annie caught a glimpse of his face, side on, and could only freeze to immobility and hold her breath as she watched him hoist Christa aloft.

Go carefully, she wanted to tell him. If Vince wakes, he'll see it's not just bedding.

She watched and listened, hardly able to take it in. Carl's steps down both staircases, the click of the front door, a car stopping then starting up again, driving off. He'd told her he would get Christa out if she were here and he'd done just that in a move that mirrored her own aborted plan.

No time to figure it out or to puzzle over what was really going on. It was time to get herself out. She listened to the timbre of the sounds from the bed as she eased herself sideways, planning to creep out from the end of the bed nearest the door. That way she could remain out of Vince's line of sight even if he woke.

At the point of making her move, she smothered a curse. Footsteps in the hallway, climbing the stairs. She eased back under the bed.

The tread on the stairs was lighter than the others she'd heard. She hoped to hear it veer off, go somewhere else, retreat back down. But of course, it didn't. It came closer and closer and she heard the door of the anteroom swing open.

Annie had felt a weight lift when Carl had whisked Christa away but, lying still, watching intently to see whose feet would appear this time, she felt her relief drain away. Her young colleague was in as much danger as ever. The only difference now was that Annie didn't know where she was.

Tiny feet. Child's size, but not a child's feet. It must be Leah.

'You think machine's never gonna bleep, don't you?'

It was the first time Annie had heard Leah clearly. Hers must have been one of the voices raised in the earlier commotion, but Annie didn't recognize it in this clipped, precise speech. Nor did she recognize the accent, a strange mix of Yorkshire intonation and a voice that didn't get itself happily around English structure. Leah didn't sound European. The Sleeman clan, who she'd always assumed to be Yorkshire based, were an eclectic melting pot.

Vince said nothing and his wife went on, 'You think car crash victim lying on life-support waiting to give you his guts…ambulance come and whisk you off? Sad old man.'

'Surely, there's a donor on life support right now, isn't there?' Vince growled, his tone riled and heavy with distaste. Annie heard him put on a laugh. It was a mistake as it degenerated into another cadaverous coughing fit.

'If not,' said Leah, 'you dead in few days.'

She tensed as the tiny feet stepped close to the bed. Bits of the draped covers disappeared, shrinking the safe area under the bed. Leah was tucking in the sheets. Annie froze, her eyes tracking every move Leah made, ready to leap out the second she was spotted. She didn't doubt she could overpower Leah, who was smaller than she was, but Pat's fear played in her mind along with Carl's strange deference to this tiny woman. Leah would be no pushover.

The wifely concern over Vince's comfort proved short-lived, no more than a token gesture. Leah stepped back from the bed and turned towards the door.

'You been good husband,' she commented. 'Good husband to day you die.'

'Feck off!' Vince's voice rose as close to a shout as Annie had heard and immediately crippled him in another choking fit so bad that surely Leah would come back, give him some water, do something, but she just laughed softly as she left the room and pulled the door closed behind her.

Ruth Vincent

Back give her some water, no more, but she just
lay there, drifting. It was if the nurse had pulled the door
down a little way.

TWENTY-THREE

ANNIE DROVE WITH the windows down all the way back
to Hull desperate to shuck off the smell of the sick room
and worried for Christa. It wasn't until she hit the sleeping city's outskirts that at last she heard her phone beep
receipt of a text message.

Almost two hours earlier she'd practically followed
Leah back down the stairs, pausing only to be sure she
was alone in the deserted part of the house before letting
herself out of the front door and going with her original plan of hugging the wall of the building, creeping
along the front to the corner and then making a break
for the cover of the wilderness at the side. It was into the
small hours by the time she broke free, the night now
inky black, the sky a myriad of stars. But apart from the
dying man upstairs, no one was asleep. Voices floated
round from the back. Annie had tried to get a look, to
see if light from the big window would show her the
outline of Pat's car or just an empty space where it had
been. It was too dark to tell and too risky to creep closer.
They must finally have shut the curtains, which had
made her nervous. Voices shouldn't carry from within
a closed room. There must still be people out by the big
shed, though that too had lain in darkness: no sign of
the fierce light that had blazed out earlier.

She first tried to ring Carl once she was well away
from the house, but his phone went straight to voice
mail. Trying at intervals as she jogged through the

night, she eventually left a short message. 'Where's Christa? Five minutes to get back to me or else.' She tried to inject menace into her tone, hoping he'd at least ring her back. She itched to tap in Scott's number, to tell him her colleague had gone missing, drugged and kidnapped by various of the Sleemans, but what could she tell him that wouldn't be neutralized by Christa's record on the PNC and the intervention of Greaves and maybe others? She'd approached her car cautiously, but if they'd found it in the search for the car Christa had supposedly stolen, they hadn't linked it to her. It sat where she'd left it.

When at last she'd heard the text ping through, she'd pulled over to look. Yes, Carl Sleeman. *Your mates OK. Was at office all along. Been on a bender.*

Angrily, she rang straight back, but again it was voice mail, so she texted, *Bollox. If she's not OK, you're in real bother.*

His text told her one thing. He didn't know she'd been out there if he thought she might swallow the lie that Christa had been in town all the time. She gunned the car back through the empty streets, pulling up outside Pat and Barbara's office, clicking open the door as she pulled up. Then she paused. The car was still not linked to her, not by anyone who mattered. She shouldn't leave it right outside. But the extra minutes to park it on a parallel street and cut back through the tenfoot might be life or death to Christa. She had to see if she was really here. Compromising, she raced it fifty metres up the road and sprinted back, wrestled the key in the lock and took the stairs two at a time as she clattered up, seeing nothing but dark rooms above her. As she fought to unlock the door to the main office a familiar sound reached her. Gentle, rhythmic snores. She swung the door open and snapped on the light. Christa had been dumped unceremoniously on the floor. She lay curled in the foetal position, fast asleep. Annie knelt down beside her and grasped her shoulder.

'Christa, wake up. Come on. Wake up.'

Nothing. Not even a break in the rhythm of her snoring. Christa's jacket was still tied roughly round her the way Annie had left it. She untied the arms, pulled it free and laid it across the sleeping woman's shoulders. A card fluttered free of one of the pockets and settled on the floor. Annie glanced at it as she reached for the cushion from Pat's chair and eased it under Christa's head. She needed to get Christa to the hospital, to get her treated for whatever the Sleemans had pumped her full of. But she needed to know what it was, and the only person she could ask was not answering his phone to her. Her gaze rested on the office phone, but no, he'd know it could only be her. The message light blinked at her so she reached across and hit the button. A stream of calls from impatient clients came through. Pat and Barbara had missed meetings, failed to return calls, ignored emails…nothing from Carl. Annie clicked it off.

Running her hand through her hair in an agony of frustration, she looked at the now silent phone on Pat's desk and at once she was back on her feet, pulling open the drawers. Pat usually kept a spare mobile in here somewhere. Yes! She pulled it out and jabbed in Carl's number. He'd think it was Pat and he'd want to speak to her.

He answered immediately. 'Where are you?'

'It's Annie. I'm with Christa and don't you dare hang up. What's she been fed? That's all I want to know. She's bang out here.'

'Chill out, fer Chris'sakes. She's cool. They'll have

give it her intravenous. Just leave her be. She'll sleep it out.'

'I'm taking her straight to the hospital,' Annie snapped. 'And you're going to tell me what she's had so they know how to treat her.'

'Is that right? For one, I haven't a clue what she's had. I wasn't there.' That was true, thought Annie, annoyance rising at his relaxed tone. 'And for two, they'll ask you some awkward questions if you take her in.'

'Yeah, well maybe I'll tell them just where she was…' Even as she spoke the words, the scenario played in front of her. Supposing she told the tale and things went as far as an official visit to the farmhouse.

Yes, some junkie broke in…she got away…why didn't we report it? There's a dying man upstairs…enough on our plates…

Whatever they'd given Christa would likely be something that was there legitimately to treat Vince. And chances were, things wouldn't get that far. Maybe the police would take more interest in the person who brought her unconscious friend to A&E. Her mind played bits of scenes where she tried to make her story sound convincing. Pat believed she'd been hired by Vince, but that wasn't a story anyone else would believe. Barbara might know the truth but was in no fit state to tell anyone. At best, she might produce Carl Sleeman. And that wouldn't win her any brownie points in official circles.

She wanted officialdom out at that farmhouse, but not just on spec. She needed them out there knowing what they were looking for and motivated to search.

Carl's voice went on in her ear, inviting her to take Christa where she wanted, but washing his hands of the difficulties in which she'd find herself.

'I can't just leave her,' she told him.

'Stay with her, then. I'm not stopping you. It's too late now, anyway.'

Annie felt panic rise inside her as her eyes snapped to the unconscious form on the floor in front of her. 'Too late for what?'

She heard a tut of exasperation. 'Oh, not her. She'll be fine.' He hesitated, then spat out, 'You've really screwed things up for me.' With that, he cut the call.

Annie sat back with a heavy sigh and looked down at Christa, sleeping peacefully as if tucked into a comfortable bed, not lying on a cold wooden floor. The business card that had fallen from Christa's jacket lay face down on the floor. She knew she should cart her down the stairs and get her to a doctor, but Carl was probably right. Christa looked far better than she often did when conscious. Maybe she should just stay and keep an eye on her, though another night in the office wasn't what she'd planned and she wouldn't get much sleep in an uncomfortable chair, not with everything that swirled around in her head. She pulled herself to her feet and went to turn on the radiator. Pat would grumble at the cost but she couldn't let Christa lie here in the cold night air.

As she knelt to retrieve the card and put it back in Christa's pocket, Annie again shook her colleague's shoulder.

'Christa! Wake up!'

Not a murmur. She was spark out, but her breathing was normal and her pulse strong.

She glanced at the card. It was a business card with an ornate border and fancy lettering that said: *R Brocklesby Associates, Legal and Financial,* followed by a mobile number. It was the typical profile for someone in Christa's network, vaguely worded expertise and corporate identity with no contact details other than a mobile number. Annie reached for Christa's inside pocket and pulled out her phone. A search for R Brocklesby's number proved fruitless. She turned the card in her hand. R Brocklesby? The R could stand for anything. It might not even be a man and Christa might have had the card for weeks.

Using Christa's phone, she called the number. As she listened to the ringtone, Annie was aware of the heating clanking into action. Water gurgled in hidden pipes to the background purr of the boiler, usually lost amongst the sounds of the office during business hours.

On ten rings, Annie thought it unlikely she'd get an answer, but hoped for an answering service to cut in. After fifteen rings, she decided she would get neither. But on the sixteenth, the phone was answered and a bleary voice said, 'Hello?'

Although she'd half-expected it Annie felt a jolt of surprise. It was Vince's companion, Reg.

'Hello.' She kept her voice soft, barely a whisper.

'Ah, is it the little girl from the car? You've woken sooner than I expected, too soon for an old man to get some much needed sleep. Never mind. Now you tell me where you are and I'll sort things out for you. That young scamp, Carl, he forgot to tell me where he was taking you.' Behind the tiredness in his voice, Reg's tone tried for avuncular joviality.

'Come along now,' he repeated, when she didn't say anything. 'You know who I am, don't you? You can trust me. But you listen to me carefully, you mustn't trust Leah. She's not working in your interests. I'll sort things out for you. No need to worry about finance yet awhile. Now, where are you?'

'Uh… I'm not sure.' Annie played for time as she tried to work out what his agenda might be. 'I've only just woken up.' And although she knew the answer, she asked anyway, 'Who are you?'

The response was a sharp intake of breath and he snapped out, 'What's your name?'

Annie hesitated, but they knew who Christa was.

'Tell me,' he insisted. 'What's your name?'

'Christa…' Again she held off, waiting to be pushed for a surname.

But instead of that, he roared, 'I'll skin the little bleeder,' and the line went dead.

Annie stared at the handset. So much for that. She couldn't even contemplate trying to work out what that might have meant. Instead, she turned to the PC and searched for suppliers of medical trailers. She didn't find anything identical to what she'd seen in the big barn at Sleeman's place, but they came in all shapes and sizes and could be specially kitted out. Common customization seemed to be for chemotherapy and dialysis. No change from a substantial six-figure sum for one of those. As she began to dig deeper into the company websites, her mobile sang out. She reached for it and saw Pat's name on the screen.

'Pat?'

Pat's voice was breathless and hurried. 'Annie, I need your help. I—'

Then that line too went dead.

she could tell from the reeling her in. She had to

TWENTY-FOUR

ANNIE FLOORED THE ACCELERATOR. The road swept up
ahead of her in a long curve that begged for speed, so
she obliged, even though she knew she might be heading into a Sleeman trap. Not that she wasn't already
held in their grasp. They'd been reeling her in from
the start. The call from Pat might be just another dan-
gling bait to draw her in, but she didn't think so. The
tangle had begun to make sense. She wondered how she
hadn't seen it earlier. She'd left Christa sleeping like a
baby, her phone and a glass of water in reach, also a
note, *RING ME, ANNIE*, in felt tip too prominent for
Christa to miss.

As she drove her head began to spin, as though she'd
been drinking on an empty stomach. It was tiredness,
lack of anything to eat, but she daren't stop. Whatever
was going to happen was going to happen soon. She
needed to know more, to fill in some of the gaps, and
then she could get help. The latest unknown was Reg
Brocklesby, who'd put his business card in Christa's
pocket without Carl's knowledge, Annie was sure. But
he'd realized he wasn't talking to Christa. He must have
been there when they'd caught Christa breaking in, and
clocked her voice well enough to realize it wasn't her
ringing him. That was pretty sharp of him because she'd
pitched her voice low and light to imitate Christa's tone,
the line hadn't been great and the guy had clearly been

woken from a deep sleep. It didn't feel right, but maybe she was reading too much into it.

Interesting that he'd warned her off Leah. Everyone else treated Leah with respect, if not liking. She had no idea where Reg Brocklesby fitted into the picture but surmised he was one in a queue looking to profit from Vince's death. Carl Sleeman was another and his position, too, was ambiguous.

She wished it was morning, that her mind was sharper, that she'd had the chance to sleep or at least to eat. She imagined the Sleeman empire destabilized with Vince's diagnosis, feuds raging round his deathbed. But Vince Sleeman wasn't one to bow out quietly. Pat had described the whole family tribe being taken to a clinic somewhere for tests. None of them was a match, or were they? Barbara lying injured after a hit-and-run. Wasn't that the sort of event that preceded a transplant? But Barbara was recovering fast. None the less, Vince needed a liver transplant and would prolong his own life at the expense of one of his family. Pat and Barbara were only distantly related and might have expected to escape the trap. Carl, a closer blood relative, had dodged a bullet. Was that why his position seemed so ambiguous? He knew what his uncle would have done to him. But who was Reg, the guy who wanted Christa under his wing? Where did he fit?

Vince had money, influence and networks that spread far and wide. When his family couldn't provide had he set out to buy himself a new liver? Well, of course he had. But he'd have done better to travel abroad. There were places where human organs were easier to come by. She wondered that he hadn't, but maybe the disease had moved too fast. He conducted the fight of his life in one of the world's closest surveillance societies. But then Sleeman's life had been devoted to ducking under the surveillance radar and dodging the controls put in place to stop people like him.

The road was quiet and dark. Annie made herself drive faster than felt safe, knowing her reactions would be compromised if anything unexpected happened, but knowing also that she would have to slow right down once out beyond the reach of the streetlights. No proper hands-free or Bluetooth with this phone. Trying Pat's number at intervals was something else she shouldn't be doing. She might drive herself off the road. Futile anyway. Straight through to voice mail, just as it had been every time she'd tried from the immediate call-back after Pat's original call had been cut off.

Vince had discharged himself from an NHS hospital. She'd been with Pat when she'd taken the call. Yet he'd been in a private clinic at some point, too. If a potential donor went through the NHS system, you waited your turn, but a private clinic must hold more opportunity to circumvent the processes, fiddle the paperwork. But even with a clinic on side, where did the donor come from? They couldn't pluck crash victims and violent deaths off the streets, and even if they could, what chance of a match via such a random process? With Sleeman's money and contacts and complete lack of conscience, there was little you couldn't do to your fellow man.

Yeah, there are thousands of slaves hidden behind the veneer of what we call civilization.

If you were the sort of person happy to own another person as a slave, it wasn't such a leap to using their body parts for yourself. Vince hadn't waited around for the system to deliver. He'd gone out and bought his own donor. The woman from the sea.

Somewhere along the line the clinic had failed him. Vince, with his network, might buy his donor but he wouldn't buy a surgeon so easily. She thought back to Barbara's case: Hassan. It had the feel of a panicked last-minute move. You surely didn't threaten someone into doing something like this. You bribed someone ready to be bribed. There'd been no time to look up that story of corruption in the Midlands, but it had hit Pat's radar for some reason.

I don't give a damn if he's legit, I said find me something.

And the fights between Vince and Leah. Could this be Stills's civil war? Leah had wanted him in hospital. He'd kept discharging himself. He'd taken himself off the transplant list. If she were in on it, why on earth would she want him in an NHS hospital? Could it be that Leah had a conscience; that there was a line she wouldn't cross?

This was the last stretch of lit road. Up ahead, she could see the snaking line of lights fade into an inky-black mist. She hoped it was a trick of the light and not real fog. Already, tiredness had pictures dancing in front of her eyes. She clicked the buttons so that both windows slid down and she could savour a rush of air that was not as cold as she expected. What she really wanted was a bacon buttie and a strong cup of coffee. A vision grabbed her of the tiny kitchen back at the racecourse. She still had the key; still had the OK to be there. The pony camp had packed up early and gone, but the kitchen might still be stocked. Annie's mouth watered at the thought of a packed fridge. She was closer to the racecourse now than to Hull. Could she take a detour? No, she couldn't ignore Pat's call for help.

The big trailer: it had started life as some type of mobile clinic but, whatever its original purpose, Vince had had it kitted out for something far more complex. Annie hadn't found any hint that a mobile medical facility could be used for something as complex as a major transplant, but maybe that was the only option left to Vince when his tame surgeons let him down. Buy an organ donor, buy a sterile medical environment and threaten a surgeon. And why hadn't he gone abroad to a place that already had the set-up? Why had Carl Sleeman been so keen to tip her off about the horsebox that wasn't, and then done it in such a roundabout way? The argument in his driveway... Leah and Carl...the big trailer backing in, crushing the concrete surface. Why was Reg Brocklesby so keen to find Christa and so furious when he realized it wasn't her at the end of the phone?

The internal feuds in the Sleeman clan were key to it all, but she didn't know enough. And now she must stop trying to work it out because very soon she'd be close to the farmhouse entrance and didn't intend that anyone would see her arrive. That meant doing the last stretch without lights, with her head out of the window trying to make out the line of the verge whilst the darkness played patterns in front of her. The point was that Vince intended to have that woman's liver inside him and his timetable was tight. That was all she needed to know for now.

Just before the bend in the lane that would make her lights visible to anyone watching from the Sleeman place, Annie stopped the car. Her priority now was to get Pat out if she could. She wanted to save the woman from the sea who clearly had no idea of her intended fate, but there were too many holes in her knowledge. How many people was she dealing with, who were they, who was on whose side? She had barely any answers, and could only hope she had enough to persuade Scott to mobilize official help.

She pulled out her phone and punched in his number. It was the middle of the night. Scott's mobile might be switched off. He had young children who might be woken by the phone. OK, so maybe she would have an uncomfortable few moments persuading him to listen, but he would, because she had information about the woman he'd plucked off the beach. Whether he'd been taken there deliberately or had been an unwanted passenger in Greaves's car, all that mattered was that Scott felt a level of unease; a level of responsibility for the woman he thought he'd rescued. He would listen. In all the tangle of questions, there was one she wished she could answer. How long did she have? She'd heard Vince say: *there's a donor on life support right now, is there?* He hadn't meant life support. He simply meant alive and imprisoned.

'Hello?' It was a woman's voice: Scott's wife, Kate— the woman who had always insisted on treating her as a rival for her husband's affections. Annie fought back the temptation to disguise her voice, pretend to be someone else. That was a tactic that was sure to backfire.

'Uh…hello, Kate. It's Annie Raymond. Sorry to ring so late, but it's important. I need to speak to Scott.'

There was a ghost of a pause into which Annie read Kate coming abruptly awake. 'You can't. He's not here. He's on duty.'

Her heart sank. 'Can you give me a number where I can reach him?'

'I could…but I won't. Tell me what it is and I'll decide whether or not to contact him.'

Annie fought down an urge to argue with Kate, knowing it would do no good. 'OK,' she said, 'but promise me one thing. Please tell Scott but no one else. It's really important.'

'Tell me what it is.' Kate's tone was neutral, but Annie didn't doubt the underlying hostility. Kate wasn't going to promise anything. Her only other option was to try and track Scott down herself; that could take ages and alert all sorts of people.

'It's Vince Sleeman,' she told Kate. 'You've probably heard that he's on his deathbed. His liver's packing up. He's bought himself a donor. It's the woman Scott picked up four weeks ago; the one who was supposed to be handed on to Immigration. They're out at the Sleeman family home right now, all of them. They're planning to do the transplant out there.'

Kate, who had remained silent during Annie's account, gave a derisory snort at this. 'That's ridiculous. You can't do major surgery in a place like that.'

'They've bought themselves one of those big medical trailers. It's all kitted out. I've seen it. It's inside a big barn next to the farmhouse.'

'A trailer? That's not suitable for major abdominal surgery, and even if they tried it, what about the after-care? It's not feasible.'

'I agree,' said Annie. 'But Vince has given the order and they're going to try. He's probably signed his own death warrant, but then he'll be dead soon anyway. And so will she.'

After a pause, Kate rapped out, 'I'll get on to Scott. And someone's going to want your statement. Your best choice is to go straight to Queen's Gardens and wait.'

'OK,' said Annie meekly, resisting the urge to remind Kate about not telling anyone else, about the need to be quick, knowing it would only rile her more. 'You have my number.'

Dissatisfied but knowing that was the best she could do, Annie set off at snail's pace along the dark road. Knowing that activity was always centred around the back of the house, or maybe was now all concentrated on the big barn, she risked inching her car up the gravel drive, cringing as it crunched over the surface. Carefully, she backed it into the bushes where she'd hidden the other car on her first ever visit to this place. It was as close as she dared take it.

A stiff breeze blew in her face as she skirted the edge of the driveway and approached the house. It might be her imagination or maybe light was leaking from somewhere round the back, but she felt she could see the first tendrils of dawn snaking across the night sky.

No background voices this time. Apart from the breeze, there was no sound at all. The house lay in an eerie quiet after the pandemonium she'd left here a few hours ago. She made her way to the back of the big shed and to the bent panel. Looking into the dense black pool of the animal hole, she knew nothing would persuade her to go down there right now and she carried on round the far side, straining to hear any sounds.

Nothing, just the whisper of the breeze. Aware of the camera above the front elevation, she pressed herself to the wall of the barn as she reached the far corner. The darkness of the night would conceal her as long as there were no motion-sensitive lights.

The front of the barn gaped open. Annie blinked to adjust her eyes to the heavy darkness, trying to make out the shapes within. She felt her heart rate increase as she pulled out her pencil torch and clicked it on. Thick heavy coils of wire lay to one side of a huge empty space.

The trailer had gone.

TWENTY-FIVE

ANNIE STOOD DUMBFOUNDED. The trailer had disappeared. She stared into the blackness of the surrounding scrub, the thin lines of trees. It couldn't be hidden anywhere here. In the time she'd been gone, someone had driven it away. She turned and crept across to the house. It lay in darkness. At the big window, she pressed her face to the glass and peered in. A clock face glowed back at her and she could just make out Pat, still sitting in the same chair, strangely motionless. She tried to see into the corners of the room. No movement, but it was impossible to be sure. She risked tapping on the glass, softly at first and then louder. Pat didn't move.

With sudden misgiving, she grasped the handle. It wouldn't budge. The key hung tantalizingly the other side of the door. 'Pat!' she shouted, banging hard on the glass pane.

No time for subtlety now. She picked up one of the stone pots and swung it into the glass. It was a thick, double-glazed unit. Her first assault cracked the outer pane; two more attempts smashed through both. For a fraction of a second she paused as her ears rang with the deafening crash of breaking glass. Her gut told her there was no one left in the house bar Pat. Now she was sure of it, unless Vince still lay between life and death in the room upstairs.

Taking care to avoid the razor-sharp edges, she reached in and turned the key. 'Pat.' She rushed to the woman's side and shook her violently, relief flooding her as Pat groaned and half-roused before slipping back into unconsciousness. She wasn't as far gone as Christa had been, but there was no way Annie could carry her any distance, let alone all the way to the car. 'Pat, you have to wake up,' she shouted into her face.

Were they alone? No heavies here, but what if someone else had been dumped like Pat; someone now cowering at the sounds of her breaking in? She had to be sure. Fighting against an urge simply to turn and flee, to leave Pat, to leave them all, she made for the door that led to the rest of the house. She ran through, pushing open the doors one by one, flashing her torch around and closing them again. Up the stairs two at a time. The room where Christa had lain was empty. She sprinted up the short flight to Vince's bedroom. This, too, was empty; the bed neatly made, the medicines out of sight.

She ran back down to Pat and shook her again, watching her half rouse and then sink back. She felt over Pat's clothes and found her phone. It was off. Why had Pat betrayed her? She still didn't know. If anyone came now, they'd find Pat drugged, Annie's car deliberately hidden and clear signs of forced entry. They had to get out.

'Pat,' she pleaded. 'You have to wake up. I'm going to get the car. Wake up!' She took the shortest route through the big front door, stumbled as fast as she could over the rough surface of the driveway and back to the car, which she started up and threw gravel in all directions skidding it round the big house and as close to the smashed door as she could.

Pat had raised her head. She groaned as Annie dived back into the room. 'The car's just outside. Come on.

Half a dozen steps, that's all. Come on, Pat. You can do it.'

Hooking one of Pat's arms over her shoulder, she hauled her to her feet. Shouting at her, staggering under her weight, she guided her to the open door, almost fell over the small step and pushed Pat into the passenger seat of the car. Pat was semi awake now but shivering uncontrollably. Annie ripped off her jacket and bundled it roughly round her colleague before leaping round to get behind the wheel. In seconds she had the car skidding back round the house, but just as they gained the top of the driveway Annie gasped and stamped on the brake. Ignoring Pat's moan as the sudden stop banged her into the bulkhead, Annie flipped the switch to leave them in darkness. Through the trees, in the direction of the road, she saw blue flashing lights.

They couldn't get to the entrance...couldn't go back...

She set off as fast as she dared, judging the turn by memory, hearing the scrape of bushes against the car door. Just a few more metres and she'd be back at the tangle of bushes. In the blackness, she almost overshot it. No doubt now that those blue lights were coming their way. She reversed the car, forcing it into the bush, then leapt out, grabbed an armful of detritus from the ground and threw it over the front of the car.

Back behind the wheel, she kept the engine idling and reached across Pat to pull her seatbelt on. Pat lay back, her breathing high and shallow. Annie sat, immobile, staring through the lacework of leaves and branches, making out the shapes of the vehicles turning in at the bottom of the drive. She heard the crunch of wheels on gravel. Two cars and a van. They were taking this seriously. Should she stay and make herself known? It would mean trouble and explanations that wouldn't look credible, but Pat would be looked after.

Instinctively she crouched lower as the first car flew past. Its flashing blue light lit the interior of the vehicle behind. From her hiding-place in the tangle of undergrowth she saw a man in the front passenger seat crane his neck away from her, casting his glance towards the copse where Carl Sleeman had parked when he'd brought her here, a prisoner in her own car's boot. Whoever it was knew this place; knew that copse as an out of the way spot to leave a vehicle. It was a momentary glance, then he turned back to face the front, his expression grim. He was in her line of sight for no more than a second. It was enough. She'd never known him well. He'd aged in the years since she'd last seen him, but she remembered his face. He'd been a PC then, but he wasn't in uniform now.

Rob Greaves.

ANNIE FELT HERSELF sink lower in her seat and hold her breath willing them on, beyond the bend in the drive. She heard the spray of gravel, the screech of tyres. They'd made straight for the back of the house. Before she lost her nerve and whilst their vehicles were still skidding noisily about, she eased the car forward. No lights. A bump up out of the shrubbery that elicited a groan from Pat. Hanging out of her window to track the indistinct boundary between the drive and the adjacent rough ground, she kept the revs low, as quiet as she could and crawled the car towards the big gates.

Thankful for the continued breeze that rustled the high branches above them, Annie turned the car out on to the road, resisting the temptation to speed up. The breeze might mask the sound to some extent but she

knew how far sound could carry at night. Once beyond
the next bend in the lane, she risked dipped headlights
and eased the accelerator down gently, concentrating
hard on the line of the road ahead. The tarmac ribbon had frayed at the edges; farm traffic wouldn't have
helped but that huge trailer had probably left its mark,
too. If she'd had time she might be able to get out and
work out which way it had gone. Beside her, Pat groaned
and wriggled in her seat.

'You'll be OK,' Annie told her.

'Got any coffee?' Pat slurred.

'No, but we're going to get some.' Now they were
away from the farmhouse and she could use her main
beam Annie pushed the car as fast as the narrow road
would allow her. From here it wasn't that far to the
racecourse. She'd get Pat settled in one of the overflow
rooms; get something to eat and drink for them both,
then she'd find Scott.

She looked across at Pat, who lay back in the seat,
her features contorted in pain. 'Pat… Pat. Are you with
me yet?'

'Oh God,' Pat groaned. Then she stirred herself and
pointed. 'Go that way.'

Annie looked at the turn Pat indicated. 'Why? I want
to get to the main road.'

'It joins it about half a mile east. There's a truck stop.
Twenty-four hour. Coffee.'

That sounded good. As Annie turned the way Pat
indicated she glanced at the car's clock. It showed
4.56 a.m.

'Over there. Lay-by.'

The road was otherwise deserted but Annie pulled
across and up to a white catering van. Its shutters were
closed. 'Go knock,' said Pat and gave a poor imitation

of a laugh. 'He won't get many customers for coffee at this hour.'

Taking her jacket from Pat Annie reached into the pocket, but Pat raised her hand, saying, 'Don't pay the bastard. He owes me. It'll be crap, but I've got to have something.'

Annie tossed her jacket on to the back seat, climbed out and walked to the van. She, banged on the shutter without much hope, but it creaked open almost immediately and a man with a lined face looked out suspiciously. 'Yeah?'

'Can you do me a couple of black coffees?'

He looked at her as though she were mad. 'Coffee? D'you know what time it is?'

'Getting on for five o'clock. Sun'll be up soon. Can you do us any coffee or not?'

He peered past her at the car. 'Is that Pat Thompson? You should have said. She looks rough. I can do better than coffee for her. How about—?'

'Just coffee,' Annie cut across him. She carried the paper cups back to the car, passed one to Pat and took a mouthful of her own.

'Yuk!' She gagged on the lukewarm, insipid liquid and took another more cautious sip. At least it was warmish and probably had some trace of caffeine in it.

Pat grabbed the cup and gulped hers straight down. Almost at once she sat up, grabbed for the handle, pushed the door open and staggered out into the night, collapsing to her hands and knees at the road's edge. Annie watched to be sure she wouldn't tumble into the roadside ditch, then turned away, clicking on the radio to drown out the sounds of Pat losing the coffee and, she hoped, some of whatever she'd been fed back at the house. She reached into the back to fish out her phone from her jacket and tried Christa, but the call rang through to voice mail. A couple of minutes later, Pat returned on wobbly legs, looking white and shaky, but more *compos mentis*. Annie put her phone away again. 'You OK?'

'Yeah, that feels a bit better. What the hell did they feed me?'

'Not the same as Christa,' Annie said, as she pulled the car back out on to the road. 'She's still spark out as far as I can tell.'

'They injected her. I saw the syringe. I got whatever I got in my drink.'

'But why did they drug you?'

'Don't know, just to keep me out of the way, I suppose. I told you it was a bad idea to go out there. I saw it coming. Leah said she'd make me a drink. I tried to ring you…in fact, I did ring you, I remember. But then I had to cut it short when she came back. I saw the mug… don't remember much else.'

'I called you back, but your phone was off.'

'They must have done that.'

'What did they give Christa?'

'No idea,' Pat shrugged.

'Pat, why did you tell them you'd seen me?'

'I had to. I'd have had a knife between the ribs if they'd caught me out. I realized I was talking to people who knew you were still around. I thought you were there, right there, outside. It never occurred to me that loopy colleague of yours had got into the back of my car. How in hell did she do that?'

'Christa's been twocking cars since she was knee-high to a grasshopper, but in this case I think you let her in.'

'What d'you mean?'

'Do you remember in the hospital car park, a gang of kids crowding you?'

Pat nodded.

'There was one did the same to me at the same time. I'll bet you'd just clicked your key fob, opened your car. I'm not sure Christa knew which one was yours. I was following you, too, but she had them on to me as well. I got hassled just as you were getting to your car so I didn't see Christa.'

'What's happened to her?'

'Long story. She's safe enough. We have to figure out where Vince is and let someone know. Scott'll listen if I can get to talk to him. Where would they have taken Vince?'

Pat looked puzzled. 'But they're back at the house.'

Annie gave her a swift summary of her arrival and of finding the place deserted. 'You were the only person left in there,' she ended.

'And the coppers arrived, you say?'

'Yes, quite a force. I don't know if it was to do with my call to Scott's wife. I wish he'd call me back. Did they clear out because I'd been there or what?'

'Why wait till now?' said Pat. 'Christ! My head. Have you any paracetamol in here?'

Annie shook her head. Pat had no idea she'd been in the house and now wasn't the time to tell her. 'I don't know that you ought to take anything just yet. Look, I'm going to get us back to the racecourse. I've a key to the building where the grooms stay overnight. We'll get something to eat and if you can keep it down, you can probably risk taking painkillers. There's a medicine cabinet. They're bound to keep something in there. Haven't you any idea where they'd take Vince?'

'Maybe back to the clinic. That private place he'd been in.'

And why the sudden evacuation? Was it because she'd found them? Who knew that she'd been out at the farmhouse? If it were an unplanned getaway, they wouldn't be so hard to track down, not by people who had official channels at their beck and call. What could Greaves do? Sleeman couldn't have the whole of the local force in his pocket. She glanced at Pat, a miserable wreck in the seat beside her. The sooner they could get to that small kitchen and eat, the better.

Carl must have assumed Pat had dragged Christa out of the room where she'd been dumped. He'd grabbed Christa from the lion's mouth just as he promised her he would, but he saw the state she was in and knew full well she hadn't climbed those stairs by herself. Vince Sleeman was on a harsh deadline with death stalking close. He'd looked to her as though it might already be too late, but what did she know? And anyway, Vince wouldn't let that stop him. He'd make them try; make them kill the woman from the sea. She recalled something of the conversations she'd eavesdropped whilst under the bed. They didn't fit the pattern she thought she'd worked out, but she pushed them aside. She'd worked out the big picture, that was what counted for now.

'That woman's his donor, isn't she?' she asked.

'I didn't know,' said Pat. 'Truly. After they tested all of us, Leah said he'd gone on the transplant register, but it's not a kidney.'

'No, I'd figured that. He needs a liver donor.'

'And if you donate a liver…'

'You die. Yeah, I'd figured that, too. So the transplant register wasn't going to come up with anything quick enough, I suppose.'

'He wasn't even going to try. I told you before, he took himself off it, but then he took a real turn for the worse and that's when Leah took him home. There was no point trying to keep him in hospital and they've money for round-the-clock care.'

'I didn't see much round-the-clock care.'

'When? When were you there to see anything?'

Annie waved it aside. It would take too long to explain and it wasn't important now. 'Something Carl said,' she murmured to sidestep the question. 'So what do you know? Who's going to do this operation?'

'I think they were going to go abroad,' Pat said, uncertainty behind her tone. 'I don't know what stopped them. Then Vince went into hospital…in and out a time or two. There was a private clinic in the Midlands somewhere. They'd done business with them before.'

'What sort of business?'

'Drugs, I suppose, but there was talk that they'd found donors for people, found a way round the waiting lists, I mean.'

'What happened back there? Why did you go alone? We were going to go together.'

'I wasn't taking you with me. That would have been suicide for both of us. I had to go alone. Huh! So I thought. But anyway, I went to the loo and I found some paperwork. I was just nosying about.'

Annie thought back. She remembered Pat leaving the room for a few minutes. 'Upstairs or down?'

'Down. Why, what difference does it make? Anyway, I had a look round because I knew something was up. You could've cut the atmosphere with a knife. They didn't want me there. Didn't want anyone seeing

Vince. I knew what I'd found. I recognized it from the paperwork I'd seen when we'd all been at the clinic that time. Tissue matching and that. I didn't understand the medical stuff, but it wasn't hard to guess what it was about. And it had her name on it, Leah's au pair. Vitoria something or other.'

'Was it after that when you rang me?'

'Yes, that dozy mate of yours crashed the party so I assumed you were around, too. I wanted to warn you. I didn't know they'd go that far. I knew he was on the way out, but he's had his time. No one's going to shed tears and he wouldn't want them to, anyway. To start with, I didn't take a lot of notice. Vince and his tantrums. I thought it was all above board, routine stuff. And you know Vince, he won't have anyone fussing. He hated doctors of any kind, but I guess he had someone on board.'

'Hassan?'

'No, I reckon Hassan was legit, but Vince targeted him for some reason.'

'Maybe if he'd lost his original team he'd have needed a last minute sub. He's desperate. I suppose you've no idea if he found anything on Hassan?'

'We can ask Babs. She's back with us now. I'm surprised she didn't turn out to be a match for Vince. She acts just like him. She's been threatening to discharge herself, too.'

'I'd no idea she'd recovered that far. That's good.' Annie felt her mouth curve to a smile as she pulled the car off the main street and on to the road that headed for the racecourse. She'd felt a measure of responsibility for what had happened to Barbara because it was her call that had prompted it. 'Try Christa's number for me, will you?'

Pat tapped the number into her phone and put it to her ear, but after a moment, said, 'No, it's rung through to answer-phone. Shall I leave a message.'

Annie shook her head. 'No point. I just hope she's OK. Right, we're here. We'll get in and get something to eat, then I'm going to see if I can track down Scott. Oh hell!'

'What?' Pat sat up, alarmed.

'Nothing, sorry. It's just that I can see a horse in one of the stables. That means there'll be grooms here. Not to worry, the place isn't full. We'll get in through the back.'

She pulled the car round behind the stable block and led Pat through past the indoor stalls. A single horse swung its head round to watch them. That was good. A single horse probably meant a single groom or, at most two, if it were a very valuable horse. She looked it up and down and thought it rather muddy for an expensive animal, but what did she know?

'Keep quiet,' she told Pat. 'We don't want to wake anyone.'

She took Pat into one of the overflow rooms at the back of the block, tossed her jacket down on the bed and said, 'Check in there for coffee and stuff,' indicating the cubby hole with its kettle. 'And I'll nip round and get us some food.'

Leaving Pat foraging in the tiny space, Annie made her way back through the stable block, weighing up whether or not to chase Scott via Kate again.

The solitary horse again raised its head to watch her pass. Something about its outline caught her attention. She stopped to look, suddenly convinced she recognized it as one of the pony camp animals. It was certainly muddy enough. Probably it was her mind playing tricks, but she would be pleased to find Jean pottering in the kitchen, and she ran through a lightning fantasy where she talked Jean into cooking her and Pat a meal whilst she dozed at the small table.

No doubts now; dawn had begun to creep across the sky. It was still dark enough for her torch to have been useful, but it was in her jacket pocket in the room with Pat. She felt her way along the wall, noting the shapes that defined themselves in the distance; the mound of the hill that led over to the racetrack, the line of trees waving their branches along the far end of the big car park. The breeze chilled her bare arms, bringing with it a background aroma of straw, of horses and early-morning air, soon to be joined by the crisp tang of frying bacon, she hoped.

As she turned the corner she saw a Range Rover parked near the entrance to the building and, at the far end of the lorry park, the outline of a small horse box. It wasn't Jean's box; hers hadn't had writing on the side, but it was Jean's Range Rover. That meant Jean was here, probably asleep in one of the rooms, looking after the last of the pony-camp animals.

Someone was up and about. She had just slipped past the first of the windows when a light came on in one of the bedrooms further down. A silhouette grew and then shrank on the curtains. At the same time she became aware of voices. The words weren't distinguishable, but the whisper of conversation came from further down the yard. There were more people here than she'd anticipated, but that silhouette was familiar. It was Jean. She was sure of it.

Jean's car but not Jean's box. She looked across again and froze on a gasp. The encroaching dawn had misled her: shown her the outline from the wrong angle. It was

tucked into a dip near the far end of the building. She'd
seen one panel and thought she was looking at the full
length of it, but it was a monster of a vehicle and for
the first time, she saw the huge tractor unit attached.

As the implications hit her the silhouette was back at
the window. No longer alone. Distorted figures twirled
in a slow motion dance; Jean's shadowy partner dumping her inert form back on the bed; the momentary outline of an odd-shaped hand. Not a hand. A fist holding
a syringe—oh God! Then the light clicked out.

Annie threw herself at the dark corner by the rain
barrel as the door to the building opened and footsteps
thudded out. The form that strode past her hiding place,
close enough for her to reach out and touch him, was
relaxed, cupping his hands round a cigarette as he lit
up. She recognized him as the heavy who had caught
Christa. And now he was between her and her way
back to Pat; the way back to her car; the way back to
her phone.

TWENTY-SIX

ANNIE PRESSED HER back to the wall feeling completely
outgunned. Too tired to be thinking straight, she'd
walked into their midst. It was only a matter of time
before they spotted her. The wall behind her felt sharp
and scratchy, pulling at the fabric of her shirt. And
damp, too. If everyone stood just as they stood now,
meat-plate hands at the corner of the car park cradling
his cigarette, the unseen person or people talking softly
at the other side, herself pressed to the wall by the rain
barrel, the dawn would creep in and shine a spotlight
on her. Already, shapes were defining themselves as
light trickled in from the far horizon. It was an action
replay of the farmhouse shrubbery. She pulled in a deep
breath. The worst thing to do now would be a panicked,
ill-thought-out move.

Out of nowhere, the comments she'd overheard back
at the farmhouse suddenly made sense. The huge coils
of wire in the big shed. That talk about stability and
the electricity supply. Carl hysterical about having the
trailer parked in his drive. There'd been panic at some
point recently. Vince, with his plan for his own salva-
tion in tatters, had seen time running out. She could
almost hear his voice from across the years.

If you want a bloody job doing, do it your bloody self.

Usually shouted at Barbara full volume, while she
turned her nose up at him and maintained he'd given her
an impossible task. Back in the days when she'd been

the sisters' employee, when they hadn't realized she was in earshot, she'd twice heard him follow up with, *I told you to give this one to Annie!* More nails in the coffin of her relationship with Barbara, which hadn't been great from the off.

So he'd lost the contacts who would leapfrog the waiting lists for him and maybe procure him a donor. He'd done the job himself. Found his own mobile operating theatre; searched for his own surgical team; found and shipped in his own donor. But an enterprise like that couldn't be set up on a whim. It needed more than even Vince's long reach could easily muster. A reliable electricity source for one. That's what they'd been trying to sort out at the big barn. And they'd failed. Probably the mains cables were too old to give them what they needed. She wondered if that was why they'd taken it to Carl's house, to hook it up there. He'd freaked at the sight of it in his drive and it had moved off again. So Leah didn't always get her way. Again, she thought about Leah's position in all this. Wasn't she the one who'd tried to keep Vince in hospital and on a legitimate waiting list for a transplant? She'd lived with him all these years, but was this a step too far? Annie knew that the Sleemans were involved in all sorts, but she'd never had a hint that they were killers; that casual assertion Carl had given someone that he'd killed her had never seemed to have substance.

If it wasn't too late for Vitoria, and if she couldn't find a way to get back to her phone, then Leah might be the one to target.

The sentry by the corner of the building made a move. He took a final drag on his cigarette, tipped his head up towards the last of the night sky and blew out a cloud of smoke; then he tossed the butt to the ground and twisted it under his heel before walking out of sight round the building.

Annie looked the other way. The voices whispered on in the darkness but they were out of sight of the front of the building. This was her chance to move. She slipped silently along to the door and let herself in. It wasn't the ideal place to be, but at least she had some cover to plan her next move. Tiptoeing from one end of the building to the other, she checked all the rooms. The only occupant was Jean, stretched out on her back on the small bed, her arms flung over her head. There was no chance of rousing her, but Annie tried anyway, before rolling her into the recovery position. Meat-plate hands must have stationed himself inside, guarding Jean. If she hadn't woken they might have left her. Or maybe Annie had just happened along at the point when the man had gone in there to deal with her. They would need an undisturbed few hours, and Jean would have been sure to take an interest in a strange new horse box. This was the back-up plan. Somewhere a horse box could park for hours without comment; somewhere with a reliable electricity supply to hook up to.

Back in the tiny kitchen Annie daren't open the fridge door because the flash of light might show outside, but on the surface lay the remains of a sliced loaf and a pot of jam. She grabbed a slice, and using her finger to hook out a chunk of jam she smeared it on the bread and chewed hungrily. Sorry, Pat, she thought. Nothing I can do for you yet. As though the tiny amount of sustenance was enough to recharge her, two things popped up at the front of her mind. The first made her stifle a gasp. Pat! Pat wouldn't wait for long. She'd come lumbering round to see what was keeping Annie, probably flashing a torch in front of her advertising her presence for all to see. The second thought had Annie racing back to the small bedroom where Jean lay unconscious. Jean had a phone. How could she have been so dumb? It just showed what tiredness could do. She raked through Jean's pockets, through the tiny unit with its single drawer and minuscule wardrobe. There inside at a back corner sat Jean's handbag, gaping open. Annie yanked it out and peered inside, impatiently upending it on to the floor. Nothing. Meat-plate hands must already have taken it, in case Jean came to earlier than expected. After all, they thought Christa had come round and made her own escape. She looked back at the comatose form on the bed hoping Jean hadn't been given an extra large dose as insurance.

As far as she could see there was no reason for anyone to come back inside this building. The trailer was parked in the dip down by a small annexe at the far end of the lorry park. Her task now was to make her way back to the stable block and her phone.

ANNIE EASED THE door open and slipped back outside. It was quiet now, but too light to risk being able to blend with the wall of the low building. She needed better cover and needed to get away from the building's shelter so she could get a look at what was going on at the two ends. At some point, she hoped, they would all converge at or round the trailer, leaving her escape route clear. Taking a last look to be sure no one was in her direct line of sight she crouched low and ran across the dirt surface, ducking down behind Jean's Range Rover. The view wasn't a great deal better, but it felt more secure to be out in the open.

A low laugh cut through the air, followed by a burst of voices talking together. She peered out from under the car, seeing three of the heavies emerge from the direction of the stable block and…she swallowed a gasp…the woman, Vitoria, was with them, walking alongside. As they swung into view the first shaft of sunlight broke across the far horizon causing them all to shade their eyes and giving Annie a grandstand view of their faces. Relaxed and laughing, they strolled on, until Vitoria stopped abruptly. Annie judged from the angle that they'd just come in sight of the huge trailer. Voices floated across.

'…no, I would rather wait…'

'…don't worry… Leah says it's OK for you to…'

Vitoria nodded and smiled reassuringly, started off again with them, then suddenly twisted away and set off at a sprint.

It was over before Annie could think about reacting. Vitoria made half a dozen steps before one of the heavies caught her by the upper arm and spun her back round. They continued on their way, Vitoria now struggling futilely against the tree-trunk of an arm that held her almost casually as the men strode with her towards the dip where the truck was parked.

Keeping low behind the car, Annie looked across. Steps had been put up to the door of the trailer. The only way in or out. But they weren't heading there. They veered away from the trailer and made for the small annexe.

If they were to go inside they might leave the way clear for her…but no, she heard yet more voices from the direction of the stable block. How many of them were there?

She looked back towards the three heavies and saw one of them push Vitoria roughly through the door of the annexe ahead of him. The other two waited outside, and a moment later, the third re-emerged. They turned and marched back the way they'd come, apparently confident she wouldn't or couldn't get back out. Annie had concentrated on getting to a phone, but there was another way to stop them. They couldn't do anything without Vitoria. And as far as Annie could tell, Vitoria had been left alone in that small annexe.

ANNIE KNEW SHE clung by her fingernails and should get out while she could. The route over the far horizon that led to the racetrack lay unguarded. There might be people there, dog-walkers, staff doing whatever it was that racetracks needed by way of early morning maintenance. Even if not, she'd reach the road eventually, flag someone down, hitch a lift, borrow or steal a phone. What would it take? An hour at most? Her priority should be to get herself out, get help for Pat and just hope she could be in time for Vitoria. But her gut told her Vitoria didn't have an hour. As the life leached from Vince, so death crept up on the woman who'd walked out of the sea. What had she hoped for that night? Not this.

Annie was pretty sure she'd just witnessed the moment at which Vitoria realized her intended fate, but she wondered how the woman could have been so blind.

She tried to judge how the odds were stacked but it was an impossible equation to solve. Too many unknowns. No illusions about what would happen to her if she were found, but she had to try to get Vitoria out before it was too late. The leaden tiredness had gone. She felt alert and wide awake, but she knew it was a temporary adrenaline rush. It wouldn't last and it was no substitute for knowledge and preparation.

Silently and as quickly as she could, she picked her

way from shadow to shadow heading for that door. What had he done to Vitoria to stop her coming right back out? Tied her, drugged her? He'd been quick for either, which was a problem because it implied that someone else was in there to stand guard.

Yet somehow the small annexe wasn't the focus. She'd heard only snatches of conversation, their sense largely carried away on the breeze, but it would be the preparations of the trailer, securing the electricity, putting the team in place, that were priority over Vitoria at this stage. The donor would normally be on life-support, their metabolism carefully balanced by machines whilst the operating room was prepared. No need for expensive machinery for Vitoria. Her own body would do the perfect job until they were ready for her. So presumably they'd keep her free of drugs.

Annie was at the corner of the annexe now and gave a swift glance back, pressing herself against the wall as another figure hurried across the dirt yard and climbed inside the trailer. It was hard to imagine there'd be room for all the people they were going to need.

The window was covered with a ragged curtain that looked as though it had been in place for months. It had frayed at one corner and didn't reach the sill. Warily, Annie drew close and pressed her face to the glass. The inside was stacked with what looked like old boxes, garbage, a holding-place for things on their way to the recycling centre by the look of it. A movement made her jump, but she realized it was Vitoria sitting on the floor at the back of the space, twisting round, pulling at something.

No sign of anyone else in there.

She reached the door, looked back to be sure no one could see her, then turned the handle and entered in one swift move, her gaze raking round the small space, ignoring Vitoria, searching for threats.

Vitoria started up in alarm at her entrance. Annie held up her hand in what she hoped was a reassuring gesture.

Vitoria wasn't alone. The other occupant was Vince, huddled in a wheelchair, tiny and wizened. If it weren't for his rasping breaths Annie would have assumed him already dead. A thought flashed through her mind. If he were dead, the reason to kill Vitoria would have gone. How long would it take to smother a dying man? Seconds by the look of him. She turned back to Vitoria.

'You doctor?' said the woman in a small voice.

'No, no. I'm here to help you…to get you out. Let me see.'

She knelt down and saw that one of Vitoria's wrists was handcuffed to a metal water pipe. She wasted a moment rattling at the cuffs and the pipe, but it was clear they were going nowhere without tools to break through them, so she turned her attention to the piles of boxes, rifling through them for something she could use. The boxes were empties. She found an old bicycle wheel, some useless oddments and then a rusty jar labelled Hoof Oil. She struggled to undo the top. Maybe if Vitoria's wrist were slippery enough…?

She inspected the cuff. It was far too tight. It wouldn't come free without the key or some kind of tool to cut it open.

In frustration, Annie rushed to the small window to peer out, to make sure no one was on their way.

'I'll go for help,' Annie told Vitoria, who looked up at her, the beginnings of panic in her eyes.

'Find Leah,' she said. 'Leah say she keep me safe. Leah not here.'

'I know,' said Annie. 'But I'll do better than that if I can just find a phone.'

A phone! Vince wasn't a prisoner. He was here voluntarily. There was no reason he wouldn't still have his phone on him. At once, she was at the wheelchair digging in the folds of the blankets, the pockets on the chair. A sour odour of decay rose from him, making her screw up her face in disgust.

He groaned as she pushed him from one side to the other.

'What the hell...?' he growled, opening his eyes and fixing her with a glare. 'Can't a dying man have a minute's peace?'

'Your phone,' Annie spat back at him. 'I want your phone. And I'll tip you out of the blasted chair to get it if I have to.'

He made an attempt at a laugh and raised one his hands, frail and skeletal, skin translucent, the crooked index finger pointing to a battered holdall on the floor by the chair. 'In there if it's anywhere. Now, screw off!'

Annie dived for the bag, tipped it upside down and scrabbled through a heap of packets and pill bottles that tumbled out. No phone. Nothing she could use for anything useful.

'Where is it?' she hissed up at Vince.

He just gave a small shake of his head and closed his eyes.

She looked towards Vitoria who also shook her head. 'I don't seen phone.'

Time leaked away and there was nothing she could do. Again she peered through the gap in the makeshift curtain. It wouldn't be long before someone came to get Vitoria and then Vince. She mustn't be caught in here with them. She looked at the stack of boxes and at the heap of medicines all over the floor. It was pretty clear someone had been in here.

Vince's rasping breaths had turned to patchy snores. Annie looked at him. It would be pretty pointless to kill Vitoria if Vince was missing.

TWENTY-SEVEN

ANNIE WEIGHED THE OPTIONS. She could lift Vince bodily and carry him away. He was so shrivelled, she could manage him easily, except that he wouldn't come quietly. If she knew what she was doing, she might force-feed him some of the tablets she'd scattered across the floor whilst looking in that bag, but she daren't. He was too frail, too close to death, and she wouldn't be the one to finish him off. Tying him in the chair would cut down any route by which she could slip away unnoticed. If he stayed asleep, she might hide him behind the boxes and leave the door swinging open. Could she lay a false trail, the way she'd been going to do with Christa? If the door were open wide the constant rush of the breeze might mask the sound of his breathing, which was shallow enough anyway.

As a plan, it hung by a thread. She tried to imagine what might happen if they came along and Vince was missing. They'd search, but they'd know he couldn't have gone far. She couldn't rely on another lucky break like Reg's car. Unless she could engineer one, but how? Everywhere was bathed in early-morning light. No dark corners to rely on. If the chance came, if they were all distracted at this end of the lorry park, she'd sprint back to the low building, back along its length, round the corner and to the stable block and her phone.

And Pat. What had happened to Pat? Either she'd

been found or she'd fallen asleep unnoticed in that out-of-the-way room.

The rusty tin of hoof oil lay on the floor beside Vitoria. Annie's gaze zoomed in on it. She moved swiftly behind Vince, grasped the handles of the chair and manoeuvred him backwards, past Vitoria, to the far corner. She shoved the chair bit by bit, pulling boxes from behind and stacking them in front. Vince's clawlike hands gripped the chair arms convulsively, but he said nothing. He wouldn't waste his breath whilst there was no one to come to his rescue. Annie couldn't bring herself to silence him with violence. He was too close to the edge. But he could barely stay awake; his voice wasn't strong. She remembered the uproar back at the house when Christa had gone missing. If his disappearance generated the same volume of sound, his weak voice hadn't a hope of being heard.

She snatched up the hoof oil and pulled the old bicycle wheel free of the debris in the corner. There wasn't much left in the tin, but what there was pooled nicely on the floor so she could run the wheel through it and make a track towards the door. The window showed everything quiet outside, so she risked easing the door open and reaching out to continue the track in the dirt. She pulled in a breath to make sure she put sufficient effort behind the move and hurled the wheel out along the side of the building towards the grass edge. It spun across the ground and disappeared from sight. 'Vitoria,' she whispered. 'I'm going back outside. When I get the chance, I'll make a break for it. I'll bring help.'

She wasn't sure how much the woman understood, but as she reached for the door, she heard running footsteps and raised voices, so crept back, eased herself behind the stack of boxes and stood close to Vince, who

looked to be asleep again. Words floated in as the footsteps raced nearer.... *from over here...quick...sounded
like a window breaking...*.

They'd heard something. She froze, holding her
breath as the door clicked open.

A shocked intake of breath and then pandemonium...
voices shouting... Cutting through it all in hesitant tones
came Vitoria's voice, 'Woman came. Take him away.'

Annie's heart flipped over. Why was Vitoria giving
her away? But even as the thought formed, she knew
it was the right thing to do. If they thought Vince had
gone under his own steam, they'd look nearby. If they
thought he'd been taken, they'd rush off to give chase.
The fly in the ointment was the poisonous old man in
the wheelchair at her side. She swivelled her eyes down
to look at him. He couldn't have stayed asleep through
all the racket. Was he aware of her close beside him,
scared of what she'd do? But Vince Sleeman wasn't
scared of anyone, certainly not people like her. All she
could do was remain still and hope.

'When...where?' someone shouted.

'After you leave me,' Vitoria said. Annie applauded
silently. Vitoria's act was perfect.

'Why didn't you shout out?'

'Shout for who? You tie me here. Where Leah?'

'Come on! She took him this way. She can't get far.'

'If they got over the rise she could have had a car
there.'

The door slammed and Vitoria's voice murmured,
'They gone.'

Annie eased herself out and looked towards the window, not taking the risk of getting too close. She caught
a glimpse of people running. If she only had a weapon
or knew how many of them there were and where they

were, but she didn't and must improvise. Now it was light, Jean's car was no good for cover. She'd have to make it from here right to the corner in one go. But if they'd gone over the rise towards where Carl had hijacked her, they would be out of sight of the lorry park. As she crept closer, she saw another group: hard to tell how many as she watched from an acute angle through the dirty glass. They didn't come her way, but she needed them gone before she could get out without being seen.

A burst of shouting and a cry, cut off abruptly. As Annie stared, someone broke off from the group and moved out of her line of sight. The others came into better view. Two heavies and a young girl, twelve or thirteen, Annie judged, and they were dragging her towards the trailer. What on earth...? Was this some early-morning dog walker grabbed off the scrubland? What part could a young girl have to play in this charade?

'Get me water,' rasped a voice from behind the heap of boxes.

She spun round. 'There,' Vitoria pointed at a bottle of spring water on the floor.

With another glance at the two men and the girl struggling between them, Annie snatched up the bottle, unscrewed the top and pushed it at Vince—a kind of thank offering that he'd remained too comatose to give her away. He had difficulty raising it to his lips, but slurped at it thirstily, dribbling liquid down his front. As soon as the two men had the young girl inside the trailer, she would make her move.

The shadow across the window came out of nowhere, the soft crunch of footsteps just outside giving Annie barely time to leap back behind the boxes. The door clicked open again.

'Leah!' cried Vitoria. 'OK. Is OK. Is Leah.'

Reluctantly, Annie moved forward. She couldn't remain hidden in the face of Vitoria's enthusiastic urging. She faced Leah across the small space. Vitoria saw the woman as her saviour. Annie saw a long-standing member of the Sleeman clan. Even if Leah was prepared to save Vitoria, what chance did she stand against the army ranged out there?

'We meet at last,' Leah said.

Annie nodded, her gaze never leaving the woman's face.

'Leah, please,' Vitoria begged. 'Find key. This thing hurt—'

'Quiet!' Leah snapped, cutting across her. 'Where have you taken him?'

Annie swallowed. Logic told her she should be able to rush this woman and overpower her, but she took in the solidity of Leah's stance, her hand hidden in the folds of her skirt. What did she have? A gun...a blade...?

'Leah, please. We have agreed.' Vitoria spoke again, an undertone of indignation behind her words.

Leah turned to look at Vitoria, putting on a smile that chilled Annie's soul, and with panther-like speed covered the ground between them in a stride. 'I told you to be quiet,' she snapped as her small foot landed deliberately on Vitoria's free hand, twisting it into the floor.

Vitoria cried out in pain. Instinctively, Annie moved forward, only to stop as Leah swung back to her. 'Where is he?'

Annie pulled in a breath. At any second Vince would wake. She was surprised his rasping breaths weren't audible already in the quiet of the annexe. Only Leah between her and the door. Distract her with Vince. Make a run for it. Everyone else must be in the trailer or out looking for her and Vince, but they'd be back soon. As thoughts flashed through her mind, the fog cleared.

Vince isn't scared of people like me... I told you to give that job to Annie.

And she realized that Carl Sleeman had told her the truth, knowing she wouldn't believe him. Vince hadn't kept quiet because he was asleep, and Reg Brocklesby hadn't been outraged that she wasn't Christa; he'd been outraged because she wasn't Vitoria. It was the job that Vince had brought her here to do.

'Uh... Pat has him,' she said to Leah. 'We came together. We had a car over the rise. I stayed to help Vitoria. I'll show you.' She made a move towards the door, but Leah flicked her right wrist, showing a glint of steel.

With her other hand Leah reached into her pocket and pulled out a phone. Annie stared longingly. In her peripheral vision she could see Vitoria, curled over her injured hand.

She had to get Leah out of here or find some way to cover the sounds of Vince's laboured breathing. Already she could hear him. He was doing his best to keep quiet, just as he had when the heavies had burst in, but he was too ill to keep it up. She started to breathe loudly herself as though beginning to hyperventilate.

Leah shot her a suspicious glance as she spoke into her phone. 'Thompson had a car here. Her own car?' She looked the question at Annie, taking a step closer to Vitoria as she did so. Vitoria cringed. The message was clear. Annie shook her head. 'No.' It was the only safe answer. Pat's car hadn't been at the farmhouse, so one of them must have taken it. 'It's my car.'

'Registration number,' snapped Leah.

Annie gave it.

'Oh, that one's yours, is it? Might have guessed.' Leah spoke into the phone, then back to Annie. 'Where's she taking him?'

'To the nearest hospital, I should think,' said Annie, as Vitoria suddenly cried out again. Both Annie and Leah jumped at the sound. Vitoria subsided but not before shooting a look at Annie, who immediately feigned a coughing fit to cover the sounds from behind the boxes. Vince was struggling to keep quiet.

Leah glared from one to the other of them. 'Nothing,' Leah snapped into the phone. 'She's likely to head for Hull Royal. Get to her before she does.'

As Leah cut the call Annie saw a shadow outside and moved swiftly across to stand beside Vitoria. At once Leah's hand flew into view and Annie saw the blade. Annie backed further, crowding Vitoria, who hugged the wall. Leah circled round, forcing Annie further over. It was a bad move, crowding herself close to Vitoria, but Annie needed Leah to turn her back to the window and door. But Leah was quick, too quick. Annie needed another diversion.

'He's been here all along,' Annie said. 'He's there behind the boxes.'

Her speech shocked Vitoria into silence and Vince's rasping breaths filled the air. As if on cue, one of the unstable mound of boxes broke free and tumbled down, showing the corner of the wheelchair and one of Vince's wizened legs. Leah gaped and swung round to Annie in such a fury that she was a microsecond behind the curve in swinging back again as the door crashed open behind her. She turned just enough to meet the metal wrench square on the temple and went down without a murmur.

'You took your time,' said Annie to Pat.

VITORIA TURNED HER head away as Annie used the wrench to smash the water pipe at the nearest joint. Water gushed out, soaking them all as they wrestled to slide the handcuff free. Pat cleared the boxes away from in front of Vince.

'They wouldn't have persuaded the surgeon, anyway,' he rasped, as he watched them struggle to free Vitoria. 'It's not the sort of thing folks do for any amount of money if they're not minded.'

'They would,' said Pat, picking up the wrench as Annie pulled Vitoria to her feet. 'Leah went for his daughter. He'd have carved up Vitoria rather than watch them carve his child. Anyway, we'll ring people, soon as we're clear. You can get on to the proper list again.'

'Pah…' He looked disgusted and waved them away.

'My God!' Annie swung round on Pat. 'Haven't you rung anyone yet?'

'I don't want the hassle. Nor does she. We'll ring as soon as we can get a phone that can't be traced back to us.'

Annie dived to Leah's comatose form and scrabbled through her pockets. 'Come on!' she urged them. 'We need to go. We'll ring from Leah's phone.'

The three of them ran as fast as they could down the sides of the buildings. At the sound of a car engine they dived inside the grooms' block.

Annie took out Leah's phone and made the emergency call, salient facts only, refusing to give her name, knowing that someone was already on their trail, but making sure to say that Hassan and his daughter had been brought here and that Jean was unconscious in the grooms' block.

Listening to a vehicle screaming up the track somewhere behind them, Annie toyed with the idea of searching for Jean's car keys, taking her car, maybe even taking Jean. They were on the lookout for her car, now. But no, Jean's car would be missed at once; it was hard to imagine starting it up without it being heard from the trailer. Her car was tucked away where they wouldn't have thought to look. Would they?

'Did anyone see you?' she hissed at Pat as the sounds grew closer.

''Course not,' said Pat. 'Well...that is, I bashed one of them, but I put him out of the way.'

'Will they have found the car? Was he inside the stable block?'

Pat shook her head. 'I fell asleep after you left. When I woke and you weren't back I knew there was trouble, so I found a wrench and went out to look. I heard them talking. They were waiting for Leah to come back with Hassan's daughter. Hassan wasn't playing ball. Two of them went with Leah when she got back, but they left one on guard.'

Annie risked a glance at Vitoria, whose expression hardened as she listened.

Instinctively they all pulled back from the window as a car skidded round the corner on to the lorry park. It roared past the block and on down to the dip towards the trailer.

'Now,' Annie told them. This was not the time to hang around for an invitation or even to wonder who was in the car. This was their last chance to get clear.

Vitoria outstripped them both, arriving at the far corner, pressing herself to the wall and peering round, then beckoning them on. Like a true professional, thought Annie, as she guided Vitoria to the stable block, made a dash for the tiny bedroom to grab her coat and fum-

ble for the keys. As she re-emerged Pat came panting
along to join them and they raced for the back lane to
Annie's stashed car.

TWENTY-EIGHT

TWENTY-EIGHT

AS THEY SWUNG out of the lane Annie felt a surge of triumph to see a clear road ahead of her, but knew they were far from safe. And a part of her was convinced they should stay and wait for the next set of flashing blue lights to arrive. If they tried to get clear, they might yet be caught in Sleeman's web. If they stayed and handed themselves in, they were in for varying levels of trouble, but they'd be safe. Or would they?

Pat groaned from the backseat. 'Christ, I feel lousy.'

'Put your seat belt on,' Annie snapped.

'Why? You planning to run us off the road?'

Annie pursed her lips and said nothing. This mini adrenaline rush might help to keep her focused for a while, but she hadn't slept for twenty-four hours and had barely eaten anything. She was in no fit state to drive as fast as she felt compelled to do, putting distance between them and the horrors they'd left behind. Concentrate, she told herself. Get back to the city. It would be waking up now. It wasn't that far. They could lose themselves in the city.

'That was a café back there.' Pat's voice radiated indignation.

Annie kept quiet. It would be madness to stop this close. Pat knew it. She was grumpy because Annie had ordered her into the back. Pat saw the sense in it, but it hadn't stopped her muttering. Annie wasn't having Vitoria behind them both. They knew too little about her.

Vitoria twisted in her seat, looking behind. 'We've got a start on them,' Annie reassured her absently as her mind spun through the options. 'We'll keep you safe.'

'For tonight maybe,' said Pat tactlessly. 'Then what? You're illegal, I suppose?'

Annie caught Vitoria throwing a distrustful glance over her shoulder. This was a marked car, now. No time to effect a change. She had to get them somewhere safe and get the car hidden. As she thought through the places they could go, Pat quizzed Vitoria. 'How did you end up coming in the way you did, landed on some beach somewhere?'

'Family here but I not allowed visa. Rules change. Quotas.'

Annie's phone rang. She pulled it out of her pocket and saw it was Christa. A shiver ran through her. The office and Pat's flat would be the first places the heavies would stake out. Not trusting herself to concentrate on the twists of the road, she passed the handset back over her shoulder. 'Speaker phone,' she told Pat. 'And keep quiet. I'm on my own, OK?'

'Annie, is that you?' said Christa's voice, clipped and alert.

'Uh…yeah. Everything OK?'

'Yeah, yeah, no problem. Just wanted to let you know a couple of guys got in touch, pretended they had a meeting with you, wanted to know where you were.'

Annie swallowed. 'Who were they? What did they say?'

'Nothing much. I took a number, said I'd get back to them when I found you. I assume you don't want me to.'

'No, you haven't heard from me. Uh…are you OK?'

'Fine. You don't need me to do anything, do you? Only I'm in the middle of something.'

'No, no. I'll be in touch.'

Annie looked in the mirror. She and Pat exchanged a glance. Pat spoke to Vitoria as she clicked off the phone. 'Sorry, what were you saying, Vitoria? Quotas?'

Vitoria told Pat how she'd looked at alternative routes into the UK once her application to come legitimately had been turned down. 'Too much money,' she said with a small laugh, 'until I hear of scheme.' She told how word had reached her of a need for people with specific skills, which might offer another chance to cross borders legitimately.

Annie thought about making a break for it, heading for the motorway. From here she could divert through North Cave, go the long way to the M1, head back to London, leave Scott and his mates to clear up. But the Sleeman heavies, although they couldn't quite put a watch on ports, airports and major roads, could come close if they were desperate enough. While they thought there was any chance of getting Vitoria back, they'd pull out all the stops. No, their best bet was to get back to Hull; to hide in the heart of the city, but where?

'Qualification not recognize here,' Vitoria told Pat. 'Have to do top up, but they say no problem. They sponsor me.'

Pat asked about medicals. And of course there'd been a health check involving blood tests. Vitoria told Pat she'd been 'over moon' when she learnt she'd been accepted, but less so when it became clear this was no legal way in. But she was desperate to be reunited with her family. They'd even waived her fee, told her that her skills were needed and it would be a matter of just a few weeks hidden away with sympathetic people in the UK, then all the paperwork would be straightened out and she could begin her new life. 'They explain to me not contact family until paperwork finish. They good liars. I believe them.'

'Got it,' murmured Annie, swinging the car round off the main road. Maybe not the ideal destination, but it was the last place they'd expect her to go.

'I see chance to find family. New life. Stupid.'

'Where are your family?'

'I don't know.' Vitoria shook her head.

For Annie that didn't quite ring true. Surely Vitoria knew how to find her family; why otherwise had there been any need to get her agreement not to contact them for a few weeks? 'Pat runs a private detective agency,' she said. 'Right up her street, a job like that.' She said this more to hear Vitoria's reaction than as a serious suggestion, but it was Pat who responded.

'Yeah right, Babs'll love that, reuniting illegals. And who's going to pay?'

'Vince preauthorized my expenses,' Annie pointed out. 'The paperwork'll be solid. Just be creative with the wording on the invoice.'

'So you've decided it is Vince paying for you?'

'Oh yes, it was Vince all along. But someone had an iron grip on all his decisions. Would that be Reg Brocklesby?' It was a guess. Annie glanced at Pat's face in the mirror.

Pat's eyebrows rose slightly. She nodded. Their eyes met briefly and by unspoken consent dropped the topic. It would be for further exploration when they were alone.

Annie drove the car round the side streets to the back of the Premier Inn tower and up the ramp to the car park. At this time of day it was quiet, the vehicles' owners asleep on the floors above them. She led Pat and Vitoria up to the reception desk on the seventh floor.

'My colleagues would like to check in for a couple of nights,' she said, 'but first, can we get breakfast? All on my bill.' They sat at a table by the window, a dishevelled group, looking out across the Humber, watching gulls swoop onto the swirling water as a ferry emerged from the mist at the far end of the estuary.

'Are we really going to stay here? How long for? Who's going to pay?'

'Just for long enough that there's no point in slaughtering Vitoria to save Vince. Sorry,' she added, seeing the expression on Vitoria's face. 'And I told you, my expenses were preauthorized. No expense spared from either side.' She looked regretfully at the menu and sniffed at the breakfasty smells beginning to seep through from behind the scenes. They weren't yet secure enough. 'They won't find us here,' she told Pat, 'but I want to make sure. Save me toast and coffee, plenty of it. I'll be back soon.'

As she ran down to the car Annie rang a local taxi firm to pick her up round the corner from Pat's flat. If they were to try for a final chance at Vitoria it would be within the next few hours. Annie's car found by Pat's flat would be the perfect diversion.

She parked on the wrong side of the block. The neat maisonettes lay quiet. Anyone waiting would be at the other side, but they'd cruise round the area; they'd find the car. When she stepped out the stiff breeze from the estuary hit her, the fresh air making her shiver. The taxi would come to the far end of the street but she would stay out of view until she saw it.

As she scurried down the pavement a shadow from a gateway caught her eye just too late. She spun round but he had her arm in an iron grip. 'Reception party's waiting at the flat,' said Carl Sleeman, 'but I thought you might pull a stunt like this. Where is she?'

As her heart thudded with shock, just for a split second the thought uppermost in her mind was regret for the coffee and toast waiting for her back at the hotel. 'I don't know.'

He raised his eyes to heaven. 'Don't piss me about. You make any fuss and they'll hear you. They're not twenty metres away through the tenfoot.'

She felt numb, unable to marshal her wits. He probably told the truth. They were there waiting. It was the obvious place for her and Pat to take Vitoria. The road was quiet, too early on a Saturday morning for there to be people about. He frogmarched her along the street, into a driveway and pushed her towards the passenger side of a BMW X5, then jogged round to get behind the wheel. 'Get in.'

When she paused, he said, 'I'm not gonna take you anywhere you don't wanna go, but you don't wanna hang around here till they find you.'

That was true, too. 'Why would I trust you?'

He shrugged. 'Why not? I got that dopey mate of yours out, didn't I?'

The sound of a car made her turn. There, passing the far of the road, was her taxi. She saw it pull up. Could she outrun him? He wasn't holding her now. Get there first, leap in, tell the driver to drive? As she watched two figures appeared in front of the taxi, one of them walking to the driver's door and leaning in.

Her gaze met Carl's. 'You didn't tell him where you were going, did you?' he asked.

She stared back at him. Tiredness had crept into every fibre of her being. The cool breeze ripped through her like icy daggers stippling her skin. Had she said where she was going? They usually asked when you booked a taxi.

'I don't know,' she whispered. 'No…no, I don't think so. No! I didn't. I said the station.' The relief was enormous. Yes, she'd said the station.

'If you don't get in,' he said, 'I'm leaving without you.' She climbed in. 'Keep your head down. It don't matter if they see me.'

She waited until he'd driven them out of the waterfront estate and back to the main road. 'Where are you taking me?'

'I'll drop you wherever you want, but we're gonna talk first.'

His phone rang. He drove one-handed while he answered it, listening for a while, then saying, 'They're headed for the flat. Might be there already. Keep yer head down. I'll look out for the car.'

He clicked off the phone and said, 'That'll keep them quiet for an hour.'

'Isn't it too late?' she said.

'Oh yeah, way too late, but with Leah out cold and Reg gone to ground, it's a bit Wild West just now. Give it a few hours. So where is she?'

She ignored the question and asked one of her own. 'Whose side are you on?'

'My own.'

Fair enough. 'All that play-acting at the pony camp, that was to have an excuse to bring me here, wasn't it?'

He slowed, glanced in the mirror and bumped the car up off the road on to a patch of waste ground outside a disused factory. Annie tensed as he reached in his pocket, but he pulled out a tobacco pouch and rolled himself a cigarette, proffering the pack to her.

'No thanks. I don't.'

'What d'you mean, excuse? We didn't bring you for that. We just shelled out enough money so that boss of yours would send you. I had to clear the place in case they needed it; get the kids to take stuff and that, but we thought it'd be useful if you had a handle on it, just in case.'

Annie took this in. 'Vince brought me here to find Vitoria, didn't he?'

Carl nodded.

'And Christa?'

'I said that was a bad idea, but he said you needed some help; said the odds were stacked against you too far.'

Annie looked out at a wall of cracked windows that had once let light into a bustling factory. 'Why not be upfront? Why not tell me?'

'He said you wouldn't work for him; said you'd help Pat out, but you'd be off like shit off a shovel if you thought you were working for him.'

'If you'd been upfront, I'd have told you to go to the police with it.'

'Yeah, like that would have worked!'

Annie thought about the civil war in the Sleeman clan. Vince with no one left to rely on except Carl, who wanted to be on side but had to watch his own back, which was why he'd never been straight with her. Whichever side won, he wasn't leaving evidence that he'd acted for the other. He'd kept pointing her in the right direction but always leaving room for it to have been nothing to do with him. And maybe Vince had had the mystery Reg Brocklesby on his side, too. She'd never known that much about Vince Sleeman but remembered his intolerance of any mention of illness or medics. 'He was scared of what she wanted to do, wasn't he? Vince, I mean.'

'Oh yeah. Said he'd kill himself with a blunt knife before he had someone else's guts inside him. He wouldn't stay in hospital or go on that transplant list.'

'So why was Leah so determined to cure him?'

'He hasn't left everything the way she wants it. She don't need long, but she needs longer than he's got to make sure she'll have full control once he's gone.'

'So what stopped her doing what she liked? He was in no fit state.'

'Reg. He holds Vince's will and all the paperwork.'

Annie looked again at the dark windows of the derelict factory where shattered glass reflected the early-morning sun. Reg Brocklesby seemed an unlikely candidate for the power behind the throne. 'I'm surprised she didn't just work on Reg.'

Carl gave a wintry laugh. 'She tried. Everyone tries, but Reg is untouchable. He has something on everyone. Even Leah. I never used to believe it, but I do now. She wouldn't go near him.'

So the bottom line was that Vince was dying too quickly for his wife's purposes. And she'd gone to extraordinary lengths to give him more time. 'What if it had worked? What if he'd had his transplant and recovered?'

'She'd have worked round him one way or another, then she'd have done him in. She wouldn't have risked him putting her through this again.'

Leah would have slaughtered Vitoria to give Vince long enough to be talked round and then she'd have disposed of him without a thought. 'She's worse than he is!'

He looked at her as if to say, have you only just worked that out?

'What do you want from me, Carl?'

'I need a bit of play-acting. I've done what I could for Vince. I kept you alive even after they knew you were on to them.'

Barely, thought Annie, thinking of the car by the graveyard.

'I showed you where to go. I took you to the house. I even got Reg out there so I could get your stupid mate out.'

Annie thought back to the sound of Carl's car racing up the drive, stopping briefly and then coming round the back. 'You brought Reg with you?' she asked. 'So there'd be a missing car. It was him who knocked on the front door.'

He smiled briefly. 'We've pulled that one before. Your mate's not the first one we've pulled out of there.'

Remembering Reg's comment, she murmured, 'So his car ended up in a ditch somewhere?'

'Not this time. No need. Too much else going on.' He turned away from her, looking back towards the main road as he drew smoke in from the fag end of his roll-up before flicking it out into the air. 'She's a nasty piece of work. Even Vince couldn't always stop her. And if you wanted my opinion, not that I'd give it, then I'd say you want to look under that barn floor. It's had a bit too much concrete put down over the years, patchwork and all. If you were to talk to your mates, that's where you should be telling them to look.'

He talked her through what he wanted. Then they climbed out and stood beside the car. She ranted at him, told him Pat was safe in hospital, no thanks to him. He growled at her to tell him where Vitoria was, and she told him Vitoria was in the hands of Immigration, soon to be deported but safe from the Sleemans. Then his tone changed. He began to wheedle her. 'Tell me where you took her. Who did you hand her to...when? Come on, what harm will it do now? You're the one with the gun. What am I going to do?'

'OK,' she said. 'I don't see what harm it'll do. And if you try to bust her out, you'll end up behind bars, which is just where you need to be. Give me that pen. I'll write it down for you.'

He held up his hand as he stopped the recording. 'That'll do.'

Annie didn't think it would convince anyone, but Carl seemed happy enough. Now, apparently, he had to get round to a mate's house to get a convincing soundtrack behind the recorded words. 'While the hired muscle chased false trails, you found me and got the info, is that it?'

'Yeah, more or less. It'll keep me the right side of her once she's calmed down.'

'But why do you even want to be the right side of her? Isn't now the time to bail out?'

'When he's six feet under and she's well behind bars, then maybe I'll think about it. Until then, she's gonna be the one with the clout.'

It was tempting to give in and let him drive her back to the hotel, but he was still on no one's side but his own and she couldn't trust him, so she insisted he left her there on the waste ground. She watched his car all the way down the dual carriageway until it disappeared from sight, then she began the walk back towards town, calling a taxi to meet her at the Sportsman pub on the old Hedon Road.

TWENTY-NINE

ANNIE EMERGED FROM a deep sleep, enjoying the warmth of a shaft of sunlight that lit the room. She sank into the comfort of the bed, running a mental inventory of aches and pains. Nothing too bad. A glance at the digital display on the TV showed her it was not quite midday. She'd slept for less than five hours but had slept well. She, Pat and Vitoria had agreed to meet in the restaurant around lunchtime. Annie lay still, feeling properly rested, relaxing into the knowledge that something nasty had been circumvented. A second later she was bolt upright. This wasn't over yet. What in hell were they to do with Vitoria?

She was pleased to find Pat on her own in the seventh-floor restaurant, toying with a menu and looking out across the Humber, where the sun snaked silver and gold coils across the water's surface. 'We need to talk about Vitoria. Any sign of her yet?'

'Let her sleep,' said Pat. 'The poor kid must be shattered. What are you thinking?'

'She needs to sit tight here a while longer. Carl talked about it being like the Wild West out there, but it'll settle once Leah's back in control and it's too late for Vince.'

Pat slapped the menu on to the table. 'I knew that all along,' she said, her face scrunched in annoyance. 'I could kick myself. Did you see the look he gave me last night when I was yapping on about transplant registers?' Pat gave a huff of irritation and looked at the menu again. 'He'd no more consent to a transplant than fly to the moon. I knew that!'

'I wish I'd worked it out earlier,' said Annie.

'Did you ever come across a guy called Stills?'

Annie felt her eyes widen but tried not to show surprise. 'I met him once.'

'He rang Babs a month or so ago, asked about Vince; about him not wanting to stay in hospital, refusing to go on the transplant register, all that. He asked her if Vince wanted to get better. She said, of course he did. But he didn't, not like that. We should both have figured it.'

'How did he know about Vince?'

'He and Stills go way back.'

So Stills had tested the waters with Barbara, but known they were just the nonentities in the game, the sisters always on the periphery of the real family business. Nonentities or not, they'd been used by both sides. Leah had them digging dirt on Hassan which they'd failed to do, and Vince had engineered Annie back into their midst, having more faith in her abilities than theirs. But who else did he have? The enigmatic Reg Brocklesby quietly wielding power behind the scenes, but unable to stop Leah, and Carl, the nephew who owed him some loyalty, but who daren't do anything other than hedge his bets at every turn.

Vince knew Carl couldn't fight Leah on his own, so he'd had Annie brought in to work for the Thompsons, who were small fry on Leah's radar. He knew she wouldn't work for him, but she would do her best for Vitoria once pushed in the right direction. No one had trusted anyone. So much for her theories about Barbara being in on it, though that phone call had panicked someone. It annoyed her that Vince hadn't bothered to hide that he was paying for her, knowing she'd never

believe it. It looked as though Greaves had been working for Vince, too, trying to get Vitoria out of Leah's
clutches and to the safety of deportation. No doubt Reg
Brocklesby had something on Greaves, gambling debts
or some such, like Pat had said. Enough to stop him mo-
bilizing official help to intercept Vitoria. No one had
anything on Scott. He'd simply walked into the middle
of it that night and Greaves had had to busk it. She supposed she should tell Scott about Greaves, but wasn't
sure he'd believe her.

'Vince had to go along with Leah,' Pat said, 'or she'd
have whipped him off abroad.'

'All he had to do was put the trip off until it was too
late for him to survive the journey.'

Pat shook her head. 'No, he was wilier than that. I
reckon he found that place in the Midlands, went along
with all the arrangements and then had someone shop
them. He didn't count on Leah trying a DIY job.'

'It was pretty Wild West even before yesterday,'
Annie commented, thinking of all the contradictory
threats and bribes flying about; Vince having Vitoria
intercepted; Leah grabbing her back. And Carl, rushing from pillar to post taking orders from both sides,
but even he had balked at the attempt to set the trailer
up at his place and having two murders—Vitoria and
Vince—committed on his doorstep. The farmhouse
was the preferred venue; quiet, out of the way, but with
inadequate utilities. The racecourse must have been
the last-ditch fall-back option, the place where a box
could be parked without comment. A week with no
race meetings, the venue booked out to the pony camp
with Carl on hand to clear them out. It had probably
been his idea to tip off Jean and then push her in the
Thompsons' direction. Was it bad luck that her call to

the police resulted in Greaves going out to see her, or was he on the lookout for anything concerning the mysterious Lance Malers?

There was a thing. 'Pat,' she said. 'I don't think Scott had made the link. I don't think he knew that Lance Malers was Carl.'

Pat shrugged. 'Probably not. Lance was supposed to keep his nose clean and stay under the radar. An insurance persona as it were.'

Annie nodded. She and Pieternel held such insurances, too. 'Well, he's cashed that in. I'm going to get Vitoria,' she said, standing. 'We need to work out what we're going to do.'

'Can you ring up to my colleague's room?' she asked the man at the reception desk.

He turned to pluck an envelope from the shelf behind him. 'Your colleague checked out, Miss Raymond. She said to give this to you or Miss Thompson when you asked for her.'

Annie's heart lurched. Had someone found them? 'Was anyone with her? Did anyone call here for her? When did she check out?'

'Uh...no, she was on her own. When you went up to your rooms after breakfast, she came straight back down.'

Annie ripped open the envelope. It contained a single sheet of paper.

Thank you. Best I go alone now. V

She took it across to Pat, who said, 'Solves what to do about her, anyway.'

Annie opened her mouth to point out that Vitoria was penniless, friendless and being hunted by a pack that would rip her to shreds, but on the point of speech, she held back, remembering Reg Brocklesby. *I'll sort things*

out for you. No need to worry about finance yet awhile.
He'd wanted Vitoria under his wing. He thought Carl
had snatched the chance to grab her away from Leah.
People like Reg Brocklesby didn't draw breath unless
there was a payout. Maybe Vitoria wasn't as defence-
less as Annie had thought, not now they'd given her a
head start. She'd have to hope so, because there was
precious little she could do for her now.

'I'd normally have popped into the office Saturday
morning,' said Pat, 'but may as well give it a miss. Shall
we get lunch?'

'Well...there was something else. I didn't want to
worry you before but I rang into the office answer
phone. It was jam-packed. Clients all playing hell with
you and Barbara for missed appointments and late reports. I think we'd better go in. I'll help you try and
clear up.'

'Oh, lawd, I'd kind of blanked all that out.'

Pat looked so crestfallen that Annie relented and
said, 'Half an hour either way won't make any difference. Let's do lunch. Then we'll go to the office, get to
know the worst and find ourselves some coffee while
we talk about how to tackle it.'

After they'd eaten Annie drove them through town,
up along the course of the river Hull. She thought back
to Pieternel's message. Mike would be over from Zurich in a week or so. She'd go to the airport to meet
him. That would surprise him. She felt it bad planning
to go off to enjoy herself leaving Pat with this wreck
of a business, but she'd give her a day or so, try to get
her back on her feet. It was a relief there'd been no link
with the job back in London. Anyone trying to lure the
company into a breach of their professional code would
never have sent Christa away. With a guilty start, she

realized she hadn't given Christa a thought since the call last night. The poor girl must be suffering a monumental hangover from whatever she'd been fed.

As they pulled up by the office and made their way inside, voices and the sound of a radio met them. Annie walked in ahead of Pat and they both stood rooted to the spot. Barbara sat at one of the desks, the phone to her ear, her hand raised imperiously to shush Annie and Pat. One side of her face bore the shadow of a waning black eye; otherwise she looked the same as ever.

'Yes, exactly,' said a clipped voice from the far side of the room, making Annie and Pat turn in unison to stare at Christa who stood by the filing cabinet, her mobile to her ear. 'I'm on my way with it now,' she went on. 'These things are best done face to face in my experience.'

As Barbara ended her call, Christa clicked off her phone, gathered up a stack of papers and turned to Barbara. 'I'm off out to the Joynsons. I'll call in for the Proctor report on the way back and shall I bring you a sandwich and some coffee?'

'Thank you, Christa,' said Barbara beaming her a smile.

'Hi Annie,' Christa acknowledged her as she pushed past. 'Can't stop. Catch up later.'

Pat stared aghast at her sister. 'You shouldn't be here. You're not well enough. You discharged yourself, didn't you?'

'It's a good job I did. Just look at all this mess. And did I hear right that you dragged Annie out to see Vince? As if he'd want her at his sickbed. And you know what Leah's like. She'll be grumpy about it for an age.'

'I didn't…well, we had to… Vince…well, Leah—'

'And thank heavens for Christa Andrew. I don't

know where she came from but she's been efficiency itself. There were clients threatening to sue from all angles this morning. With her help I've held back the tide. We're keeping her on. I've already hired her so no arguments. Annie can go and we'll try and recoup whatever Vince paid her.'

The phone rang and Pat sprang forward, but Barbara glared at her. 'I'll deal with it.'

Pat drew back and turned to Annie. 'What's with Christa?' she asked.

'Whatever they pumped into her out there; that and a full fifteen hours' sleep. It's cleared her system. This is how she is when she's clean. I've not seen her like it for ages.'

'But yesterday…'

'Whatever they gave her it was a massive dose, and with whatever was already in her…' She shrugged and left the rest unsaid, but wondered if Christa's theatrical ebullience might be covering huge lapses in her memory. Which wouldn't, she mused, be such a bad thing.

'Will it last? Will she stay clean?'

Annie shrugged. 'On past experience, a week, ten days. Who knows?'

'… I shall look forward to it,' purred Barbara's voice as she replaced the handset in its cradle, her professional smile freezing into a scowl as she turned back to face them. 'And on top of all that,' she scolded, 'I hear there's been a ruckus out at Vince's. The last thing he needs when he's as ill as he is.'

'Uh… What's happened?'

'Some gang of Vince's hired muscle got above themselves. Injured Leah apparently, but she's all right. Some bother with illegal immigrants. Poor Leah got wind of it and went after them. She called the police but one of them attacked her before anyone got there.'

Poor Leah! Annie and Pat exchanged a glance. Annie wondered, had Leah really managed to keep her nose clean after all this? But who was going to say anything against her? Hassan hadn't seen her. His young daughter had, but Annie supposed she'd talk her way out of that; say she'd been forced to do whatever she'd done. And after all, the emergency call had come from Leah's phone. It was too late for Leah for keep Vince alive. Annie was surprised the debacle at the racecourse hadn't killed him off, but it wouldn't be long.

As Annie thought through the implications of Vince's impending death, she slipped out of the office to the comparative privacy of the landing, cradling her phone and thinking through the call she had to make to Scott to arrange to meet him one last time before she left.

Without ever properly thinking it through, Annie had always assumed that whole strata of wheeling and dealing would die with Vince; that whole areas would clean themselves up. Not a bit of it, she knew now. It would be a far dirtier game once Leah had fought it out with Reg and taken charge. Reg Brocklesby might hold all the cards on paper, but Leah wielded the power; Leah was the one with the army at her back. Annie shuddered at the thought of the carnage that would ensue, with worse to come once Leah had established her position. From the first time she'd met him all those years ago, Annie had wanted to see Vince Sleeman wiped off the map of this area. She'd always known it was a goal way beyond her means, but it wasn't beyond everyone's means if they struck fast and took advantage of what would be a small window of opportunity whilst

Leah and Reg were focused on each other and the outer strands of Vince's enterprises were adrift and in chaos.

Scott might not be the ideal contact for this, but he was straight and he wasn't stupid. Annie had promised to pass on the information that came to her through unofficial channels as long as he was open with her. She wasn't certain he'd kept to his side of the bargain but that didn't matter now. He'd know what to do with the pointers she could give him; how to take advantage of the unstable Sleeman empire while Vince hovered between life and death. Then there were Carl's hints about where the bodies were buried. They might not be reliable, but she'd pass them on.

Not wanting to be cornered into a discussion she wasn't yet ready to have, she sent him a text, telling him to be at the Humber Bridge country park at three o'clock. It would take no more than half an hour to debrief him, and then she'd be on the road and heading back south, knowing she'd finally closed a Chapter that had opened when she'd first arrived at Hull's Paragon station seven years earlier.

She would let the Thompsons reap the rewards of Christa's temporary normality. They needed all the help they could get. She slipped the phone into her pocket and stepped back into the office to hear Barbara snap at Pat, 'You can go downstairs and see what's come in the post. It hadn't arrived when I got here.'

As Annie entered Barbara's attack swung round to her. 'I found that poor girl on her own. Coping extraordinarily well. If Vince had only sent her in the first place. It's all very well for you two. We'd all like to spend a day in the countryside. What have you been doing out there? Lazing about gossiping, I suppose, not an awkward character in sight, and we've had them by

the dozen. Well, don't just stand there.' The glare turned
again to Pat. 'Go on!'

With the barest of glances signalling assent between
them, Pat and Annie turned and left the office together,
ignoring Barbara's tetchy, 'It doesn't need both of you,
for heaven's sake!'

'Coffee?' said Annie as they made their way down
the stairs.

'Lead me to it, kid,' replied Pat.

* * * * *

ABOUT THE AUTHOR

PENNY GRUBB IS a novelist and an academic who teaches and researches creative and academic writing techniques. For six years to 2013 she was Chair of the Authors' Licensing and Collecting Society, the largest writers' organisation in the world. Her Annie Raymond mystery series has been published in the UK, USA and Canada. Buried Deep is her first police procedural. Penny is winner of an international crime fiction award from the Crime Writers Association.

Find out more about Penny at www.pennygrubb.com.